The New York Times

IN THE HEADLINES

Political Extremism

HOW FRINGE GROUPS OPERATE

THE NEW YORK TIMES EDITORIAL STAFF

Published in 2020 by New York Times Educational Publishing in association with The Rosen Publishing Group, Inc.
29 East 21st Street, New York, NY 10010

First Edition

The New York Times
Alex Ward: Editorial Director, Book Development
Phyllis Collazo: Photo Rights/Permissions Editor
Heidi Giovine: Administrative Manager

Rosen Publishing
Megan Kellerman: Managing Editor
Julia Bosson: Editor
Greg Tucker: Creative Director
Brian Garvey: Art Director

Cataloging-in-Publication Data
Names: New York Times Company.
Title: Political extremism: how fringe groups operate / edited by the New York Times editorial staff.
Description: New York : The New York Times Educational Publishing, 2020. | Series: In the headlines | Includes glossary and index.
Identifiers: ISBN 9781642823158 (library bound) | ISBN 9781642823141 (pbk.) | ISBN 9781642823165 (ebook)
Subjects: LCSH: Radicalism—United States—History—Juvenile literature. | Right and left (Political science)—Juvenile literature.
Classification: LCC HN90.R3 P65 2020 | DDC 303.48'4—dc23

Manufactured in the United States of America

On the cover: Battle lines form between white nationalists, neo-Nazis and members of the alt-right and anti-fascist counterprotesters at the entrance to Emancipation Park during the Unite the Right rally, Aug. 12, 2017, in Charlottesville, Va.; Chip Somodevilla/Getty Images.

Contents

CHAPTER 2

Anti-Abortion Extremists

CHAPTER 3

Second Amendment Extremists

CHAPTER 5

Animal Rights and Ecological Extremists

Introduction

AMERICA IS UNDER threat from extremists. But depending on your political beliefs, it might come as a surprise to learn that more people have been killed by far-right and white nationalist extremists than Islamic radicals since 2001. When most people think of extremists, the first things that come to mind might be religious extremists, particularly those who have brought their beliefs toward violent ends. But extremism itself refers to anyone who espouses radical or fanatical positions, religious or otherwise.

In American politics, extremism most often takes on the form of those who advocate for recognition of single issues. The articles in this collection explore extremists of gun rights, animal rights and the environment, as well as groups who fanatically oppose the expansion of the government and a woman's right to choose. It also touches upon a growing contingent of extremist actors, white nationalists and far-right movements.

The antigovernment movement has been around nearly as long as the founding of the country, and was first expressed when Thomas Jefferson disagreed with Alexander Hamilton about the fundamental role of the federal government. In modern times, the antigovernment movement has cropped up largely in relation to disputes over land ownership and taxation.

The antigovernment movement shares some overlap with gun rights extremists, who argue that the right to bear arms is one of the primary aspects of American democracy. However, as mass shootings have become a frighteningly regular part of American life, these advocates have begun to feel a new urgency to defend the future of America as a gun-wielding nation.

STEPHEN CROWLEY/THE NEW YORK TIMES

A hat with the slogan "Make America Great Again" during a campaign event for Donald Trump in Raleigh, N.C. Mr. Trump voiced the bewilderment and anger of whites who do not feel at all powerful or privileged.

For the anti-abortion activists who oppose a woman's right to choose under any circumstances, the act of terminating a pregnancy amounts to murder. This might explain some of the more extreme actions its supporters have taken in order to prevent abortions from happening in states in the South and the middle of America, ranging from extremely prohibitive legislation to threats of violence — some of which have even been carried out. For these radicals, it is a matter of life and death.

White nationalists are an extremist group that has a long history in America, with a prominent presence since the Civil War and Reconstruction. However, since the election of Donald Trump, whose rhetoric echoes some of the talking points used on far-right websites, this group has grown louder and more visible. In August 2017, a rally organized by an alt-right organization was met with protests that quickly turned violent, leading to the death of one counterprotester.

This led Americans to wonder where these extremists came from and how they could be stopped.

It is a favorite criticism on both sides of any issue to call those at the opposite end of the political spectrum "extremists," whether or not that is based on reality. Some arguments could be made in favor of political extremism: In a two-party system in which policies are watered down by compromise, taking an extremist stance is a way of edging progress forward in a useful direction. But, of course, taking an extremist position often results in a shutting down of discourse and an end to compromise. And ultimately, violence has not been proven to effectively do anything but spread harm.

The 21st century seems to be a century of extremes, fueled in part by the advent of social media and algorithms that filter news in order to feed individual biases and stoke animosity. The rise of extremism can feel frightening, but as the antigovernment extremists demonstrate, these forms of extremism have been part of American culture since the founding of the nation. As time goes on, it will continue to be a fact of our lives.

CHAPTER 1

Antigovernment Extremists

In 2014, a cattle rancher from Nevada named Cliven Bundy led an armed protest against the Bureau of Land Management. This followed nearly two decades of disagreement, with Bundy asserting that the government had no right to regulate public land. Bundy represents a strain of antigovernment extremism that dates back to the country's founding. The articles in this chapter examine the enduring prevalence of this movement.

Two States, Two Gatherings and a Lot of Antigovernment Sentiment

BY MICHAEL JANOFSKY | MAY 15, 1995

CORNISH, N.H., MAY 13 — Some brought family members, some their friends, some just the gun racks in the back of their pickup trucks.

From all over New England, they arrived for a rally of the Patriots movement, about 100 true believers, some of them members of the armed groups that call themselves militias, but nearly all united in the belief that the American political process has broken down, that elected officials no longer respond to the people and that citizens need to defend themselves against Federal agents abusing their power.

"The overarching reason we're here is that we know the problems we're facing," said Barry Buswell, a 36-year-old logger from the far northern New Hampshire town of Pittsburg, about 140 miles away.

"The only way we can solve them is to stick together. We know a lot more than most Americans."

It seemed an odd and curious event for Cornish, a scenic place populated by millionaires, artists, farmers and factory workers. It is not a town so much as a collection of close-by dots on the map — Cornish Center, Cornish Mills, South Cornish — midway up the Connecticut River on the state's western edge.

Just above Cornish Mills, the longest covered wooden bridge in the nation, built in 1866, connects New Hampshire with Windsor, Vt., and folks along the east bank love to brag that J. D. Salinger lives nearby. They all know where, of course; they just will not tell outsiders.

Privacy, like gun ownership, is a cherished notion in New Hampshire, where there is no state income tax or sales tax. Its motto is "Live Free or Die," and more than a few attending the rally talked about how G. Gordon Liddy, the right-wing radio talk-show host, was right when he recommended shooting Federal agents if they tried to break down your door.

"I don't preach violence, but if they kick my doors down, I'll shoot the bastards in the head," said Leroy Crenshaw, a physical education teacher from Springfield, Mass., a guest speaker and the only black man who attended today's rally in the quaint old Cornish Town Hall. The thrust of his speech was that the Federal Government was dividing people by race to conquer them.

Although the rally had been scheduled and well publicized for months, the organizer, N. Scott Stevens, head of White Mountain Militia Information Services, said he never expected more than a few dozen people. But once the April 19 bombing of the Federal Building in Oklahoma City brought new attention to the far right, interest swelled. Mr. Stevens's event was one of the first of its kind in the nation to take place since the bombing, and he said he could scarcely get off the phone this week because of all the inquiries.

Organizations that monitor the activities of right-wing groups say the bombing is the latest in a series of events to draw new members to such groups. Others were the 1992 attempt to arrest Randall C. Weaver, a white supremacist, in Ruby Ridge, Idaho, in which Mr. Weaver's wife and son and a Federal marshal were killed, and the 1993 assault by Federal agents on the Branch Davidian compound outside Waco, Tex.

Chip Berlet, who tracks right-wing groups for Political Research Associates, a watchdog organization in Cambridge, Mass., said membership in groups that call themselves militias had not grown as quickly in New England as it had in other parts of the nation. He said he knew of one group in Maine and two in New Hampshire — Mr. Stevens's and one called the Constitution Defense Militia, run by Ed Brown, an insect exterminator from Plainfield, N.H.

Mr. Berlet described the Patriot movement as a diffuse amalgam of right-wing groups linked by antigovernment sentiments that include opposition to taxes and gun control.

He said that the movement could involve as many as five million people through such groups as the John Birch Society, the Liberty Lobby, armed paramilitary groups and some neo-Nazi organizations, but that it was hard to tell how many adherents lived in New England.

Mr. Stevens said he did not know the number of people in his group; Mr. Brown said the same. But Philip (Joe) Osgood, the Chief of the Cornish Police Department for the last 10 years, who kept an eye on the proceedings from a cruiser parked across the street, said he believed that Mr. Stevens's group had only two other members and that Mr. Brown operated alone.

"But a lot of people strongly agree with what they are saying," Chief Osgood said.

Mr. Buswell said that he was a member of a group called the Ghost Militia and that one of his reasons for attending the rally was to learn how to expand membership. He also said he disagreed with the notion that such groups are loose-knit.

"There are more of them than you think," he said. "And they're not loose. They're very tight."

Mr. Stevens, who was master of ceremonies for the rally, welcomed the crowd, mostly men, and introduced the speakers. They included

Sam Blumenfeld, a proponent of home schooling from Boston; State Representative Donald Gorman, a Libertarian, and Bruce R. Chesley, the New England field representative for Jews for the Preservation of Firearms Ownership, an organization based in Milwaukee.

Speaking to reporters before his presentation, Mr. Chesley said his organization was needed primarily because some Jewish members of Congress who favor tighter gun control measures were feeding anti-Semitism in the United States, so Jewish citizens needed to protect themselves. He cited Senator Dianne Feinstein of California, former Senator Howard M. Metzenbaum of Ohio and Representative Charles E. Schumer of Brooklyn, all Democrats.

Among the material the group offered for sale was a poster showing Hitler in a Sieg Heil salute with the words, "All in favor of gun control, raise your right hand."

Ever gracious and eager to answer questions, Mr. Stevens, 37, insisted that his group embraced no racist philosophies. Rather, he said, it served merely as an information clearinghouse for groups opposed to regulations that restrict rights defined by the Constitution.

"We view with great disdain anybody that talks about hate, violence or the overthrow of the Government," he said.

He apologized for a flier prepared by a California group that was among the materials he was selling, for 50 cents an ounce. The flier said that only white people were entitled to the full rights of citizenship.

The rally attracted a few local residents who said they had stopped by out of curiosity. Bo Rock, 67, a farmer who lives nearby, said, "I just came to see the wackos." He laughed and went inside.

But Annabelle Cone, a French teacher at Dartmouth College, was not amused. A former Brooklyn resident, she said she moved here in 1986 after being victimized by three crimes in two weeks. All the talk about guns and the need for self defense against out-of-control Federal agents frightened her.

"Ironic, isn't it?" she said. "I thought I was moving to a relatively safe, civil society."

When to Violate the Top Two Commandments of Antigovernment Crusaders

COLUMN | BY ROBERT H. FRANK | MARCH 15, 2007

WHEN ASKED TO identify the two most important items from their list of 10 public policy commandments, most antigovernment crusaders pick (1) public spending shall be kept to an absolute minimum and (2) the state shall not transfer income from rich to poor.

No government heeds these admonitions in any literal sense. Yet they have had a profound impact on public policy decisions, especially in the United States. Often, however, their impact has been the opposite of what antigovernment crusaders intended.

The problem is that many compellingly advantageous public policies cannot be enacted without violating the two commandments. Every significant policy change benefits some people and harms others. If the gains to winners substantially outweigh the costs to losers, solutions can always be found that allow everyone to come out ahead. But those solutions often involve higher taxes and income transfers to the poor.

Regulations that limit auto emissions are a case in point. Because these regulations increase car prices, legislators in most jurisdictions exempt older vehicles to avoid imposing unacceptable costs on the mostly low-income motorists who drive them. Yet the cost to society of this exemption far outweighs its benefit for the poor.

For example, although fewer than 10 percent of the vehicles in Los Angeles are more than 15 years old, these cars account for more than half the smog. Exempting the old cars thus necessitates much stricter regulations for new ones. But the cheapest ways of reducing emissions from new cars have long since been adopted. According to a RAND Corporation study, meeting air quality targets by further tightening new-car standards is several times as costly as meeting those targets by eliminating the exemption for older vehicles.

By raising taxes on high-income motorists, the government could finance vouchers that would enable low-income motorists to scrap their older vehicles in favor of cleaner used cars of more recent vintage. The required taxes would be much smaller than the resulting savings from not having to adopt such costly standards for new vehicles. Both rich and poor motorists would win.

The problem is that taking these steps would violate the two commandments. Antigovernment crusaders have prevailed for now. The ostensible champions of economic efficiency, they have kept government budgets smaller and blocked some transfers to low-income families. In the process, however, they have made everyone poorer.

Some believe that minimal government is synonymous with economic efficiency. But it is not. As the emissions example illustrates, economic efficiency sometimes requires that government play a larger role.

This example is part of a much broader pattern. In health care, for example, the private insurance system employed in the United States delivers worse outcomes at substantially higher cost than the single-payer system employed in virtually every other industrial country. But switching to the single-payer system would require higher taxes and increased benefits for low-income citizens, steps that would violate the two commandments. So for now, we remain saddled with a system that everyone agrees is dysfunctional.

In the realm of antipoverty policy, most economists agree that raising the earned-income tax credit would be the most efficient way of increasing the living standard of the working poor. Under this program, general tax revenues support income subsidies to those whose earnings fall below a given threshold. Its compelling advantage is that unlike a higher minimum wage, it does not discourage hiring. But raising taxes to increase the earned-income tax credit would violate the two commandments.

Because the most efficient antipoverty policy is deemed politically unfeasible, many economists support current legislative proposals to raise the minimum wage for the first time in a decade. If this legislation passes, antigovernment crusaders will be able to claim, truthfully, to have prevented an increase in the federal budget. But they will have won a hollow victory. For unlike an increase in the earned-income tax credit, an increase in the minimum wage not only limits job creation for the least-skilled workers, it also raises the prices of goods they produce. Over all, it would have been cheaper to raise the earned-income tax credit.

Antigovernment crusaders have also prevented the adoption of energy policies that would produce better outcomes for all. For example, economists of all political stripes have argued that a stiff tax on gasoline would relieve traffic congestion, reduce greenhouse gases, accelerate the development of energy-saving technologies and reduce dependence on foreign oil. But it would also impose significant economic hardship on low-income families, making it necessary to increase transfer payments to those families. Both the tax on gasoline and the transfers to low-income families would be clear violations of the two commandments. And so gasoline taxes continue to be far lower in the United States than in other industrial countries.

That democratic forces limit the economic hardship that government can impose on low-income families is a good thing. But sometimes imposing hardships on those families would create far larger gains for society as a whole. In such cases, we can always devise solutions that make everyone better off. But it is impossible to put these solutions into practice without violating the two commandments.

Is it better to solve a problem by spending two extra dollars in the private sector than by spending one additional dollar in the public sector? The two commandments insist, preposterously, that it is.

Economic efficiency is a worthy goal because when the economic pie grows larger, everyone can have a larger slice than before. Antigovernment crusaders deserve credit for emphasizing the importance of this goal. But as events of recent years have repeatedly demonstrated, they are often the biggest obstacles to its achievement.

ROBERT H. FRANK, an economist at the Johnson School of Management at Cornell University, is the author of "The Economic Naturalist," which will be published this spring.

A Defiant Rancher Savors the Audience That Rallied to His Side

BY ADAM NAGOURNEY | APRIL 23, 2014

BUNKERVILLE, NEV. — Cliven Bundy stood by the Virgin River up the road from the armed checkpoint at the driveway of his ranch, signing autographs and posing for pictures. For 55 minutes, Mr. Bundy held forth to a clutch of supporters about his views on the troubled state of America — the overreaching federal government, the harassment of Western ranchers, the societal upheaval caused by abortion, even musing about whether slavery was so bad.

Most of all, Mr. Bundy, 67, who was wearing a broad-brimmed white cowboy hat against the hot afternoon sun, recounted the success of "we the people" — gesturing to the 50 supporters, some armed with handguns and rifles, standing in a semicircle before him — at chasing away Bureau of Land Management rangers who, acting on a court order, tried to confiscate 500 cattle owned by Mr. Bundy, who has been illegally grazing his herd on public land since 1993.

"They don't have the guts enough to try to start that again for a few years," Mr. Bundy said in an interview.

Mr. Bundy's standoff with federal rangers — propelled into the national spotlight in part by steady coverage by Fox News — has highlighted sharp divisions over the power of the federal government and the rights of landowners in places like this desert stretch of Nevada, where resentment of Washington and its sprawling ownership of Western land has long run deep.

His cause has won support from Senator Rand Paul, the libertarian Republican from Kentucky who is likely to run for president. Senator Dean Heller, a Nevada Republican, referred to Mr. Bundy's supporters as "patriots." Senator Harry Reid, the Nevada Democrat who is the Senate majority leader and has a long history of pushing for protection of public lands, denounced the rancher's supporters as "domestic terrorists."

RONDA CHURCHILL FOR THE NEW YORK TIMES

Sympathizers have embraced Mr. Bundy as a symbol of their anger and a bulwark against federal abuse.

The dispute spilled over this week into Texas, where Greg Abbott, the attorney general and a Republican running for governor, challenged the Bureau of Land Management on reports that it was looking to claim thousands of acres along the Red River.

For now, Mr. Bundy appears to have won, forcing the government to back down after its rangers were met with armed Bundy supporters this month.

"The gather is now over," said Craig Leff, a deputy assistant director with the Bureau of Land Management. "Our focus is pursuing this matter administratively and judicially."

But if the federal government has moved on, Mr. Bundy — a father of 14 and a registered Republican — has not.

He said he would continue holding a daily news conference; on Saturday, it drew one reporter and one photographer, so Mr. Bundy used the time to officiate at what was in effect a town meeting with supporters, discussing, in a long, loping discourse, the prevalence of abortion, the abuses of welfare and his views on race.

"I want to tell you one more thing I know about the Negro," he said. Mr. Bundy recalled driving past a public-housing project in North Las Vegas, "and in front of that government house the door was usually open and the older people and the kids — and there is always at least a half a dozen people sitting on the porch — they didn't have nothing to do. They didn't have nothing for their kids to do. They didn't have nothing for their young girls to do.

"And because they were basically on government subsidy, so now what do they do?" he asked. "They abort their young children, they put their young men in jail, because they never learned how to pick cotton. And I've often wondered, are they better off as slaves, picking cotton and having a family life and doing things, or are they better off under government subsidy? They didn't get no more freedom. They got less freedom."

A spokesman for Mr. Paul, informed of Mr. Bundy's remarks, said the senator was not available for immediate comment. Chandler Smith, a spokesman for Mr. Heller, said that the senator "completely disagrees with Mr. Bundy's appalling and racist statements, and condemns them in the most strenuous way." A spokeswoman for Mr. Abbott, Laura Bean, said that the letter he wrote "was regarding a dispute in Texas and is in no way related to the dispute in Nevada."

The crowds may be beginning to dwindle, but for much of the past two weeks, here at Mr. Bundy's ranch in Bunkerville, 80 miles northeast of Las Vegas, the rancher has been a celebrity, drawing hundreds of supporters, including dozens of militia members, many carrying sidearms, and members of Oath Keepers, a militia group, who have embraced him as a symbol of their anger and a bulwark against federal abuse.

He was honored at a celebratory party on Friday night attended by 1,500 people, who wore "domestic terrorist" name tags, listened to cowboy poetry and ate hamburgers, hot dogs and Bundy beef. "This is the beginning of taking America back," said Shawna Cox, who had come from Kanab, Utah, to support him.

Mr. Bundy, whose family has grazed cattle here since they homesteaded in the 1870s, owes the government more than $1 million in grazing fees. He stopped paying after the bureau ordered him to restrict the periods when his herd roamed the 600,000-acre Gold Butte area as part of an effort to protect the endangered desert tortoise.

Mr. Bundy's case happened to heat up around the time that Mr. Paul, building the foundation for a presidential campaign, struck a chord with some members of the Republican Party with warnings about governmental overreach. Mr. Paul's latest book is titled "Government Bullies: How Everyday Americans Are Being Harassed, Abused and Imprisoned by the Feds." In the Bundy standoff, Mr. Paul has criticized the federal government as overreaching with its use of regulations, but cautioned against any violence or lawbreaking.

Rob Mrowka, a senior scientist with the Center for Biological Diversity, which has been battling to get Mr. Bundy to move his cattle in deference to the tortoises, said the standoff had come to symbolize divisions across the country about the role of government, particularly here in the West.

"It's symbolic of the polarization and divide within the country that we saw starting with the Obama election," he said. "This is merely a surrogate for bigger issue and topic in America today — it's the whole idea of federalism versus states."

The federal government owns 85 percent of the land in Nevada, a statistic repeatedly noted by Mr. Bundy's supporters as they denounced the actions of the government. Six cattle, including two that had Bundy brands, died during the attempt to collect the animals.

"Western states don't have the control over their land that Eastern states have over their land," said Ivan Jones, 60, a brick mason who came here from Northern California. "Someone like the Bundys, they have been here for generations, before the B.L.M. was ever created, using this land to graze their animals. And the B.L.M. comes in and changes the rule. A small little rancher trying to make a living and they come in like big bullies."

Toby Purvis, 51, an electrician who came here from Farmington, N.M., called the bureau operation "a land grab."

"This is happening all over the country right now," he said.

Mr. Bundy's case is clearly divisive. About 16,000 ranchers across the country pay relatively modest fees for their herds to use public land. The Nevada Cattlemen's Association, while expressing sympathy with some of Mr. Bundy's complaints, pointedly did not endorse his methods.

"This should not be confused with civil disobedience," Mr. Mrowka said. "This is outright anarchy going on here."

Mr. Bundy disputes the legitimacy of both the bureau and the courts that have ruled against him. "I'll be damned if I'm going to honor a federal court that has no jurisdiction or authority or arresting power over we the people," he said.

Still, as Mr. Bundy surveyed the dusty landscape last weekend, the only sign of law enforcement was Brad Rogers, the sheriff of Elkhart County, Ind., who had flown 1,800 miles to stand in solidarity with the embattled rancher.

With the rangers gone, "I don't feel any threat — that's a big change," Mr. Bundy said. At the same time, he said he saw no reason for his supporters to leave. "As long as we are getting together as a group and as long as we feel good about being here, we are going to be here," he said.

One of Mr. Bundy's sons, Ammon, 38, a car fleet manager from Phoenix, said his father had taught the federal government a lesson. "We ran them out of here," he said, sitting in a trailer set up near one of the protesters' camp sites. "We were serious. We weren't playing around."

But Alan O'Neill, who had a similar struggle with Mr. Bundy when he was superintendent of the Lake Mead National Recreation Area, expressed concern that the government had backed down.

"He calls himself a patriot, and says he loves America," Mr. O'Neill said. "And yet he says he won't follow any federal laws. You just can't let this go by, or everybody is going to be like, 'If Bundy can break the law, why can't I?' "

LYNNETTE CURTIS contributed reporting from Bunkerville.

Wildlife Refuge Occupied in Protest of Oregon Ranchers' Prison Terms

BY LIAM STACK | JAN. 2, 2016

FEDERAL OFFICIALS SAID Sunday that no federal wildlife employees were in danger after a group of armed activists and militiamen protesting the prosecution of two ranchers took over a remote federal wildlife refuge in the rural southeastern corner of Oregon over the weekend.

A building at the refuge seized on Saturday afternoon by the group houses the offices of the Malheur National Wildlife Refuge, and is operated by the United States Fish and Wildlife Service, about 30 miles southeast of Burns, in Harney County. A representative of the Fish and Wildlife Service said the agency was monitoring the situation. "While the situation is ongoing, the main concern is employee safety and we can confirm that no federal staff were in the building at the time of the initial incident," the press officer said.

The occupation began after a demonstration on Saturday in support of Dwight Hammond, 73, and his son Steven Hammond, 46, who were to report to California prison after a federal judge ruled that the sentences they had served for arson were not long enough under federal law.

Among the occupiers were Ammon and Ryan Bundy, two sons of Cliven Bundy, a Nevada rancher who became a symbol of antigovernment sentiment in 2014, according to The Oregonian.

"We're planning on staying here for years, absolutely," Ammon Bundy told The Oregonian in a telephone interview. "This is not a decision we've made at the last minute." The two men refused to provide details on how many people were taking part in the occupation, but militia members claim there are as many as 150 people at the refuge.

In a telephone interview Sunday morning with CNN, Mr. Bundy said his group wanted the federal government to restore the "people's constitutional rights."

"People need to be aware that we've become a system where government is actually claiming and using and defending people's rights, and they are doing that against the people," he said.

A lawyer for the Hammonds said, however, they did not welcome the Bundys' help, according to The Associated Press.

"Neither Ammon Bundy nor anyone within his group/organization speak for the Hammond family," the lawyer, W. Alan Schroeder, wrote to David Ward, the Harney County sheriff.

An email to the sheriff seeking comment was not immediately returned.

In a video posted to Facebook on Thursday, Ammon Bundy called on the members of "different militia groups" to participate in the protest on Saturday.

"This is not a time to stand down," he said. "It is a time to stand up and come to Harney County. We need your help and we are asking for it."

The Hammonds admitted they lit fires in 2001 and 2006, but said it had been to protect their property from wildfires and invasive plant species, The A.P. said. They were convicted three years ago, and the father served three months in prison, while the son served one year.

The Harney County Sheriff's Department said the Oregon State Police was handling the incident. Beth Anne Steele, a spokeswoman for the F.B.I. in Portland, said the agency was aware of the situation, but declined to comment further.

The Bundys have been organizing opposition to the government case against the Hammonds on social media in recent weeks, which they described as a tyrannical use of federal authority.

"We're out here because the people have been abused long enough," Ammon Bundy said in a separate video posted to Facebook on Saturday.

He called the prosecution of the Hammonds "a symptom of a very huge, egregious problem" that he described as a battle over land and resources between the federal government and "the American people."

"The people cannot survive without their land and resources," he said. "We cannot have the government restricting the use of that to the point that it puts us in poverty."

Mr. Bundy described the federal building as "the people's facility, owned by the people" and said his group was occupying it to take "a hard stand against this overreach, this taking of the people's land and resources."

He said the group would remain there indefinitely and told an interviewer that he hoped more supporters would join them. "We have a facility that we can house them in," he said, referring to the occupied building.

"We pose no threat to anybody," Mr. Bundy said. "There is no person that is physically harmed by what we are doing." He added that if law enforcement officials "bring physical harm to us, they will be doing it only for a facility or a building."

However, in an interview with The Oregonian earlier on Saturday evening, Mr. Bundy and his brother said they would not rule out violence if law enforcement officers attempted to remove them from the building.

"The facility has been the tool to do all the tyranny that has been placed upon the Hammonds," Ammon Bundy told the newspaper. He said he planned to remain in the building for "years."

Cliven Bundy previously galvanized conservative critics of the federal government after a standoff with agents from the Bureau of Land Management, who attempted to confiscate cattle he had illegally grazed on federal land since 1993.

NICHOLAS FANDOS contributed reporting from Washington.

Trump Pardons Oregon Ranchers Whose Case Inspired Wildlife Refuge Takeover

BY EILEEN SULLIVAN AND JULIE TURKEWITZ | JULY 10, 2018

WASHINGTON — President Trump on Tuesday pardoned a pair of Oregon cattle ranchers who had been serving out five-year sentences for arson on federal land — punishments that inspired the armed occupation of a wildlife refuge in 2016 and brought widespread attention to anger over federal land management in the Western United States.

The case against the ranchers — Dwight L. Hammond, now 76, and his son, Steven D. Hammond, 49 — became a cause célèbre for an antigovernment group's weekslong standoff at the Malheur National Wildlife Refuge.

The occupation, led by the Bundy family, drew hordes of militia members who commandeered government buildings and vehicles in tactical gear and long guns, promising to defend the family.

During his campaign, Mr. Trump played to that sense of Western grievance, and the pardon of the Hammonds was a signal to conservatives that he was sympathetic. His pardon in August of former Sheriff Joe Arpaio of Maricopa County, Ariz., was another such sign.

The Hammond pardons were the result of a monthslong push by agricultural groups like the Oregon Cattlemen's Association, and Interior Secretary Ryan Zinke had been among the ranchers' strongest supporters, according to the association's executive director, Jerome Rosa.

Sarah Huckabee Sanders, the White House press secretary, said in a statement on Tuesday that the Obama administration had been "overzealous" in pursuing the Hammonds. "This was unjust," she said.

The pardons drew immediate criticism from environmental groups and their allies, who said they would imperil the rule of law on public lands.

"This is so very wrong," Joan Anzelmo, a former superintendent of Colorado National Monument, said in a message on Twitter. "No one is safe from from felons with friends in high places. Terrible. Dangerous. Wrong."

The federal government owns about half the acres in the West, and Obama administration policies there often angered ranchers and others who work and live on those lands. His administration blocked new coal leases, imposed moratoriums on uranium drilling near the Grand Canyon, and placed an unprecedented amount of land and sea under heightened federal protection.

Mr. Trump, in contrast, has struck a far more favorable tone toward those who want to loosen regulation on public land, and he has been aided by Mr. Zinke. In December, the president sharply reduced the size of two conservation areas in Utah, Bears Ears and Grand Staircase-Escalante national monuments. It was the largest rollback of federal land protection in the nation's history.

The Hammonds were prosecuted under a 1996 terrorism statute, passed after the Oklahoma City bombing, that imposed five-year mandatory minimum sentences for arson on federal property. Critics called the sentences too harsh.

"The Hammonds are multigeneration cattle ranchers in Oregon imprisoned in connection with a fire that leaked onto a small portion of neighboring public grazing land," Ms. Sanders said. "The evidence at trial regarding the Hammonds' responsibility for the fire was conflicting, and the jury acquitted them on most of the charges."

In a pointed criticism of the Obama administration, she added, "The previous administration, however, filed an overzealous appeal that resulted in the Hammonds being sentenced to five years in prison."

Dwight and Steven Hammond — who own about 13,000 acres of land in Eastern Oregon and once ran cattle on 26,000 acres of public land — have a history of conflict with federal officials, which indirectly led to the showdown in Oregon.

Both were convicted for a 2001 fire that burned more than 100 acres of federal land. While the Hammonds said it was devised to control invasive species, witnesses at their trial testified that it occurred after Steven Hammond and a hunting party illegally slaughtered several deer. The jury was told that Steven Hammond handed out matches and told allies to "light up the whole country on fire."

He was also convicted of setting a second fire, in 2006, which he said was meant to manage the spread of other wildfires, a common practice.

The pair was convicted in 2012 and served a short time in prison. But a federal appeals court ruled in 2015 that they had been improperly sentenced and ordered them to return to prison.

Word of this second imprisonment soon reached the Bundy family, a sprawling ranching clan based in Bunkerville, Nev., that in recent years had emerged as a symbol of the most extreme version of the push against federal land control.

Angered by the Hammond case, two of the Bundy brothers, Ryan and Ammon, traveled to Oregon and stormed the Malheur wildlife refuge in what turned into a standoff with federal officials.

Many of those who joined the protest were members of unofficial militias who carried long guns and pistols and dressed as if at war. The occupation resulted in the death of a rancher from Arizona.

The Hammonds, however, never asked for the help of the Bundys or the militia members, and amid it all, quietly headed to prison.

The pardons will shave some time off the Hammonds' sentences — Dwight Hammond has served three years and Steven Hammond has served four.

Ryan Bundy, one of the occupation leaders, hailed the president's announcement of the pardons as a victory, the latest in a string of wins for his family. Mr. Bundy was ultimately acquitted for his role in the takeover, and is now running for governor of Nevada.

"Awesome, awesome, awesome," he said. "It's been a long time coming. It's been a long time coming. That is good news."

The move also drew praise from the cattlemen's association.

"I had the opportunity to have a private meeting with him," Mr. Rosa, the group's executive director, said of Mr. Zinke. "I mentioned to him the Hammond situation. He was well aware of it, agreed that the Hammonds were good people, and said he would talk to the president and give his blessing to release the Hammonds from prison."

Representative Greg Walden, Republican of Oregon, also lobbied aggressively for the pair's release.

But some conservation groups strongly opposed the decision.

"Pardoning the Hammonds sends a dangerous message to America's park rangers, wildland firefighters, law enforcement officers and public lands managers," Jennifer Rokala, executive director of the Center for Western Priorities, said in a statement. "President Trump, at the urging of Interior Secretary Ryan Zinke, has once again sided with lawless extremists who believe that public land does not belong to all Americans."

The Hammonds are the sixth and seventh people to receive pardons from Mr. Trump. In all his pardons, Mr. Trump bypassed the typical process (a five-year waiting period is required for requests to be made to the Justice Department) and passed over the more than 10,000 pardon and clemency applications. The president has the power to pardon anyone sentenced for a federal offense.

EILEEN SULLIVAN reported from Washington, and **JULIE TURKEWITZ** from Denver. **EMILY COCHRANE** contributed reporting from Washington.

Antigovernment Obsession Preceded Las Vegas Shootings

BY IAN LOVETT | JUNE 9, 2014

LAS VEGAS — Before 6 on Sunday morning, just hours before they killed two police officers and a civilian in a display of antigovernment violence, Jerad and Amanda Miller left their two beloved cats with Kelley Fielder, the next-door neighbor with whom they had been staying. Ms. Miller, 22, promised to return later. Mr. Miller, 31, did not. He gave Ms. Fielder a tearful hug, and said, "I got to do what I got to do."

" 'The revolution has begun' — that's what he kept saying," Ms. Fielder said Monday. "All Jerad wanted to do is talk about overthrowing the government. I thought he was talking smack."

But rather than idle talk, Sunday marked a bloody end to what neighbors described as Mr. Miller's obsession with overthrowing the government.

The couple set off on foot from their apartment building — she with a handgun in her purse, and he with at least one shotgun and hundreds of rounds of ammunition in a backpack, the police said. Just before noon, the couple entered a CiCi's Pizza parlor, where Mr. Miller shot one officer in the head. Then the couple opened fire on the other.

They draped one officer's body in a swastika and a yellow "Don't Tread on Me" flag that has been adopted as a symbol of the Tea Party. On the other, they pinned a note warning of "the beginning of the revolution," a phrase they also shouted, the police said.

They promptly crossed the street to a Walmart, where Mr. Miller fired a single shot and continued shouting about revolution to terrified shoppers. One man at the checkout area who was carrying a handgun tried to stop Mr. Miller, but did not notice that Ms. Miller was working in concert with her husband; she shot the man dead. The couple proceeded to maraud through the store until the police trapped them at the back. There, Ms. Miller fatally shot her husband before shooting herself in the head.

Documents the police found in Ms. Fielder's apartment, where the Millers had been staying for the last two weeks, indicated that they may have planned even greater destruction: A search warrant inventory said that the authorities had seized "numerous papers including detailed plans to take over a courthouse and execute public officials."

On Saturday, the day before the shooting, Mr. Miller posted an ominous message on his Facebook page: "The dawn of a new day. May all of our coming sacrifices be worth it."

Though the police said they believed the Millers acted on their own — and that the officers they killed were targeted at random — the authorities are investigating the couple's ties to other antigovernment groups.

This year, in what may have amounted to an attempt to join a revolution, the couple were believed to have briefly joined the antigovernment militia assembled at the Nevada ranch of Cliven Bundy, who became a symbol of opposition to the government this spring for his refusal to pay grazing fees for his cattle on federal land. The couple dressed in camouflage and carried coolers full of guns and ammunition, neighbors said, and Ms. Miller even left her job at Hobby Lobby. Mr. Bundy said Monday that militia members had told him about a couple on the ranch who "made radical comments" and had said the man admitted to being a felon and carried arms. Members were concerned, Mr. Bundy said, and he believes someone asked them to leave.

"We believe this is an isolated act," said Kevin McMahill, an assistant sheriff with the Las Vegas Metropolitan Police Department. But he added, "There is no doubt that the suspects have some apparent ideology that's along the lines of militia and white supremacists."

Sheriff McMahill said that investigators believed the Millers set out on foot from their apartment building on Sunday morning, carrying with them a rifle, multiple handguns and hundreds of rounds of ammunition. He did not know if the guns were purchased legally or by whom. Ms. Fielder said that she believed the guns were registered to Ms. Miller, and that the couple had said they were for self-defense.

It was around 11:20 a.m. on Sunday when the Millers reached the CiCi's Pizza, where Officers Alyn Beck, 41, and Igor Soldo, 31, were eating lunch. Mr. Miller shot Officer Soldo in the back of the head at close range. Officer Beck then tried to draw his weapon, but Mr. Miller shot him in the throat. The couple fired several more rounds into Officer Beck when he did not die immediately, Sheriff McMahill said.

After taking the officers' weapons and ammunition and covering their bodies in antigovernment paraphernalia, the Millers crossed the street to the Walmart. Mr. Miller fired a round and announced: "Get out! This is a revolution. Police are on the way."

Amid the pandemonium, Joseph Wilcox, 31, who had been in the checkout line, approached Mr. Miller brandishing a weapon, the police said. Ms. Miller pulled a pistol out of her purse and fatally shot him in the midsection, the police said.

"He died attempting to protect others," Sheriff Douglas C. Gillespie said of Mr. Wilcox. "His death is completely senseless."

Police officers soon entered the Walmart and, after several exchanges of gunfire, surrounded the Millers in the back of the store. Ms. Miller had been shot, the police said, and Mr. Miller used items from the store to build a makeshift wall to give them cover. Before a SWAT team arrived, however, Ms. Miller fired several shots at her husband, killing him, and then killed herself.

The couple had moved to Las Vegas in January, and their Facebook pages featured dewy-eyed photos of their wedding in September 2012. She was from Indiana, he from Indiana and Washington State. A string of arrests and at least one felony conviction followed him through both states.

In only a few months in the modest apartment building where they lived here, they made little secret of their distaste for government and their desire to foment revolution.

Their posts on Facebook sometimes threatened violence, and last month, Mr. Miller used the website to ask people to send him "a rifle to help stand against tyranny." Neighbors said Mr. Miller talked incessantly to anyone who would listen about the evils of welfare or President Obama. He worked as a street performer, and would often dress as Batman or the Joker; Ms. Miller would sometimes accompany him dressed as the villain Harley Quinn.

Sheriff McMahill said that the police believed the Millers may have moved in with Ms. Fielder in recent weeks because their own apartment had become unsanitary.

Ms. Fielder said she never believed the Millers would actually act on any of their talk of revolution. She said Ms. Miller's parents called her on Monday morning, trying to confirm that it was indeed their daughter who had been involved.

"They were horrified," Ms. Fielder said. "I feel hurt and disgusted. I have to live with this on my shoulders now. I should have called the cops, but I didn't know they were going to do this."

TIMOTHY WILLIAMS contributed reporting from New York. **ALAIN DELAQUÉRIÈRE** contributed research from New York.

Nashville Suspect Once Called Himself a 'Sovereign Citizen,' Police Say. What Is That?

BY JESS BIDGOOD | APRIL 23, 2018

WHEN THE MAN suspected of killing four people at a Waffle House in Nashville on Sunday was arrested last year in Washington, he called himself a "sovereign citizen," according to a police report.

The suspect, who was identified by the authorities as Travis J. Reinking and taken into custody on Monday, was arrested in July after he insisted on a meeting with President Trump and crossed a security barrier at the White House, the report said.

The suspect "stated he wanted to speak to the President and said he was a sovereign citizen and has a right to inspect the grounds," the report said.

There is an antigovernment ideology by that name that is identified by the Federal Bureau of Investigation and the Anti-Defamation League as an extremist movement. But it is not known whether Mr. Reinking, 29, had ties to the movement, and investigators have not publicly identified a motive for the mass shooting in which he is accused. An expert on extreme ideologies cautioned against linking Mr. Reinking to the movement without additional evidence, and Don Aaron, a spokesman for the Metropolitan Nashville Police Department, said Monday that he did not know "about the sovereign citizen issue."

Here is a look at the phrase and the movement.

WHAT IS A SOVEREIGN CITIZEN?

People who identify as sovereign citizens in the movement generally do not believe federal, state and local governments hold legitimate power over them, and they sometimes turn to cumbersome legal actions or take more violent actions as they flout authority. The movement has its roots in white extremist groups such as the Posse Comitatus of the 1970s, according to the Anti-Defamation League, which wrote in a 2012 report that the group was in the midst of resurgent growth.

"From every quarter, there have been more violent confrontations, more threats and acts of intimidation and harassment, and more scams and frauds," the report said.

Mark Pitcavage, a senior research fellow with the Center on Extremism at the A.D.L. who has tracked the movement for about 25 years, estimated that about 200,000 Americans identify as sovereign citizens. Mr. Pitcavage said the movement tends to gain more acolytes during periods of economic struggle — as it did during the recession and farm crisis in the early 1980s, and after the foreclosure crisis and the Great Recession in 2009. The movement appeals to the financially desperate, the 2012 report said, because it offers the government or banks as a scapegoat for financial struggle and because its supporters sometimes offer solutions for those difficulties, which can turn out to be scams or frauds.

Sovereign citizens believe the federal government has been infiltrated by a nefarious conspiracy rendering it illegitimate, and often do not pay taxes or meet other obligations. Sometimes, they file a flurry of nuisance lawsuits or liens in an effort to harass public officials — a tactic the authorities have termed "paper terrorism."

Experts say sovereign citizens are not organized under a single umbrella, but operate as a loosely affiliated network of individuals and groups.

WHAT ARE SOME WAYS SOVEREIGN CITIZENS HAVE CLASHED WITH THE LAW?

Because they do not believe in governmental authority, sovereign citizens sometimes set up their own juries or make their own currency — which has led some to face charges like impersonating a police officer or fraud, Mr. Pitcavage said.

Sovereign citizens dismiss the power of the government, but sometimes become deeply familiar with its inner workings, studying legal code and familiarizing themselves with bureaucracy in their efforts to undermine it. They have turned to nuisance lawsuits to harass local officials. In 2013, a couple who had lost their home to foreclosure and who identified with the sovereign citizen movement were sentenced to 23 months in prison after they filed billions of dollars in liens and other claims against local officials. A year earlier, The Albany Times-Union reported that a member of a school board in Ravena, N.Y., was a sovereign citizen who owed back taxes and had demanded $1 million from his town, claiming a copyright infringement.

In 2015, according to the F.B.I., three sovereign citizens who had fraudulently claimed ownership of 70 foreclosed properties and then filed false tax forms against numerous local officials were charged with crimes including conspiracy and bank fraud. (The three pleaded guilty in 2016 and received sentences ranging from a day to eight years in prison.)

In some cases, sovereign citizens have been involved in violent confrontations with the authorities. In 2010, a father and son described by the F.B.I. as sovereign citizen extremists shot and killed two Arkansas police officers during a traffic stop. The Times-Picayune reported that some of the men linked to the 2012 killing of two sheriffs' deputies in Louisiana had ties to the sovereign citizen movement, according to the authorities. And Gavin Long, who killed three law enforcement officers in Baton Rouge in 2016 before dying in a shootout with other officers, was part of a group that held such beliefs.

UNDER WHAT CIRCUMSTANCES DID MR. REINKING USE THE TERM?

In July 2017, Mr. Reinking described himself as a "sovereign citizen" who had the right to inspect the grounds of the White House, according to a police report from the Metropolitan Police Department in Washington.

Hate group experts caution against drawing firm conclusions from a line in police reports without more context. As public awareness of the sovereign citizen movement has grown since the 2010 killings of the police officers in Arkansas, some criminal suspects have inaccurately been linked to the movement.

"Based on that one very fragmentary thing in a context where you can imagine one generically using a phrase like sovereign or sovereign citizen," Mr. Pitcavage said, "I'm quite cautious."

After Mr. Reinking's arrest in Washington last year, the F.B.I. passed on information about him to local authorities in Illinois, where he had lived for most of his life, and where he was ordered to complete 32 hours of community service at a Baptist church in Morton, Ill.

The F.B.I. closed its investigation of Mr. Reinking in October.

How Sovereign Citizens Helped Swindle $1 Billion From the Government They Disavow

BY ASHLEY POWERS | MARCH 29, 2019

ONE DAY IN 2015, Barbara Lavender's husband returned from a U.F.O. conference and handed her a business card. It bore a red theater-curtain background, a vintage microphone and gold-and-white lettering that read: "Sean David Morton, Radio Host, Public Speaker, Author, Director, Screen Writer, Actor." The polymathic Mr. Morton, Jeff Lavender told his wife, was U.F.O. royalty.

Mr. Morton had spent years whisking E.T.-obsessed tourists to Area 51 for $99 a pop, then leveraged his following into stints on the wee-hours conspiracy show "Coast to Coast AM" — at one point, the nation's No. 3 talk-radio program. He dabbled in other fringe arts, such as remote viewing and psychic predictions about earthquakes, elections and the stock market. But by the time Mr. Lavender saw him talk in Southern California, Mr. Morton had shifted to something truly fantastical: instant debt relief.

He'd been peddling a workshop called "The Sovereign Factor: The Revolution Starts With You" — a nod to what is known as the sovereign citizens movement. A loose network of perhaps tens of thousands of far-right antigovernment extremists, sovereigns share certain conspiratorial beliefs and, sometimes, a desire to profit off a government whose legitimacy they deny.

"Do you realize," read Mr. Morton's workshop description, "you are ALL considered 'Incompetent,' 'Wards of the State,' 'Residents' and the 'Chattel Property' of the US Federal government, until you declare your Emancipation? Learn all the secrets about how to get the government off your back and out of your life once and for all!!" One of these secrets was called the "bond process." By submitting the right set of papers, Mr. Morton said, you could wipe out your mortgage, tax bills and student loans.

Mr. Morton's message had appeal beyond the tinfoil-hat crowd. In America after the Great Recession, plenty of people with upside-down mortgages and student debt were inclined to believe anyone offering help. Ms. Lavender, listening to her husband recap the workshop, was intrigued. Years earlier, she'd borrowed $48,000 to help her son attend college. She and her husband had worked in the mortgage industry in Southern California for decades, but educational debt was unfamiliar terrain. "I had never gone to college myself," she told me recently. "I took out a loan I shouldn't have." Ms. Lavender lost her job and deferred the payments, and the interest kept piling up. By the time she held Mr. Morton's business card in her hands, she owed $70,000.

She realized a U.F.O. gathering was an unusual venue for debt-relief advice. Her husband's annual get-togethers with the "X-Files" crowd were a hobby for him, and a good-natured punch line for their family. But the size and intractability of her loan balance weighed on her; also, she trusted her husband, and he thought Mr. Morton's bond process was worth checking out. She told me, "I think he probably was enticed by it because it might have been a little tiny kick in the pants to the government."

As the Lavenders came to discover, sovereign fraudsters are the snake-oil salesmen of our time. Peddling a bouquet of grifts as varied as tax fraud and real estate scams, they prey on our suspicion of institutions, financial illiteracy, greed and despair. You don't even have to buy into sovereign dogma to get swindled. You just need to be, as Ms. Lavender was, in debt. From 1990 to 2013, far-right extremists carried out more than 600 financial schemes that resulted in criminal charges, according to the researchers who run the U.S. Extremist Financial Crime Database, which is affiliated with the National Consortium for the Study of Terrorism and Responses to Terrorism and is the only clearinghouse of its kind.

MINH UONG/THE NEW YORK TIMES

That adds up to — conservatively — public losses of $1 billion. The majority of perpetrators were either sovereigns or their ideological cousins, tax defiers. Fraud is to them what cross-burning is to white supremacists: an expression of belief.

1. WHAT SOVEREIGN CITIZENS BELIEVE

Sovereigns, who sometimes call themselves "freemen" or "state citizens," have no foundational document, but broadly they subscribe to an alternate version of American history. The tale can vary from sovereign to sovereign, but it goes roughly like this: At some point, a corporation secretly usurped the United States government, then went bankrupt and sought aid from international bankers. As collateral, the corporation offered the financiers ... us. As sovereigns tell it, your birth certificate and Social Security card are not benign documents, but contracts that enslave you.

There is, they believe, a pathway to freedom: Renounce these contracts or otherwise assert your sovereignty. (Mr. Morton said he once told the Social Security Administration, "I don't want this number.") Then no one — not the taxman, not the police — can tell you what to do. Not all sovereigns are con men, but their belief system lends itself to deceit. You might declare yourself a "diplomat" from a nonexistent country. (Mr. Morton represented the Republic of New Lemuria and the Dominion of Melchizedek.) Or start a fake Native American tribe. Or blow off a court case because the American flag in the courtroom has gold fringe. Some sovereigns have even lashed out violently at law enforcement officers, which is why they're considered a domestic terrorism threat.

Many sovereign myths hark back to the creation, in 1913, of the Federal Reserve. "It was this weird, complicated instrument for controlling the monetary system. People saw it as sinister," the author J. M. Berger told me. In a recent paper, Mr. Berger traced the circulation of these ideas, in part, to a company named Omni Publications, which was something like the Infowars of the middle of the 20th century. One Omni title, "The Federal Reserve Conspiracy," claimed that "enemy aliens" had infiltrated the banking system, and that their biographies could be found in "Who's Who in American Jewry." (Sovereign lore is often rooted in anti-Semitism.) By the 1970s, the intellectual father of the sovereign citizen movement, William Potter Gale, helped spread this type of falsehood to a larger audience.

The founder of the antigovernment group Posse Comitatus, Mr. Gale aligned himself with an emerging movement of tax protesters who argued, for instance, that paying taxes was a form of involuntary servitude. In turn, he introduced them to his warped version of America, where patriots establish their own legal system and hang those who defy it. Mr. Gale's specific gift was wrapping nonsense in enough legalese that it sounded real. "If you have this movement that offers you essentially a lot of magic words that you can say to get out of trouble, that's going to really appeal to people who are desperate and angry," Mr. Berger said. Mr. Gale's outreach was a success. Over time, the line between thousands of tax protesters and Posse members blurred.

Take “redemption” — a theory popularized, in part, by a Gale associate. Remember how the corporation-slash-fake-government used us as collateral? According to sovereign lore, this means the government set up secret accounts in our names. Some believe they contain the oddly specific amount of $630,000. (To be clear, this is “pure fantasy,” according to the Internal Revenue Service.)

One way sovereigns try to make the imaginary money real is by abusing legitimate I.R.S. forms. Law-abiding taxpayers use Form 1099-OID, for example, to report “original issue discount” income. But some sovereigns write in fake OID income, and fake withholding, in order to claim illegitimate refunds. If you file such a return, you risk at the very least a large fine. Yet from 2012 to 2014, according to the Treasury Inspector General for Tax Administration, the I.R.S. received close to 7,000 sham OID filings.

Chronically underfunded and understaffed, I.R.S. investigators refer only about two dozen sovereign-scam cases, on average, for prosecution each year. The agency sometimes misses returns that should raise suspicion. For example, in 2016, the I.R.S. discovered a sizable redemption scheme — but only after processing 207 bogus returns and disbursing more than $43 million. That’s another reason these strange theories persist, and have begun to leach out of the sovereign network and into the general population: Sometimes, improbably, they work.

2. ‘THEY JUST WENT BERSERK’

Mr. Morton was born in 1958, and his comfortable childhood in Northern California was a tutorial in how to make a sales pitch. His mother, Maureen Kennedy Salaman, was — as San Francisco magazine once described her — a “millionaire evangelical alternative-medicine fanatic” who promoted questionable cancer treatments.

She was also a member of the John Birch Society, the far-right group known for its paranoid anticommunism, and she stockpiled beans, grains and ammunition in case of a Russian invasion. In

1984, she was chosen as the vice-presidential nominee for the Populist Party, a favorite of white supremacists. (Its presidential candidate the following cycle was the former Ku Klux Klan grand wizard David Duke.) In her acceptance speech, she warned the crowd: "We're up against the most evil and powerful conspiracy the world has ever known."

When Mr. Morton reached adulthood, he sold unorthodox beliefs from behind a suburban-dad veneer: a flop of dark hair, a round, clean-shaven face, and a button-down-and-khakis wardrobe. He was charismatic but also childlike, friends said, his ego easily bruised. He branded himself an investigative reporter within the U.F.O. world, and in the 1990s, when Mr. Morton appeared on "The Montel Williams Show," he made outrageous claims — more than 100 alien species had visited Earth! — with the certainty of a Nobel laureate. "I got close enough to one of these things that was floating around in the desert to actually get my face burned by it," he said.

Even other U.F.O. enthusiasts considered him a kook, but Mr. Morton's fans didn't care. The truth was out there — and Sean David Morton had it. Branding himself a prophet, he plumbed the new-age convention circuit alongside specialists in animal telepathy, chakras, hauntings, angelic gemstone messages and the afterlife. Near the end of the millennium, at a convention in Las Vegas, a blue-eyed, reddish-haired woman approached him. Back in Utah, Melissa Thomson had grown up in a Mormon home and married at 22; she worked in banking and, in her spare time, doted on her pedigreed cats, even serving as treasurer of the local Cat Fanciers group. The "Coast to Coast" program was her escape, and she spent hours fan-girling over Mr. Morton, a frequent guest.

At the Las Vegas convention, Ms. Thomson apparently had one goal: to meet her idol. "It was love at first sight," Mr. Morton said. She soon left her husband and joined Mr. Morton in Southern California. Her oldest brother, Robert, told me, "The more we found out, the more we warned Melissa that he is just not a decent person at all. But he promised her movie roles; they'll inherit Mommy's home in Atherton, her condo in Tahoe. All she could see was dollars." When they got married, her family refused to attend.

(Through her lawyer, Ms. Morton declined to comment. Mr. Morton did not respond to multiple requests for comment, although he said on YouTube last fall that The New York Times was conducting a "massive smear campaign" against him. Unless otherwise noted, all of his quotes in this article are from court records.)

The Mortons lived in Hermosa Beach, a surf spot about 20 miles from downtown Los Angeles. Next to its mini-palaces, their oatmeal-colored apartment building resembled servants' quarters, but it was a short stroll to the Pacific Ocean. Mr. Morton welcomed his new wife's bushy-tailed Norwegian forest cats — when a new litter arrived, more than a dozen scampered around the apartment — and in turn she oversaw the administrative side of being Sean David Morton. He shilled conspiracy fiction ("The Dark Prophet — Veil of the Anti-Christ"); CDs ("Everything You Wanted to Know About the Future Vol. 2"); a $65 newsletter with thousands of subscribers ("TOMORROW'S HEADLINES TODAY!").

Either this wasn't particularly lucrative, or it wasn't lucrative enough to replicate Mr. Morton's childhood wealth. From the outside, it was hard to tell. "He was always asking me to try and help him to do something so that he could raise some money," said Susan Shumsky, a fellow fixture on the new-age circuit. "Like, 'Let's do a trip to Peru so I can have some money. Let's do a tele-seminar so that I can make some money.' " Ms. Morton's pedigreed kittens, which sold for hundreds of dollars each, apparently kept them solvent. At various points, she also dog-walked and worked at Disneyland. Their friend Will Chappell said, "It was him leading the charge, him leading the family. She did what was necessary to accomplish his goals."

Early in their relationship, a website called UFO Watchdog — "Exposing the Parasites, Delusional Personalities, Morons and Frauds Currently Clouding the UFO Issue" — dismantled much of Mr. Morton's official biography. Mr. Morton sued; the case was dismissed. But in an email included in the case file, Ms. Morton waved off the findings: "I would only be concerned if Sean DIDN'T have critics. Some of the greatest people in history have had people attacking them at every step. It just means that Sean is doing something right and trying to make a difference in the world."

By 2006, the couple was expecting a windfall. Ms. Salaman was in poor health; when she died, Mr. Morton assumed he'd inherit some of his mother's fortune. But their relationship, already frosty, iced over in her final weeks. Ms. Salaman didn't even want her son and his wife to visit. She cut them both out of her will, even as she kept a $100,000 trust for her Great Dane, Duke.

"They just both went berserk," Ms. Morton's brother recalled. "It's just been scam after scam after scam."

3. A DEPOSIT FROM THE GOVERNMENT FOR HALF A MILLION DOLLARS

While the sovereign citizen movement is inherently not organized, some members of the firmament become known as gurus, and are vectors for spreading the ideology. Mr. Morton often lectured at the Living Temple, a new age shop just south of Hermosa Beach. The owner favored a black T-shirt with five flying saucers and the admonition "KEEP LOOKING UP," and yoga music ommed through a clutter of apothecary bottles, bags of herbal something, miracle-cleanse guidebooks and crop-circle DVDs.

One day, most likely in 2008, a man named Brandon Adams started showing up. Like Mr. Morton, he was a budding sovereign amplifier — but he was so much younger that his untucked button-downs looked like an attempt at playing dress-up. His family ran a local tax-prep business. "His whole thing was the banks," Mr. Morton said later. "What he considered the great criminal conspiracy between the Internal Revenue Service and the banking cartels." Mr. Morton quickly got him a speaking slot.

Some of Mr. Adams's talks were recorded. Pacing in front of a few dozen people, scribbling phrases and stick figures on a whiteboard, he wove a dark tale. The secret bankruptcy. The people-as-collateral. Then, a twist: The banks were skimming money from — or "fractionalizing" — every transaction we make. He told the group they could reclaim the funds via Form 1099-OID.

From a folding chair, Mr. Morton — looking grayer and rounder than during his "Montel Williams" days — asked Mr. Adams if anyone had really gotten a big refund that way. Yes, Mr. Adams said. "The funny thing is, watch how quiet people start to get when they're not so sure about the process and they do start getting the returns." Laughter. "They've got that mentality: 'I'm not going to say I just got two hundred and fifty grand.' "

The audience lapped it up. This was America during the financial crisis: The banks had been bailed out, but not homeowners, and the era of Tea Party rallies and Occupy Wall Street encampments was imminent. It wasn't too much of a leap to suspect that Washington was in cahoots with the likes of J.P. Morgan. Mr. Adams's Living Temple talks drew large enough crowds that he moved to a bigger venue and sold private coaching for $200 an hour. "It became a movement, really," Mr. Morton said. (Mr. Adams did not respond to multiple requests for comment.)

In the spring of 2009, under Mr. Adams's tutelage, the Mortons tried the OID scheme themselves. Mr. Morton filed four years of returns — from 2005 to 2008 — and claimed nearly $4 million in refunds. His wife filed a 2007 return and claimed about $12,000. "I never, ever, ever in any of this thought that I was breaking a law," Mr. Morton later said. "I thought that this was the law." His faith was bolstered when, that April, he got a refund for one of his returns: a direct deposit to their Washington Mutual account of $480,322.55.

4. RICH PEOPLE FIND LOOPHOLES. WHY NOT US?

In 2010, the Securities and Exchange Commission went after the Mortons for a different scheme — one with no connection to sovereign ideology. Mr. Morton had used his unconventional celebrity a few years earlier to begin an investment club, where he would channel his psychic powers into predicting foreign currency markets. It's a risky type of trading, but Mr. Morton bragged that his forecasts were so accurate that even Henry Paulson, then the Treasury secretary, relied on them.

After hearing Mr. Morton promote the fund on "Coast to Coast," a man from Washington State invested $217,000. An elderly New York woman parted with $20,000. "He's promising the stars," recalled Tim Saunders, an Alaska electrician who poured in his life savings of $135,000. "Yeah, my greed came out, and I felt I needed more, and quickly." In all, more than 100 people invested $6 million. Mr. Morton sank only half of it into foreign-currency trading — nearly all of which he lost. At least $240,000 was funneled to a nonprofit the Mortons set up, and authorities don't know where the rest is. In 2013, the S.E.C. won an $11.5 million judgment against him. (Ms. Morton was a relief defendant, meaning she was accused only of profiting from the scheme.)

The Mortons filed for bankruptcy, but repeatedly misled the government — for instance, when they claimed not to have bank accounts. A court eventually denied their discharge, meaning they couldn't get rid of their debt. They were also tossed out of their beach-adjacent apartment. "Bottom line," Ms. Morton told the bankruptcy trustee one day, "I just want to be able to get a decent job, have a nice place to live, pay my taxes, and just have my life back."

It was around this time that the Mortons turned to hawking the debt-erasing sovereign scheme known as the "bond process." Over two years, they helped people around the country send nearly two dozen fake bonds to the I.R.S., Quicken Loans, PennyMac, Bank of America, Chase Bank and the treasurer's office in Contra Costa County, California. Early in 2015, Barbara Lavender, the woman whose husband met Mr. Morton at a U.F.O. conference, gave him a call.

Ms. Lavender is 61 and a front-desk clerk at an adult school. When I met her last year in Hemet, Calif., nearly 90 parched miles east of Los Angeles, her ranch-style home was trimmed in red Christmas lights.

We chatted at her kitchen table, with her 14-year-old dog, Remy, curled at our feet. She explained that when she spoke to Mr. Morton over the phone, he avoided talking about sovereign ideology. Instead, he said she could purchase a portion of a bond that he held — and almost magically make her educational loan disappear.

To wipe out her $70,000 balance, he suggested Ms. Lavender should send him $2,500, or less than 4 percent of what she owed. She and her husband believed Mr. Morton had discovered the sort of workaround rich people find. "You know," she testified later. "You hear it all the time: 'wealthy with tax loopholes,' and that kind of thing."

The bond looked authentically bureaucratic, with a formal scalloped border. It was really certificate paper from Office Depot. The accompanying paperwork said that the student loan company was entitled to be paid back from a fund that, in reality, the United States taps to help stabilize foreign currencies. Mr. Morton said he warned Ms. Lavender: "Look, I don't know if this is going to work. I'm not a lawyer." He added, "It's all going to depend on whether or not they accept it."

A month after the Mortons mailed the bond package, Ms. Lavender checked her educational loan balance, saw it hadn't budged and wrote Ms. Morton an email. She didn't get a response. Ms. Lavender sent follow-up after follow-up. "This is beginning to feel increasingly more like a scam," she wrote that October, "where we were bilked out of hard-earned money we did not have to spare."

Ms. Morton finally replied and said she'd been recovering from knee surgery. Ms. Lavender sent an almost apologetic response. Her attention was elsewhere — her husband had died suddenly from a brain mass. "Once you hear from Sean, can you let me know what he thinks we should do next?" she wrote. "With my husband gone, this debt is now an even greater burden for me as he was the main breadwinner."

Nothing came of the exchange. That winter, two men in jackets showed up at Ms. Lavender's home and questioned her about the Mortons, the bond process, the outcome. Afterward, Ms. Lavender took one of their business cards to her nephew, who works for the local sheriff's office. Yes, he reassured her. They really are from the I.R.S.

5. THE CONSPIRA-SEA CRUISE

On Jan. 31, 2016, a nearly 200-foot-tall, white-and-blue cruise ship called the Ruby Princess docked at the Port of Los Angeles. About 100 guests on board had paid $3,000 each for what was marketed as the Conspira-Sea Cruise — a weeklong jaunt through Mexican waters and American paranoia, from "Vaccinations: Do You Really Know What's Coming Through That Needle?" to "Conspiracy to Steal Your Body and Soul." As the Mortons prepared to disembark, they were arrested by federal agents.

After years of digging by I.R.S. investigators, the Mortons faced a suite of charges related to their tax filings and fake bonds. Once off the Ruby Princess, where Mr. Morton had led a workshop called "From Fascism to Freedom," they were separated, patted down and asked what medications they took. Mr. Morton said to ask Melissa about his. An agent did. "Cyanide," she said, seething. On the way to jail, she added, "Do me a favor and tell Sean this: 'Thank you and I'll see you in the next life.' "

Their trial began just before Tax Day, 2017. The prosecution told a simple story of greed. "I submit the I.R.S. was a slot machine," one prosecutor, Valerie Makarewicz, said. "Keep hitting spin. Keep playing until you hit that jackpot." The same day the Mortons got their $480,322.55 refund, she said, they went to the bank and drained nearly all of their account. Once the I.R.S. realized its mistake and tried to recoup the money, the Mortons filed two more rounds of bogus returns and a set of fake bonds.

Ms. Morton's lawyer presented a good-faith defense. She was under the thrall of sovereign gurus, he said, "people who kind of strutted back and forth on the stage with an answer for everything." He showed the jury 37 pages of perfect-cursive notes Ms. Morton took at a Brandon Adams lecture. "In this courtroom, it's obviously nonsense. But at that time, people believed it, and Melissa Morton believed it."

Mr. Morton represented himself. "I'm not a rapist, a thug, a war criminal," he said during his opening statement. "I didn't run a Nazi concentration camp and murder millions of children."

Serving as his own lawyer also meant he cross-examined witnesses. "Are you familiar with the bankruptcy of the United States in 1933?" he asked the government's fraud expert. It was a reference to the sovereign conspiracy theory.

"No," the witness said. "I'm not."

During his closing argument, on the trial's fourth day, Mr. Morton told the jury about the Norwegian forest cats. Earlier in the week, he said, he and his wife tried to save a premature kitten. They stayed up late, swaddled her in cloth, fed her milk with an eye dropper. The kitten died anyway. Ask yourselves, he implored the jurors, "Do we send these nice people who care for kittens and raise cats to jail forever?" The panel deliberated for two hours. When they returned, Ms. Morton greeted them with a hopeful smile. The verdict: guilty on all counts. She fainted.

Around this time, other prominent sovereigns were facing a reckoning. A court had permanently barred Mr. Adams from preparing tax returns or promoting the OID scheme; he ended up in prison for peddling fake money orders. Another guru on the Conspira-Sea Cruise named Winston Shrout (workshop: "Conspiracy of the Court System") was awaiting trial in Oregon.

Mr. Morton's sentencing was set for that June. But when the 11 a.m. hearing started, he didn't show.

6. A POST-ECLIPSE, POOLSIDE BUST

Agents spotted him that afternoon outside a Domino's in Hermosa Beach, a gray hood and sunglasses shrouding much of his face. He hopped in his white Ford Escape and headed south. The next morning, he tweeted a plea for donations: "Melissa (and the cats) need help relocating."

Two months passed. Mr. Morton resurfaced via video on a friend's online talk show, "Project Camelot" ("Getting the Truth Out One Whistleblower at a Time"). His hair was mussed, as if he'd been startled awake, and he wore a headset, a black V-neck and dark-rimmed glasses that he took on and off.

His version of "hello" was ripping his judge and prosecutors as "the biggest gang of criminals you're ever going to see." Soon, he turned his attention to the impending solar eclipse. "This is one of the biggest turning points in American history!" he said. The video clocked more than 40,000 views. It was vintage Sean David Morton, which is to say it was impossible to tell what, if anything, he believed.

I once asked Will Chappell, who has known the Mortons for more than a decade, whether they were actual sovereign dogmatists. He said, "She definitely believed in the story that Sean was telling. I believe that Sean believed in the story that he was telling. A little bit, I believed in it." And now, after their convictions? "Melissa, of course, knowing what she knew now, she would have been gone a long time ago. I think Sean would have still done what he did. He still thinks he just missed a step."

The solar eclipse took place in August, the week after Mr. Morton's on-the-lam interview. Though Ms. Morton promised the court she would have no contact with her fugitive husband, the couple rendezvoused at a hotel just outside Palm Springs. That morning, after the moon briefly blotted out the sun, Mr. Morton was lounging poolside in swim trunks, purple mountains arrayed above him, eclipse glasses at his side. An I.R.S. agent walked up. It was over.

At their sentencing, Ms. Morton distanced herself from him. "I am a living embodiment of 'love is blind,' " she wrote to the judge. "If I ever questioned the teachings and processes by others, I was told, who was I to question others who were far smarter than I? There were thousands of attendees to the workshops and seminars. It was so convincing, well-organized and very believable. How could thousands of people be wrong?" She was sentenced to two years in prison and has filed an appeal. Behind bars, she passed time taking classes — résumé-writing, watercolor-painting, embroidery — and watching the Food Network; she was recently transferred to a halfway house. Emails posted on the Project Camelot site suggest she and her husband are still in touch.

Mr. Morton was sentenced to six years in prison. He's representing himself on appeal, and in court papers he argued that he'd been "improperly profiled" as a "terrorist sovereign citizen." On Project Camelot, he's unrepentant — even sharing a pardon request he said he sent to President Trump.

"It's because of my work in RADIO and TV INVESTIGATIVE JOURNALISM that DEEP STATE forces within the D.O.J. put my wife and I in prison for YEARS!" he wrote. Of course, he had a suggestion for how to correct this injustice: donate to his PayPal account.

CHAPTER 2

Anti-Abortion Extremists

There are few issues as divisive in American society as that of abortion. Pro-life activists assert that life begins at conception and argue that abortion equates to murder, creating a deeply felt moral imperative to stop abortions at all costs at any stage of pregnancy. On the other side, pro-choice activists defend legalized access to abortion services and seek to protect a woman's right to choose when and whether to carry a pregnancy to term. The articles in this section trace the actions of anti-abortion activists, ranging from protests and political lobbying to violence.

Tracing the Path of a Hard-Line Foe of Abortion

BY JAMES RISEN | NOV. 6, 1998

WASHINGTON, NOV. 5 — In July 1988, when Randall Terry drove through the night from his home in Binghamton, N.Y., to Atlanta to start the series of anti-abortion protests that would finally put his new hard-line group, Operation Rescue, onto America's front pages, James Charles Kopp was in the van riding alongside him, said former leaders of Operation Rescue.

And when Mr. Terry was arrested on the first day of Operation Rescue's "Siege of Atlanta," Mr. Kopp followed him into jail, said the leaders, who spoke on the condition of anonymity. Along with more than 100 other Operation Rescue members, according to some people who were there, Mr. Kopp remained in jail for 40 days and adhered to Mr. Terry's orders not to give a real name to the police or courts.

After his release, Mr. Kopp returned to Operation Rescue's Binghamton headquarters, and was there working alongside Mr. Terry as the group's power and influence in the anti-abortion movement surged in late 1988 and 1989, according to the former leaders of Operation Rescue.

Now, Mr. Kopp is being sought by Federal and local law enforcement authorities for questioning as a material witness in the murder of an obstetrician who performed abortions in the Buffalo region. The authorities also say he may have information that will help solve four other sniper attacks on doctors who performed abortions in Canada and upstate New York. Some abortion-rights groups are seizing on Mr. Kopp's role in Operation Rescue to raise new questions about the connections between the recent anti-abortion violence and the hard-line anti-abortion protest groups that burst onto the national scene in the late 1980's.

For years, the Federal Bureau of Investigation and the Justice Department have looked in vain for evidence to determine whether a national conspiracy might be behind a series of clinic bombings and shootings of doctors and other clinic staff members that began in the early 1990's. A Federal grand jury in Alexandria, Va., that looked into conspiracy allegations was disbanded without finding a national underground.

But some Federal law enforcement officials say they hope that Mr. Kopp may help provide such a link. The announcement that law enforcement officials are looking for him was made as Attorney General Janet Reno has prepared to revive an interagency task force to look once again for possible conspiracies behind anti-abortion crimes.

"This is the first time that we have had so many connections between the violence and these groups like Operation Rescue that we have been concerned about for so long," said Ann Glazier, director of clinic defense for Planned Parenthood.

Federal law enforcement officials and the authorities say Mr. Kopp is not now a suspect in the sniper attack on Oct. 23 that killed the obstetrician, Dr. Barnett A. Slepian near Buffalo. But they say Mr. Kopp's car was seen near Dr. Slepian's home in Amherst, N.Y., in the weeks before the doctor was shot.

One day after issuing a warrant for Mr. Kopp's arrest as a material witness, law enforcement officials from at least 10 agencies spanning the United States and Canadian border still had not located Mr. Kopp today. But law enforcement officials said that they were pursuing many tips, including about 400 that have poured into the F.B.I.'s information line: (800) 281-1184.

Police have looked at photographs of abortion protesters and clinic workers in Buffalo and around the country, and they are also reviewing hundreds of hours of videotapes of demonstrations in search of Mr. Kopp's face.

At this point, officials consider the shooting of Dr. Slepian to be connected to three attacks in Canada and one in Rochester on doctors who provide abortions. The five attacks, all since 1994, occurred in the weeks leading up to Nov. 11, Veterans Day — called Remembrance Day in Canada — a holiday that some anti-abortion groups regard as a memorial day for unborn children. But the attacks were spread over four years and 3,000 miles, from Vancouver, British Columbia, to Buffalo.

As is the case with many early veterans of Operation Rescue, Mr. Kopp was transformed into a hard-core anti-abortion militant in jail in Atlanta in 1988, according to many people who were in jail with him and who insisted on anonymity. It was while he was in Atlanta's Key Road Detention Facility that Mr. Kopp took the nickname "Atomic Dog," which he used so that he could follow Mr. Terry's orders and not give the authorities his true identity.

Kept separate from the general jail population and housed together as a group, the Operation Rescue members underwent an extraordinary period of personal bonding. During their days in jail, Mr. Terry and others led all-day prayer services as their followers huddled around, and many Operation Rescue veterans later described the experience in spiritual terms.

Some who were there have described their time in Key Road as an addictive experience, one that turned at least a few into full-time protesters who ultimately drifted into a new and militant anti-abortion subculture. The anonymously written Army of God manual surfaced as a guide for extremists on how to make bombs and perform other acts of anti-abortion violence, and its acknowledgments are full of nicknames and coded references to people and events known only to those who were involved with Operation Rescue in Atlanta and to the group's experience in jail at Key Road. Mr. Kopp's nickname, "Atomic Dog," is listed prominently.

Along with Mr. Kopp, others who were in jail in Atlanta and who eventually drifted into anti-abortion extremism include Shelley Shannon, later convicted in the 1993 shooting of a doctor who performed abortions in Wichita, Kan.; John Arena, later convicted in a series of acid attacks on abortion clinics, and the Rev. Norman Weslin, a Roman Catholic priest who later founded and led the "Lambs of Christ."

Operation Rescue veterans say that Mr. Kopp became close to Father Weslin in jail in Atlanta and, after working for a time at Operation Rescue headquarters and later with a group of anti-abortion advocates in Pittsburgh, he became closely associated with the Lambs of Christ.

The Lambs of Christ was one of the first of a new brand of anti-abortion groups in the late 1980's and early 1990's to use Kryptonite locks to attach themselves to cars to make it more difficult for them to be moved by the police. After being arrested, the members of the Lambs of Christ refused to cooperate with the police or the courts, going completely limp so that they had to be carried by the police and prison guards.

The Lambs of Christ have been active in Vermont, near Mr. Kopp's last known address in St. Albans, according to the former leaders of Operation Rescue and members of other anti-abortion groups.

Eventually, Mr. Kopp joined others who traveled to Europe to conduct clinic blockades, but several Operation Rescue veterans insist he has not maintained contact with current or former leaders of Operation Rescue for several years.

Shift in Virginia on Abortion Bill

BY SABRINA TAVERNISE | FEB. 22, 2012

GOV. BOB MCDONNELL of Virginia backed down on Wednesday on a bill requiring women to have a vaginal ultrasound before undergoing an abortion. It was a sudden change of position for a conservative governor who is viewed as having political ambitions on the national stage.

The bill had drawn intense national attention in recent days, with a large protest by women's health groups over the weekend and spoofs on left-leaning television shows.

In a political year that was supposed to be all about the economy, this was the second instance in a month in which a public outcry organized in part by women's health advocates through social media caused a reversal on the issue of abortion.

The governor's decision not to support the bill capped several days of brinkmanship in which opponents of the measure lobbied furiously against it, galvanizing opposition by drawing on the image of male lawmakers mandating a procedure that requires inserting a probe into the vagina. One Democrat was prompted to denounce it as a "rape" bill.

Opponents presented what they said were 33,000 signatures protesting the measure. At the same time, the mostly Republican supporters in the legislature kept putting off debate on the measure, raising suspicions that the governor might be balking.

Finally, on Wednesday afternoon, Mr. McDonnell, a rising star in the Republican Party who is often talked about as a candidate for vice president, told Republican delegates to make changes that softened the requirements in the legislation. Some political analysts speculated that the decision was made with an eye to a broader national audience that might not look favorably on the passage of such a conservative bill.

This month the Susan G. Komen for the Cure foundation yielded to pressure by affiliates and women's rights advocates and reversed its decision to largely end decades of partnership with Planned Parenthood.

In Virginia, in a written statement issued minutes before the House of Delegates was to debate the bill on Wednesday afternoon, Mr. McDonnell said that after discussion with doctors, lawyers and legislators, he had concluded that amendments were needed. He called for changes stipulating that the ultrasound be abdominal rather than vaginal. A doctor would be required to offer the next level of ultrasound, most often vaginal, but a woman would be free to reject it.

"Mandating an invasive procedure in order to give informed consent is not a proper role for the state," the governor said in the statement.

The Family Foundation, a strong backer of the ultrasound bill, made reference to the Komen decision in a note to supporters blasting Mr. McDonnell's reversal, saying that it was "extremely disappointed in this outcome," particularly, it said, "given the strong pro-life credentials of this governor."

The change — which passed the House in a vote of 65 to 32 — softens the bill considerably, but did not abolish the requirement that women have an ultrasound. If it is signed into law, Virginia would become the 10th state to require such procedures, though the requirement has been stayed by court rulings in two states, Oklahoma and North Carolina.

Specifically, the bill's new wording would require a doctor to offer the woman a different type of ultrasound if the fetus is not viewable through an abdominal screening, but not require her to have one.

That opponents of the bill were successful in getting the language softened was a major success for them, particularly considering that vaginal ultrasounds are often administered before abortions anyway. A spokeswoman for Planned Parenthood said the group routinely includes ultrasounds "as part of the thorough medical practice of abortion care," and gives the woman the option of viewing the image. But the group said a legal requirement that women undergo such a

LUKE SHARRETT FOR THE NEW YORK TIMES

A George Washington impersonator prayed Wednesday outside the legislative chamber as debate on the bill continued.

screening was politically motivated and "is the very definition of government intrusion."

Supporters of the bill hoped such a requirement would lead some women to change their minds about having abortions, as vaginal ultrasounds usually show detailed images. Many women's advocates called the bill an effort to shame women and said it intruded on their privacy.

Republicans, for their part, said the bill had been blown out of perspective by Democrats and liberal groups. State Senator Richard Black said that he participated in a call-in event on Wednesday morning with hundreds of constituents and that just one mentioned the ultrasound bill.

Abortion legislation was a "tiny part" of the larger body of hundreds of bills in play in the legislature, State Senator Steve Martin said. "It's simply not a primary focus," he said. "It only appears to be because people call me from New York newspapers acting as if it's some big deal."

Democrats savored their victory, giving a news conference after the House debate, but said they were hoping the bill would still be killed.

"This is definitely a retreat for the governor," said State Senator Janet Howell, a Democrat from Northern Virginia. "The national spotlight and ridicule has had an impact. The Republicans are scrambling for an out."

But there was some concern among Democrats over a companion bill in the State Senate that has language identical to that in the old version. It is unlikely Senate Republicans would openly defy the governor and pass that bill, but Democrats said they were watching closely.

Besides, they said, the watered-down bill is still objectionable. "It's still putting up a barrier to a woman trying to exercise her constitutional right," said Delegate Charniele Herring, a Democrat.

In yet another twist, the Republican sponsor of the Senate bill, Jill Vogel, said she would withdraw the legislation altogether, though it was not clear whether the rules would allow her to do so after its passage.

Delegate Bob Marshall, a Republican who had supported the bill, said the companion measure, which is due to be voted on as early as Thursday in a Senate committee, might not clear that hurdle, raising the specter of complete collapse of the ultrasound bill and giving Mr. McDonnell a way out of having to sign it.

"This is a high-stakes game," Mr. Marshall said. "Everything is on a razor's edge."

Most political analysts agreed that Mr. McDonnell was seeking to defuse an embarrassing and unmanageable situation — especially at a moment when he seems to be shifting his gaze to a national, and more centrist, audience.

"Pragmatism trumped ideology today," said Daniel Palazzolo, a professor or political science at the University of Richmond.

ERIK ECKHOLM and **JENNIFER PRESTON** contributed reporting.

Senate Candidate Provokes Ire With 'Legitimate Rape' Comment

BY JOHN ELIGON AND MICHAEL SCHWIRTZ | AUG. 19, 2012

KANSAS CITY, MO. — In an effort to explain his stance on abortion, Representative Todd Akin, the Republican Senate nominee from Missouri, provoked ire across the political spectrum on Sunday by saying that in instances of what he called "legitimate rape," women's bodies somehow blocked an unwanted pregnancy.

Asked in an interview on a St. Louis television station about his views on abortion, Mr. Akin, a six-term member of Congress who is backed by Tea Party conservatives, made it clear that his opposition to the practice was nearly absolute, even in instances of rape.

"It seems to me, from what I understand from doctors, that's really rare," Mr. Akin said of pregnancies from rape. "If it's a legitimate rape, the female body has ways to try to shut that whole thing down. But let's assume that maybe that didn't work or something: I think there should be some punishment, but the punishment ought to be of the rapist, and not attacking the child."

The comments, made during an interview with KTVI-TV that was posted on Sunday on the station's Web site, provoked howls of outrage from Democrats and women's rights organizations. Senator Claire McCaskill, the Democrat who will face Mr. Akin in the November election, immediately took to Twitter with a blunt response. "As a woman & former prosecutor who handled 100s of rape cases," she wrote, "I'm stunned by Rep Akin's comments about victims this AM."

Mr. Akin quickly backtracked from his taped comments, saying he "misspoke."

"In reviewing my off-the-cuff remarks, it's clear that I misspoke in this interview, and it does not reflect the deep empathy I hold for the thousands of women who are raped and abused every year," Mr. Akin, who has a background in engineering and is a member of the House science committee, said in a statement. "I recognize that abortion, and particularly in the case of rape, is a very emotionally charged issue. But I believe deeply in the protection of all life, and I do not believe that harming another innocent victim is the right course of action."

The Republican presidential ticket of Mitt Romney and Paul Ryan was quick to distance itself from Mr. Akin's remarks.

"Governor Romney and Congressman Ryan disagree with Mr. Akin's statement," the campaign said. "A Romney-Ryan administration would not oppose abortion in instances of rape."

Ms. McCaskill, who is seeking a second term in the Senate, is seen as one of the most politically vulnerable Democratic incumbents on the ballot this fall, beset by her ties to President Obama and tens of millions in dollars spent against her by outside advocacy groups.

Mr. Akin, 65, won the Senate Republican primary this month with strong support from Missouri's religious conservatives. But he was also helped by Ms. McCaskill, whose campaign spent nearly $2 million on ads portraying Mr. Akin as ultraconservative. It was a clear attempt to bolster his candidacy among more conservative primary voters while gambling that the independents and moderate Republicans needed to win the election would be turned off by his views on social issues.

Political observers have said Ms. McCaskill's best chance of defending her seat, and perhaps the Democrats' majority in the Senate, is to paint her opponent as extreme.

"Claire McCaskill will certainly amplify this remark, make sure everybody's heard it," said Dave Robertson, a professor of political science at the University of Missouri-St. Louis.

Mike Talboy, the Democratic minority leader in the Missouri Legislature, said that he had spoken to members of both parties about Mr. Akin's comments and had found uniform outrage.

"Nobody has defended him," Mr. Talboy said. "That, I think, is pretty telling."

Brian Walsh, the communications director for the National Republican Senatorial Committee, declined to address what impact Mr. Akin's comments might have on the Senate race. But he wrote in an e-mail that "Congressman Akin did the right thing by quickly correcting the record and acknowledging that he misspoke." He said the election would be a referendum on Ms. McCaskill's voting record and support for the president's agenda.

If this state is truly aligning itself with more conservative values, some believe that Mr. Akin's comments might actually help him politically.

Jamie Tomek, president of the Missouri branch of the National Organization for Women, who lives in the county where Mr. Akin grew up and says she knows his parents, said she was not surprised by the statement and did not think it would cost him much ahead of the election.

"He is very far right and very likely to make those types of statements," Ms. Tomek said.

JOHN ELIGON reported from Kansas City, and **MICHAEL SCHWIRTZ** from New York. **REBECCA BERG** contributed reporting from Washington.

New Frontiers of Extremism

EDITORIAL | BY THE NEW YORK TIMES | AUG. 20, 2012

REPUBLICANS ARE FRANTICALLY trying to get Representative Todd Akin to drop out of the United States Senate race in Missouri after his remark about abortion and rape, but not because it was offensive and ignorant. They're afraid he might lose and cost them a chance at a Senate majority next year. He would surely be replaced by a Republican who sounds more reasonable but holds similarly extreme views on abortion, immigration, gay rights and the role of government because those are the kinds of candidates the party nominates these days in state after state.

Like many Republicans, including the vice presidential candidate, Paul Ryan, Mr. Akin opposes abortion even when a woman has been raped. But, in an interview that was aired on Sunday, Mr. Akin went further and decided to explain his position by saying that pregnancy rarely results from rape because "if it's a legitimate rape, the female body has ways to try to shut that whole thing down."

His comments betray more than a remarkable unfamiliarity with the human reproductive system. They expose a widely held belief among many fierce abortion opponents that a rape exception will be abused by women whose rapes were not "legitimate." This came up last year, for example, when the Indiana House was debating a stringent abortion restriction and Republicans objected to a rape exception. State Representative Eric Turner said the exception was a "giant loophole" that could be abused by a woman who falsely claimed she had been raped.

The principal difference between Mr. Akin and most other Republican candidates is that they would be more decorous in inventing reasons to strip women of their abortion rights. One of the two candidates Mr. Akin defeated in the Republican primary last week supported the overturn of Roe v. Wade; the other supported a constitutional amendment saying life begins at conception.

All three positions are outside the mainstream of American opinion, but they are pretty much in the dead center of Republican thinking. Mr. Ryan has said he doesn't believe in a rape exception when outlawing abortion, and he worked with Mr. Akin in the House in trying to narrow the definition of rape so Medicaid would pay for fewer abortions of poor women. Mitt Romney says he supports a rape exception, but many of the politicians he has invited to speak at next week's Republican convention disagree with him.

As several recent Republican primaries demonstrated, the party continues to nominate Tea Party candidates who create increasingly ludicrous definitions of "far right." Ted Cruz, who won the Senate primary in Texas and is all but certain to be elected, favors the closure of the Departments of Energy, Commerce and Education, along with the Transportation Security Administration and, naturally, the I.R.S. He says he is very worried that the United Nations is trying to ban golf courses and paved roads.

Ted Yoho, who won a Congressional primary in northern Florida, wants to abolish the income tax and replace it with a sales tax, believes life begins at conception and considers gun ownership a "birthright."

The Republicans pressuring Mr. Akin to leave the race didn't seem to care when he said he doubted that Medicare was constitutional or warned that same-sex marriage would destroy civilization. If the party wanted to end these kinds of embarrassing moments, it could return to the days when it nominated mainstream candidates.

Why Abortion Is Not Like Other Issues

COLUMN | BY DAVID LEONHARDT | JULY 13, 2013

WASHINGTON — It's no secret that the Republican Party differs with public opinion on some of the day's biggest issues. Be it on gun control, immigration, same-sex marriage or high-end taxes, the party has advocated a position at odds with the beliefs of most Americans, polls show. This disconnect has helped Democrats win the popular vote in five of the last six presidential elections.

The recent acrimony in the Texas Legislature, with Republicans pushing a restrictive abortion bill, seems to provide a new example. It has allowed Democrats to cast Republicans, once again, as out of the mainstream.

Yet abortion is not quite like those other issues.

On abortion rights, both parties have a claim on public opinion. Maybe more to the point, both can make a strong case that the other party has an extreme view. Abortion is the relatively rare issue in which the cliché is true: public opinion does actually rest about midway between the parties' platforms.

As a result, abortion occupies a different place in the Republicans' continuing struggle about whether and how to modernize their party. On a set of other social issues related to the increasingly diverse American population, the party clearly faces big challenges. The two fastest-growing ethnic groups — Latinos and Asian-Americans — are decidedly liberal. Younger white adults also lean left. My colleague Nate Silver estimates that in the year 2020, ballot initiatives on same-sex marriage would pass in 44 states, based on the direction of public opinion. The only six states where the initiatives would likely fail are solidly Republican Southern states.

Anyone following the Texas abortion debate through social media could easily imagine that the issue belongs in the same category. During her filibuster against the bill, State Senator Wendy Davis inspired a hashtag — #StandWithWendy — and a Twitter explosion. An often overlooked aspect of social media, however, is that it still skews slightly liberal.

Nationwide, polls consistently show that people are no more "pro choice" than "pro life," when asked to choose a label. More detailed questions yield similar results. And women are no more in favor of abortion rights than men. "Abortion is not heading in either party's direction," says Andrew Kohut of the Pew Research Center.

About 60 percent of Americans favor access to abortion in the first trimester (or first 12 weeks) of pregnancy, but close to 70 percent think it should be illegal in the second trimester, according to Gallup. Likewise, a recent National Journal poll found 48 percent of respondents favoring, and only 44 percent opposing, a House of Representatives bill that would ban abortions after 20 weeks of pregnancy except in cases of rape and incest.

"About 8 in 10 Americans believe abortion is taking a life," said Ed Goeas, president of the Tarrance Group, a Republican polling firm. "What you then have is a discussion about when it is acceptable."

Perhaps the best weapon of abortion rights advocates is their opponents' extremism. The Texas bill, for instance, would close most of the state's abortion providers and ban the procedure after 20 weeks, without exceptions for rape or incest. A clear majority of Americans support such exceptions, as well as those for the health of the mother, polls show.

Ilyse Hogue, president of Naral Pro-Choice America, says that while she is distressed by the recent spate of state laws, she thinks her side will ultimately benefit from the new focus on the issue. Not only do many abortion opponents favor tough restrictions on the practice; they also oppose in vitro fertilization, some forms of contraception and stem-cell research. Ms. Hogue argues that many Americans will find these arguments "wing-nutty."

But supporters of abortion access have their own challenges. The issues on which it's easiest to predict the future of public opinion generally involve individual rights. Over time, rights — suffrage for women and blacks, job opportunities for Irish, Jews, Latinos and other ethnic minorities, marriage for interracial and same-sex couples — tend to expand in the United States.

In the debate over abortion, unlike the debates over immigration and marriage, both sides can easily claim the mantle of individual rights. Supporters can maintain that women deserve the right to make decisions about their bodies at any point in a pregnancy — and that many abortion opponents change their position when facing a real-life decision.

Opponents can counter with increasingly clear images from sonograms, often showing decidedly human forms on the cusp of viability. Opponents can also point to the specter of eugenics: one study has found that prenatal screening caused births of children with Down syndrome to be 49 percent lower than they otherwise would have been, even as medical advances have sharply extended the lives of people with the disorder. When fetuses with Down syndrome are aborted, it is typically after the first trimester.

Those dueling claims probably mean that the debate over abortion is here to stay. As Mr. Kohut notes, polls show that young people — despite their general liberalism — are divided, much as their parents and grandparents have been.

If the issue presents either Republicans or Democrats with a political opportunity, it is one they will both struggle to exploit, given the passionate feelings of their bases. But the opportunity does exist.

Most Americans are uncomfortable with abortion yet believe there are circumstances — and not just a narrow few — when it should be legal. They believe that women should have control over their bodies and also that an abortion is akin to a death. Where they struggle is in deciding when each principle deserves to take priority.

DAVID LEONHARDT is the Washington bureau chief of The New York Times.

Planned Parenthood and the Tinderbox of Abortion Rhetoric

COLUMN | BY EMILY BAZELON | NOV. 30, 2015

ABORTION OPPONENTS HAVE been quick to distance themselves from the Nov. 27 shooting at a Planned Parenthood clinic in Colorado Springs, which left three people dead. The anti-abortion groups lining up to condemn the violence included the Center for Medical Progress, which released videos in July accusing Planned Parenthood of selling fetal parts and tissue. Planned Parenthood denied making sales, saying one of its 700 health centers was being reimbursed for supplying fetal tissue to researchers, who have used fetal cells to produce lifesaving vaccines and treatments. But the doctor caught on camera spoke in graphic medical terms while sipping wine over lunch, and the videos prompted five separate congressional investigations into Planned Parenthood's practices. Testifying before a House committee in October, the group's president, Cecile Richards, said it would continue facilitating the tissue donations, with patients' consent, but stop accepting reimbursements. The Center for Medical Progress called this "an admission of guilt."

In police custody in Colorado Springs, the suspect in the shootings, Robert L. Dear Jr., seemed to refer to the videos when he said "no more baby parts," in response to questions about the shootings. Dear's phrasing, intentionally or otherwise, echoed the declaration of the Republican presidential candidate Senator Ted Cruz in September: "We are now a nation that harvests the body parts of baby boys and girls." A banner at anti-abortion rallies read, "Planned Parenthood sells baby parts." Some of the language was a good deal stronger: Charmaine Yoest, president and chief executive of Americans United for Life, said in September, "Now is the time to hold Planned Parenthood accountable for these atrocities." Another Republican candidate, Carly Fiorina, said on television during a debate that the video showed a fetus with "its heart beating, its leg kicking, while someone says we have to keep it alive to harvest its brain." The video does not actually depict this.

Over the weekend, Democrats and Republicans clashed over the inflamed rhetoric. When Senator Barbara Boxer of California called for an end to "demonizing" Planned Parenthood, Representative Marsha Blackburn of Tennessee told her to "stop playing politics with this tragedy." On Fox, Fiorina picked the same word as Boxer, but turned it against pro-choice advocates. "This is so typical of the left to immediately begin demonizing a messenger because they don't agree with the message," she said.

Before the shooting, abortion opponents like Cruz, Yoest and Fiorina weren't advocating violence, of course. They were calling on Congress to investigate and stop funding Planned Parenthood. The group doesn't receive federal money to pay for abortions; Congress has barred that since 1977 (except in the rare case of rape, incest or saving the life of the mother). But Planned Parenthood receives $450 million in federal funds annually, mostly from Medicaid, to provide health care like birth control and testing for sexually transmitted diseases to low-income women.

Abortion opponents have every right to lobby to take the funding away, and to use whatever language they choose in doing so. The First Amendment protects them. But that doesn't mean that the killings necessarily came from nowhere, or that no one cautioned that the recent burst of angry accusations carried a physical risk. In September, the F.B.I. warned of an uptick in attacks against abortion facilities, singling out "lone offenders" using tactics "typical of the pro-life extremist movement." After the shooting, Vicki Saporta, president of the National Abortion Federation, said in a statement: "We have seen an unprecedented increase in hate speech and threats against abortion providers. We have been quite worried that this increase in threats would lead to a violent attack like we saw today."

There's a logic to violence at abortion clinics, however twisted. Before he shot and killed Dr. George Tiller, an abortion provider in

Kansas, in 2009, Scott Roeder contributed to a newsletter, Prayer and Action News, which has argued that killing an abortion provider is justifiable homicide. David Leach, publisher of the newsletter, said of Roeder's act, "There is Christian Scripture that would support this." Roeder invoked his religious beliefs at trial and explained, "There was nothing being done, and the legal process had been exhausted, and these babies were dying every day." In March 1993, Randall Terry, leader of the anti-abortion group Operation Rescue, said: "We've found the weak link is the doctor. We're going to expose them," at a rally in southern Florida. A few days later, Dr. David Gunn, an abortion provider, was shot and killed outside his clinic in the state.

The history of opposition to abortion is punctuated by killings — 11 over the years, including the ones in Colorado Springs. In other contexts, we don't shy away from the link between extremism, tinged with religious fervor, and violence. In June, when Dylann Roof was charged with killing nine African-Americans in a Baptist church in Charleston, S.C., his record of racism was part of the news coverage. Many Americans draw a straight line from jihadist promises of martyrdom to radical Muslim terrorism. Opposition to abortion is an issue with cognizable moral claims on both sides. Still, the question is whether it is really more tenuous to connect Dear's decision to open fire at the Colorado Springs clinic and the gruesome accusations against Planned Parenthood.

Abortion is an American tinderbox. A small spark can light a big fire in a country with ample access to guns and far less to mental-health care. In my reporting, I've noticed a sharp rise in the targeting of Planned Parenthood in recent years. It dates to another video, shot in 2011 on hidden camera by the group Live Action and released by the activist Lila Rose, of a woman posing as a prostitute, visiting clinics with a man posing as her pimp. At a New Jersey clinic, a manager suggested the pair could lie to avoid laws requiring the reporting of a minor having sex with an adult. The manager was fired. Still, Republicans in Congress opened investigations of Planned Parenthood that time too, along with the first measure to strip the organization of funding. Then, as now, it was a presidential election season, and denouncing (or defending) Planned Parenthood served as a political ritual. This year, Cruz called for shutting down the government over the issue.

Defunding threats don't have to succeed to make an impact. Among other things, the funding fight reinforces Planned Parenthood's status as "the abortion giant," in Yoest's words, as Jill Lepore pointed out in a history of the organization in The New Yorker. When I interviewed Yoest for an article three years ago, she compared her group's budget with Planned Parenthood's and said, "Just think how different it would be if we had all that money to spend."

On this front, state by state, Yoest's allies are gaining. Over the past year, the journalist Meaghan Winter investigated crisis pregnancy centers, which oppose abortion but advertise free "options counseling," along with pregnancy tests and ultrasounds. Winter found that crisis pregnancy centers now outnumber abortion clinics nationwide by three to one. "Eleven states fund them directly, sometimes with federal funds, and often through programs intended for low-income women and children," she wrote in a recent Times Op-Ed.

Questioned on Sunday about Dear's reference to "no more baby parts," Cruz cited a claim that Dear was registered to vote as a woman and called him a "transgendered leftist activist." There's no more evidence for this characterization than there was for Fiorina's video claims. But it was handy, in the moment. In the past four years, Planned Parenthood's opponents have concluded they can wage political warfare by creating a swirl of negativity around the organization with extreme rhetoric. The most vitriolic of them have marked off an increasingly narrow space for themselves, embracing the language of brutality and violence while disavowing real violence when it occurs.

EMILY BAZELON is a staff writer for the magazine and the Truman Capote fellow at Yale Law School.

An Abortion Ban's Bogus Arguments

EDITORIAL | BY THE NEW YORK TIMES | MAY 14, 2015

FOR THE SECOND TIME in two years, the House voted Wednesday to pass legislation that would ban almost all abortions 20 weeks or more after fertilization. The bill, called the Pain-Capable Unborn Child Protection Act, claims that "an unborn child is capable of experiencing pain at least by 20 weeks after fertilization," though medical evidence does not support this.

Of course, the bill is not really about scientific findings of any sort. It is simply another attempt by conservative Republicans to undercut women's constitutionally protected reproductive rights. A 20-week abortion ban would be a restriction before fetal viability that violates the Supreme Court's ruling in Roe v. Wade.

The House passed a 20-week ban in 2013, but the Senate never voted on it. House Republicans had planned to vote on a 20-week ban again this January, but that was stalled when some Republican members objected to the bill's language prohibiting rape victims from getting an abortion unless they had reported their rape to the police.

The measure gained momentum after The New England Journal of Medicine published a study indicating that a tiny number of babies born at 22 weeks can survive if given intensive medical treatment. Representative Diane Black of Tennessee, one of the bill's sponsors, released a statement last Friday saying, "Science tells us that, after 20 weeks, babies can feel pain and are increasingly able to live outside the womb."

The modified bill now allows rape victims to obtain an abortion if they've received counseling or medical care at least 48 hours before the procedure. It does not make an exception for the health of the mother, as current law requires. It permits an abortion after 20 weeks only if the mother's life is in danger, which could mean a woman with health problems would have to wait until her pregnancy threatened her life.

The bill also lacks an exception for fetal abnormalities, some of which are detectable only late in a pregnancy. It is unlikely to pass the Senate. If it does, the White House has made it clear that President Obama will veto it.

The increasingly onerous restrictions imposed on abortion at the state level may actually be causing some women to delay their procedures into the second trimester and beyond.

One 2013 study found that women who sought abortions after 20 weeks were more than twice as likely as women who sought first-trimester procedures to report that difficulty traveling to a clinic delayed them. They were also more than twice as likely to be delayed by problems with insurance coverage.

Making it hard to get an abortion early in a pregnancy — by restricting the use of health insurance for abortion, closing clinics and mandating waiting periods — and then banning the procedure after 20 weeks would essentially prohibit abortion for those with limited resources. This, of course, is what many Republicans in Congress want, but it would be disastrous for American women and families, especially those who cannot afford to travel long distances or pay for medical procedures out-of-pocket.

Affirmative Action for Reactionaries

OPINION | BY MICHELLE GOLDBERG | MARCH 30, 2018

ALTHOUGH I'M A squishy-hearted liberal, I have a soft spot for dyspeptic reactionaries like H. L. Mencken and V. S. Naipaul, men — they're almost always men — who speak to a dark, misanthropic corner of my soul. Thus I occasionally read Kevin Williamson, a truly vicious but sometimes bracing writer, when he was at National Review.

Where his words resonated with me, it would make me aware of hidden currents of cruelty in my own thinking. I grew up in a conservative rust belt suburb and hated it, and I loathe populist sanctimony that treats my stultifying hometown as more authentically American than the vibrant city I escaped to. So I felt a guilty shudder of satisfaction reading Williamson's vituperative 2016 attack on the dysfunctional small towns that supported Donald Trump. ("If you want to live, get out of Garbutt.")

The way Williamson's contempt spoke to me made me think about how my fury over Trump's rise, and my devotion to cosmopolitanism, was curdling into the very elitism people like me are constantly accused of. The ability to prompt such uncomfortable self-recognition is a good quality in a polemicist. So I almost understand why The Atlantic magazine, seeking to add a provocative right-wing voice to its roster, recently hired Williamson.

That hiring has set off the latest uproar over which conservatives belong in the opinion sections of elite mainstream publications, including, of course, The New York Times. These controversies are, naturally, of particular interest to people who write for opinion sections, and so receive disproportionate media coverage. But there's a broader significance to these recurring fights, because they're about how we decide which views are acceptable at a time of collapsing mainstream consensus. The intellectual implosion of the Republican Party, it turns out, creates challenges for liberals as well as conservatives, because suddenly it's not clear which views a person who aspires to fair-mindedness needs to grapple with.

The progressive objection to Williamson lies in the demeaning ways he's written about poor people, black people, women, and trans people. He described an African-American boy in East St. Louis sticking out his elbows in "the universal gesture of primate territorial challenge." Defiantly using male pronouns in a piece about the trans actress Laverne Cox, Williamson wrote, "Regardless of the question of whether he has had his genitals amputated, Cox is not a woman, but an effigy of a woman." Feminism, he wrote, is a "collection of appetites wriggling queasily together like a bag of snakes." He tweeted that women who have abortions should be hanged, later clarifying that while he has doubts about the death penalty, "I believe that the law should treat abortion like any other homicide."

In some ways I appreciate Williamson's honesty in admitting where his anti-abortion agenda leads. More abortion opponents should be willing to acknowledge that treating abortion as murder necessarily means treating women as murderers. All the same, I understand why many people are furious that the storied Atlantic magazine would give a perch to a man who traffics in crude stereotypes, and who thinks that the nearly one-quarter of American women who have had abortions deserve to die. "Too many men in power don't care," feminist Jessica Valenti wrote in despair. "To them, our lives and freedom are just abstract concepts — things to be debated rather than understood as a given."

The backlash against Williamson, in turn, has occasioned self-pity among some members of the conservative intelligentsia, who feel victimized by a concerted campaign to write them out of mainstream public life. In National Review, Williamson's friend and former colleague David French demanded, "Decide now, progressives, do you want any serious intellectual media space where conservative and progressive ideas clash?"

Personally, I do. But which conservative ideas?

In "Age of Fracture," an intellectual history of the late 20th century, the Princeton professor emeritus Daniel T. Rodgers described how the salience of ideas in American politics took on "new breadth and intensity in the last quarter of the twentieth century. Novel forms of intellectual production and dissemination — more politically oriented think tanks, new journals of scholarly debate and opinion, more argumentatively structured media — now began to move ideas more aggressively into circulation." Ideology was obviously not the only thing that drove politics — money and group interests were, as ever, important. But to understand national politics, you had to understand certain conservative ideas.

Trump put an end to that. The field of ideas has gone from being the ground on which politics are fought to a side in politics, which is why it's so difficult to find serious intellectual Trump defenders. Trump has resentments and interests, but not ideology; he governs more as a postmodern warlord than a traditional party leader. Few things signal the irrelevance of ideas to his presidency like the appointment of John Bolton as national security adviser. Bolton's relentless advocacy of regime change contradicts the isolationism Trump touted during the campaign. Trump called the Iraq war a "disaster"; Bolton is one of few who continue to defend it. Yet Bolton's appointment isn't discordant, because he and Trump are both belligerent bullies, and in this administration stylistic similarities matter more than policy details.

Inasmuch as there are ideas bound up with Trumpism, they are considered too disreputable for most mainstream publications. An opinion section that truly captured the currents of thought shaping our politics today might include Alex Jones, the conspiracy-mad Sandy Hook truther; the white nationalist Richard Spencer; and CliffsNotes fascist Steve Bannon.

Most supporters of liberal democracy, on the right as well as the left, realize that once we treat issues like religious freedom and the desirability of racial equality as matters for debate rather than as first principles, we are lost. But because there's now so little correlation between the political arena and the intellectual one, the question of which conservatives liberals ought to engage becomes subjective and arbitrary.

Williamson was hired at The Atlantic not just for being an energetic writer, but in the name of ideological diversity. "If we are going to host debates, we have to host people who actually disagree with, and sometimes offend, the other side," wrote Atlantic editor in chief Jeffrey Goldberg — no relation — in a memo to his staff. "Kevin will help this cause."

But Williamson, perhaps to his credit, doesn't really represent a "side." His ideas — with their combination of laissez-faire capitalism and harsh moralism — are fairly marginal. If they're going to be defended, they should be defended on their own terms, not as representing an important tendency in our civic life. But on their own terms, they are very hard to defend.

Editors can't escape the fact that, even when they want to broaden the conversation, their choices make a statement about where the parameters of acceptable argument lie. I'd have thought that supporting the execution or mass incarceration of women by the millions would put a writer, even one capable of enjoyably caustic prose, well outside those boundaries. I'd like to hear a serious argument about why it doesn't. Somehow, Williamson's champions don't seem to want to have that debate.

MICHELLE GOLDBERG became an Op-Ed columnist for The New York Times in 2017 and was part of a team that won a Pulitzer Prize in 2018 for public service for reporting on workplace sexual harassment issues. She is the author of three books: "Kingdom Coming: The Rise of Christian Nationalism," "The Means of Reproduction: Sex, Power, and the Future of the World," and "The Goddess Pose: The Audacious Life of Indra Devi, the Woman Who Helped Bring Yoga to the West."

The Outrage Over Kevin Williamson

OPINION | BY BRET STEPHENS | MARCH 30, 2018

DEAR KEVIN,

You *had* the right to remain silent. Now every word you've ever uttered, and every one you ever will, can and will be held against you.

I'm sorry to have to write you, for two reasons. Sorry, first, that you have to endure having your character assailed and assassinated by people who rarely if ever read you and likely never met you. Sorry also that your hiring as a writer for The Atlantic has set off another censorious furor in media circles when surely there are more important subjects on this earth.

Then again, as my colleague Michelle Goldberg noted Friday, the question of what counts in mainstream media as "acceptable argument," and what doesn't, is not a small one. Every society is civilized, or blinkered, by its choice of moral and political taboos. Too many taboos blunt and bury thought. Too few coarsen and cheapen it. Part of the art of culture — and of editing — lies in finding the path between.

The case against you, as best as I can tell, rests on three charges. You think abortion is murder and tweeted — appallingly in my view — that doctors and women should perhaps be hanged for it. You believe "sex is a biological reality" and that gender should not be a choice. And you once boorishly described an African-American boy in East St. Louis, Ill., "raising his palms to his clavicles, elbows akimbo, in the universal gesture of primate territorial challenge."

Oh, another thing: As a NeverTrumper, you're guilty of being insufficiently representative of contemporary conservatism. Had you been a Trumper, doubtless you would have been dismissed as a moron unworthy of the pages of The Atlantic.

Weighed against these charges are hundreds of thousands of words of smart, stylish and often hilarious commentary, criticism and reportage. How many of the people now demanding your firing read your unforgettable description of Steve Mnuchin's "Scrooge McDuck-style sphincter-clenching," or of Anthony Scaramucci's "batty and profane interview in which he reimagined Steve Bannon as a kind of autoerotic yogi"?

Shouldn't great prose and independent judgment count for something? Not according to your critics. We live in the age of guilt by pull-quote, abetted by a combination of lazy journalism, gullible readership, missing context, and technologies that make our every ill-considered utterance instantly accessible and utterly indelible. I jumped at your abortion comment, but for heaven's sake, it was a *tweet*. When you write a whole book on the need to execute the tens of millions of American women who've had abortions, then I'll worry.

We also live in an age — another one — of excommunication. This is ugly because its spirit is illiberal, and odd, because its consequences are negligible. Should The Atlantic foolishly succumb to pressure to rescind your job offer, you'll still be widely read, presumably at National Review. If you're really the barbarian your critics claim, you're already through the gates.

The real question, then, isn't what kinds of arguments are "acceptable." It's what kinds are, or ought to be, acceptable to liberals. In The Huffington Post, one writer proposes that the answer is none. This is the liberalism of the 9-year-old sticking fingers in his ears and saying: *nah-nah-nah-nah-nah*. Anyone still wondering how Donald Trump became president need look no further.

The wiser test of acceptability is whether an argument is thoughtful, thought-provoking and offered in good faith. That holds true even if the views aren't politically representative. Last I checked, you and I were hired as columnists, not party ideologues or demographic segments.

It also holds true whether or not a given opinion is offensive. Offensive to tens of millions of intelligent and morally sincere Americans is the idea that abortion ought to be legal at all, much less in the second or third trimester. If those Americans can make their peace with pro-choice writers like me, the least liberals can do is not make war on pro-life writers like you.

That doesn't mean there ought to be limitless tolerance for every shade of opinion: There are cranks and haters both left and right, and wise editors should not give them a platform. But your critics show bad faith when they treat an angry tweet or a flippant turn of phrase as proof of moral incorrigibility. Let he who is without a bad tweet, a crap sentence or even a deplorable opinion cast the first stone.

Worse, they foreclose the possibility of learning something useful from someone smart. Learning does not require agreement. There's a reason this section of the newspaper is labeled "Opinion," not "Affirmation," "Reinforcement," or "Emotional Crutch." Liberals used to know that. What happened?

My guess is that you'll find working for The Atlantic a discipline and a joy. It's not always easy to write for an audience whose views you rarely share. It's not always fun to hear back from them, either. But the result will be sharper writing by you, a broader understanding for them, and more competition for us. Congrats.

BRET L. STEPHENS joined The New York Times as an Op-Ed columnist in April 2017. His column appears Thursday and Saturday.

Among the Abortion Extremists

OPINION | BY ROSS DOUTHAT | APRIL 7, 2018

A FEW WEEKS AGO, The Washington Post's deputy editorial page editor, Ruth Marcus, wrote two columns explaining why, had either of her children been diagnosed with Down syndrome in utero, she would have accepted the "ghastly" nature of a second-trimester abortion and terminated the pregnancy. She conceded that people with Down syndrome can be happy and fulfilled, that both they and their parents might be understandably disturbed by the way abortion can effectively cull them from the world. But she concluded with self-acknowledged bluntness: "That was not the child I wanted."

I know Marcus a little, having chatted with her amiably a few times many years ago. She seemed like a lovely person, like so many of my pro-choice friends; indeed, people who believe firmly in an absolute or near-absolute right to an abortion are effectively my people in a certain tribal way, given that I'm a Connecticut Yankee raised by Bill Clinton-voting boomers and educated in the modern meritocracy. I like these folks; I think they mean well; I try to listen to their arguments with the respect that the sincere and intelligent deserve.

But I also think that they are deceived by a cruel ideology that has licensed the killing of millions of innocents for almost 50 years. In the language that the respectable use to banish views without rebuttal, I regard them — friends and colleagues and faithful readers — as essentially *extremists*, for whom the distinctive and sometimes awful burdens that pregnancy imposes on women have become an excuse to build a grotesque legal regime in which the most vulnerable human beings can be vacuumed out or dismembered, killed for reasons of eugenics or convenience or any reason at all.

I am sharing these reflections in the context of the latest media war over whether a particular conservative columnist should be hired by a particular establishment publication — in this case Kevin Williamson, a National Review scribe with a brilliant pen and a long paper trail of insults and wild opinions, who was boldly hired by The Atlantic and then quickly jettisoned, after it came to light that he had not only suggested hanging as a penalty for abortion in a since-deleted tweet but also more carefully defended the idea of someday prosecuting women who obtain abortions the way we prosecute other forms of homicide.

From my own anti-abortion perspective, this opinion makes Williamson an extremist as well. When American laws restricted abortion they generally did not impose such penalties, and today's pro-life movement likewise generally rejects the idea of prosecuting women. This position often gets cast as inconsistent by pro-choicers, but I think it represents the incorporation by pro-lifers of the points that my pro-choice friends actually get right — that pregnancy is unique in ways that mitigate culpability and make it unwise to treat abortion like a normal homicide, that the government can only go so far in restriction without becoming a reproductive police state — without making the literally fatal mistake of believing these things also require a civil right to kill your unborn child.

Now: The fact that Williamson is an extremist doesn't change the fact that to hire him for his pen and then fire him for having expressed an extreme opinion was stupid and gutless — akin to hiring Christopher Hitchens and then firing him for antireligious bigotry (and yes, Hitch was a bigot, but worth publishing anyway), or adding Hunter S. Thompson to your masthead and then dropping him because it's pointed out that he writes under the influence of drugs. But still there is a part of me, as someone whose goal is to persuade liberal readers to reconsider their pro-abortion views, that's glad Williamson won't be carrying the pro-life flag at The Atlantic, out of fear that his extremities could make the work of persuasion harder.

Another part of me, though — the more important one — thinks that this is a case study in exactly the problem establishment editors are trying to address by widening their pool of writers: the inability of contemporary liberalism to see itself from the outside, as it looks to the many people who for some reason, class or religion or historical experience, are not fully indoctrinated into its increasingly incoherent mix of orthodoxies.

By this I mean that my pro-choice friends endorsing Williamson's sacking can't see that his extremism is mirrored in their own, in a system of supposedly "moderate" thought that is often blind to the public's actual opinions on these issues, that lionizes advocates for abortion at any stage of pregnancy, that hands philosophers who favor forms of euthanasia and infanticide prestigious chairs at major universities, that is at best mildly troubled by the quietus of the depressed and disabled in Belgium or the near-eradication of Down syndrome in Iceland or the gendercide that abortion brought to Asia, that increasingly accepts unblinking a world where human beings can be commodified and vivisected so long as they're in embryonic form.

All this extremism has its reasons, as those tenured philosophers will be happy to explain. But everyday liberalism is sufficiently muddled between semi-Christian ideas and a utilitarian materialism that mostly the system is defended by euphemism and evasion, and by a failure to imagine oneself as all of us once were: tiny and dependent and hidden, and yet still essentially ourselves.

Williamson, who was put up for adoption in poor-white Texas just before Roe. v. Wade was decided, had personal reasons to make that imaginative leap, and it carried him all the way to an eye-for-an-eye impulse in response. His views are not common among pro-life writers, they rather deliberately give offense, and I have no doubt they would make inter-office events more uncomfortable than, say, my interactions with Ruth Marcus.

But if they are "callous and violent," to use the pursed-lip language of Williamson's firing, they reflect back an essential fact about our respectable reproductive rights regime — which is justified with the hazy theology of individualism, but implemented with lethal violence against the most vulnerable of human bodies every single day.

ROSS DOUTHAT joined The New York Times as an Op-Ed columnist in April 2009.

What Happens When Abortion Is Banned?

OPINION | BY MICHELLE OBERMAN | MAY 31, 2018

THE WORLD OF illegal abortion today looks nothing like the way it did 45 years ago.

When I first visited Chile, in 2008, it was one of a handful of countries in the world that banned abortion in all cases, without exception. Given that hundreds of women a year died from botched illegal abortions in the United States before Roe v. Wade, which legalized the procedure in 1973, I expected to find hospitals in Chile overflowing with dying women. Instead, I found that abortion drugs have dramatically altered the situation.

I've spent the past decade studying abortions in Latin American countries where abortion is always, or almost always, illegal. Yet, abortion in these countries remains commonplace. It is vastly safer than it was in the past, thanks to a revolution that has replaced back alleys with blister packs ordered online. But this revolution has come with unexpected consequences — for the doctor-patient relationship and for law enforcement.

Whether we're marching with coat-hanger posters or passing laws that outlaw the procedure earlier and earlier, we fight over abortion in the United States as if we know what will happen if it's banned. But as we inch closer to potentially allowing states to recriminalize the procedure — with laws that ban abortions after six weeks, as in Iowa, and even seek to effectively ban the use of abortion-inducing drugs — we would do well to look past our southern border to consider what happens when abortion actually is illegal. It's not the outcome anyone is looking for.

Abortifacient drugs have become so readily available in places like Chile and El Salvador that it has become impossible to enforce abortion bans. That was also the case in Ireland, where by some accounts, before last month's legalization vote, at least two Irish women a day were self-administering abortions using pills.

The most widely available abortion drug in Latin America, misoprostol, is commonly used to treat ulcers. Although less effective than the combination of mifepristone and misoprostol used in the United States, misoprostol taken in the first trimester causes an abortion in approximately 90 percent of cases. In Brazil, where abortion is all but banned, experts estimate there are about a million illegal abortions each year; around half of them are induced using abortion drugs. Efforts to restrict access to misoprostol will fail not simply because it costs pennies to make, but also because it saves lives. The World Health Organization lists misoprostol as an "essential medicine" for treating miscarriages, and the drug has been credited with reducing deaths from illegal abortions.

But if abortion drugs have reduced the risk of death from illegal abortion, they have also generated new concerns: When abortion is a crime, the emergency room can become the scene of a criminal investigation, and doctors the detectives.

If a woman takes the wrong drug or the wrong dosage, particularly too late in pregnancy, she is likely to wind up in the emergency room, bleeding. There is no ready way for doctors to tell the difference between the hemorrhaging from a natural miscarriage and that from an induced abortion. But this hasn't stopped governments from tasking them with trying.

There are two ways to enforce laws against abortion: prosecute doctors or prosecute women. Historically, as well as in most countries today, abortion prosecutions typically target the doctor. This practice is endorsed by today's anti-abortion movement, which regularly proclaims that women are abortion's "second victims," deserving compassion rather than punishment.

Abortion drugs complicate this strategy. When no doctor is involved, the woman who uses abortion drugs might seem less like a "second victim" and more like a criminal.

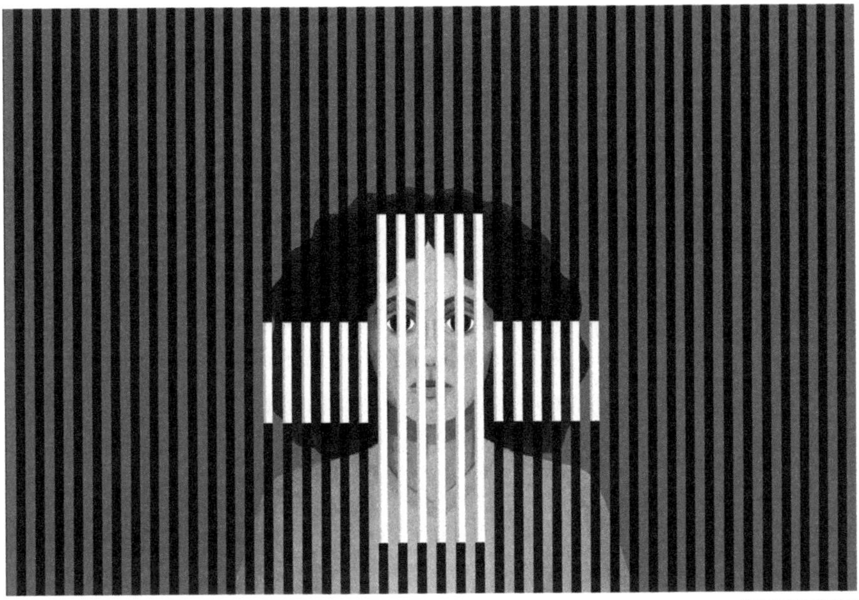

ELENI KALORKOTI

In Chile, the small number of abortion prosecutions annually typically target doctors. El Salvador prosecutes women. Government officials there have toured the country's hospitals to inform doctors of their duty to report women suspected of having induced their miscarriages. Not only does this policy violate near-universal norms of patient confidentiality, but because doctors have no reliable way to tell a natural miscarriage from an abortion, reports are made on the basis of suspicion. Whom do doctors tend to suspect most readily? Poor women.

The only comprehensive investigation of El Salvador's experience in enforcing its abortion ban, a study that traced all 129 abortion-related investigations in the country from 2000 to 2011, found that while public health care centers reported their patients, not a single accusation against a woman originated from a private doctor or hospital. Doctors may suspect wealthier patients of inducing a miscarriage, but they report only poor patients. Confidentiality has become a commodity.

The effects of poverty follow the woman to the courthouse: In case after case, Salvadoran judges have wrongly convicted poor women of crimes when the only real evidence against them is that they had a miscarriage.

The risk of being accused of a crime injects fear and distrust into the doctor-patient relationship, leading some women to postpone or forgo necessary care. The law also creates a dilemma for doctors, who told me they fear both being reprimanded for failure to report patients suspected of abortion and being sued for reporting.

Americans should care what happens under Latin American abortion bans not just for the sake of the women who live there but also because they provide a glimpse of what could be our future.

The fight over abortion includes the passing of laws intended to restrict access. In the 45 years since Roe v. Wade legalized abortion, states have enacted more than 1,200 anti-abortion laws — more if one counts federal regulations such as the Trump administration's recent decision to deny family planning funds to organizations that provide abortions. In anticipation of a shift on the Supreme Court, states are lining up laws, like Iowa's, that take direct aim at abortion.

Court fights are inevitable, yet it's clear that even a substantial legal victory for abortion opponents will not be as effective in combating abortion as they imagine — not just because a woman who wants to terminate her pregnancy will find a way, but also because abortion drugs make finding that way easier than ever. In the internet age, trying to stop abortion by closing clinics is like trying to eradicate pornography by seizing magazines.

But there will still be consequences. Doctors will find themselves torn between norms protecting confidentiality and the pressure to report their patients; the pressure to treat women themselves as criminals is likely to grow, intensifying an existing pattern of charging poor minority women with crimes arising from miscarriages, stillbirths or perceived risks taken while pregnant.

Knowing all of this — that banning abortion will not make it go away and that without doctors to charge, law enforcement will wind up targeting the poorest, most marginalized women — our battle over legalized abortion seems misguided. The rise of abortion drugs simply throws into sharper relief what we have always known: Abortions rates are driven not by legality but by economics. Half of the abortions in the United States take place among women below the federal poverty line.

People of good faith on both sides of the abortion war know that the best way to lower abortion rates is to deal with what causes women to want to abort in the first place. Rather than ending abortion, criminalizing abortion will merely create new ways in which the state can intensify the misery of the poorest among us.

MICHELLE OBERMAN is a law professor at Santa Clara University and the author of "Her Body, Our Laws: On the Front Lines of the Abortion War, From El Salvador to Oklahoma."

CHAPTER 3

Second Amendment Extremists

Gun rights activists have long rallied behind the National Rifle Association. But as mass shootings have become an increasingly regular part of American life and culture, the battle lines have become more sharply drawn. As a growing consensus has been reached that guns need to be more strictly regulated, the movement to protect the second amendment has maintained a vocal presence. The articles in this chapter speak to the powerful contingency of gun rights extremists.

The National Regulation-Resisters Association

OPINION | BY CHARLES M. BLOW | JAN. 30, 2013

SOMETIMES COMMON SENSE isn't a common trait.

Wayne LaPierre, the National Rifle Association's executive vice president, is a shining example of this. He continues to voice resistance to even the most basic kinds of changes in existing gun policy, changes that almost all Americans support, changes that would have little impact on the rights and ability of sane, law-abiding citizens to purchase legal weapons.

First, some background.

The White House released its plan to reduce gun violence two weeks ago, a month after the horrific school shooting in Newtown, Conn.

The plan covered closing loopholes in the background check system, banning assault weapons and high-capacity magazines, as well as improving school safety and mental health services.

Public opinion polls suggested that people generally supported the president's plan.

A Gallup poll conducted the day after the president presented his plan found that 53 percent of Americans would want their representatives in Congress to vote for it.

An ABC/Washington Post poll last week found that 53 percent of Americans favored it.

And a Pew Research Center poll last week found that a majority of Americans thought the plan was about right or didn't go far enough. Only 31 percent thought that it went too far.

In fact, one of the greatest points of agreement among Americans is the need for universal background checks, as the president proposed.

A Gallup poll released last week found that 91 percent of Americans would vote to "require criminal background checks for all gun sales" if they could.

From a public relations perspective, trying to find some common ground on this issue with the public would seem a no-brainer. Not so for the No Brain-ers.

On Wednesday, at a Senate Judiciary Committee hearing on gun violence, LaPierre, as is his wont, gave a rambling, twisted argument against, that's right, universal background checks.

LaPierre said during the hearings:

"My problem with background checks is you are never going to get criminals to go through universal background checks. All the law-abiding people, you'll create an enormous federal bureaucracy, unfunded, hitting all the little people in the country, will have to go through it, pay the fees, pay the taxes."

He continued:

"We don't even prosecute anybody right now that goes through the system we have. So, we're going to make all those law-abiding people go through the system and then we aren't going to prosecute any of the bad guys if they do catch one. "

So LaPierre's argument, if I can follow this spiral of spuriousness, is that if we don't prosecute "bad guys," then there is no use in checking buyers in the first place so that "bad guys" could be identified and prevented from making the purchases. As best I can tell that seems to be it, and if that is it then I say: you can't be serious.

Senator Dick Durbin, a Democrat from Illinois, shot back:

"Mr. LaPierre, that's the point. The criminals won't go to purchase the guns because there'll be a background check. We'll stop them from original purchase. You missed that point completely. It's basic."

The room erupted in applause.

Universal background checks would seem a basic and exceedingly reasonable proposal. I would add that there should also be universal prosecutions for being intentionally misleading during those checks. But LaPierre is a different kind of person. His interests are not the same as most Americans'. His organization and the majority of so-called "pro gun rights" groups are in the business of unfettered gun proliferation as a means of increasing gun industry profit.

This is about money, pure and simple.

Wednesday morning, before LaPierre's testimony, the Republican Joe Scarborough of MSNBC said on his show:

"You know what the greatest danger to that Second Amendment right and that guarantee is right now? Extremism from the survivalist wing of the N.R.A. that impacts Republicans' policies nationwide and moves the Republican Party so far away from mainstream America that they lose the House, they lose the Senate again in '14, and they lose the presidency again. And the next president will be Democratic."

I would have to agree with that.

LaPierre is fanning paranoia because it helps grow the N.R.A.'s membership rolls and helps the N.R.A.'s friends and benefactors in the gun industry. And the N.R.A. uses its war chest to scare cowering politicians into taking unreasonable positions.

But extreme resistance to change is no longer acceptable with most of the public. People want action. They're demanding it. Extreme resistance in this climate could prove more politically poisonous, particularly to some Republicans, than upsetting the N.R.A.

At this moment you have an outraged public against the gun profiteers and the gutless politicians. I believe in the end the people will win.

CHARLES M. BLOW has been a New York Times Op-Ed columnist since 2008. His column appears on Monday and Thursday.

Some Extremists Fire Guns and Other Extremists Promote Guns

OPINION | BY NICHOLAS KRISTOF | JUNE 16, 2016

OVER THE LAST two decades, Canada has had eight mass shootings. Just so far this month, the United States has already had 20.

Canada has a much smaller population, of course, and the criteria researchers used for each country are slightly different, but that still says something important about public safety.

Could it be, as Donald Trump suggests, that the peril comes from admitting Muslims? On the contrary, Canadians are safe despite having been far more hospitable to Muslim refugees: Canada has admitted more than 27,000 Syrian refugees since November, some 10 times the number the United States has.

More broadly, Canada's population is 3.2 percent Muslim, while the United States is about 1 percent Muslim — yet Canada doesn't have massacres like the one we just experienced at a gay nightclub in Orlando, Fla., or the one in December in San Bernardino, Calif. So perhaps the problem isn't so much Muslims out of control but guns out of control.

Look, I grew up on a farm with guns. One morning when I was 10, we awoke at dawn to hear our chickens squawking frantically and saw a fox trotting away with one of our hens in its mouth. My dad grabbed his .308 rifle, opened the window and fired twice. The fox was unhurt but dropped its breakfast and fled. The hen picked herself up, shook her feathers indignantly and walked back to the barn. So in the right context, guns have their uses.

The problem is that we make no serious effort to keep firearms out of the hands of violent people. A few data points:

- More Americans have died from guns, including suicides, since just 1970 than died in all the wars in U.S. history going back to the American Revolution.

• The Civil War marks by far the most savage period of warfare in American history. But more Americans are now killed from guns annually, again including suicides, than were killed by guns on average each year during the Civil War (when many of the deaths were from disease, not guns).

• In the United States, more preschoolers up through age 4 are shot dead each year than police officers are.

Canada has put in place measures that make it more difficult for a dangerous person to acquire a gun, with a focus not so much on banning weapons entirely (the AR-15 is available after undergoing safety training and a screening) as on limiting who can obtain one. In the United States, we lack even universal background checks, and new Harvard research to be published soon found that 40 percent of gun transfers didn't even involve a background check.

We can't prevent every gun death any more than we can prevent every car accident, and the challenge is particularly acute with homegrown terrorists like the one in Orlando. But experts estimate that a serious effort to reduce gun violence might reduce the toll by one-third, which would be more than 10,000 lives saved a year.

The Orlando killer would have been legally barred from buying lawn darts, because they were banned as unsafe. He would have been unable to drive a car that didn't pass a safety inspection or that lacked insurance. He couldn't have purchased a black water gun without an orange tip — because that would have been too dangerous.

But it's not too dangerous to allow the sale of an assault rifle without even a background check?

If we're trying to prevent carnage like that of Orlando, we need to be vigilant not only about infiltration by the Islamic State, and not only about American citizens poisoned into committing acts of terrorism. We also need to be vigilant about National Rifle Association-type extremism that allows guns to be sold without background checks.

It's staggering that Congress doesn't see a problem with allowing people on terror watch lists to buy guns: In each of the last three years, more than 200 people on the terror watch list have been allowed to purchase guns. We empower ISIS when we permit acolytes like the Orlando killer, investigated repeatedly as a terrorist threat, to buy a Sig Sauer MCX and a Glock 17 handgun on consecutive days.

A great majority of Muslims are peaceful, and it's unfair to blame Islam for terrorist attacks like the one in Orlando. But it is important to hold accountable Gulf states like Saudi Arabia that are wellsprings of religious zealotry, intolerance and fanaticism. We should also hold accountable our own political figures who exploit tragic events to sow bigotry. And, yes, that means Donald Trump.

When Trump scapegoats Muslims, that also damages our own security by bolstering the us-versus-them narrative of ISIS. The lesson of history is that extremists on one side invariably empower extremists on the other.

So by all means, Muslims around the world should stand up to their fanatics sowing hatred and intolerance — and we Americans should stand up to our own extremist doing just the same.

NICHOLAS KRISTOF has been a columnist for The New York Times since 2001. He covers human rights, women's rights, health and global affairs.

A Pistol for Every Bar Stool

OPINION | BY GAIL COLLINS | JUNE 16, 2016

THE NATION HASN'T exactly joined hands in a united response to the Orlando massacre. But since this terrible mass shooting happened in one of the most weapons-friendly places in the country, maybe we can at least all agree that having wildly permissive gun laws does not make a city safer.

O.K., probably not.

On Wednesday, Donald Trump took time out from vilifying Muslims and put some of the blame on gun control. If the patrons of Pulse, the gay bar in Orlando, had been carrying concealed weapons, he said, they could have taken control of the situation. The gunman would have been "just open target practice."

(This was at the same speech where he congratulated himself for his stupendous relationship with the gay community, suggesting he didn't "get enough credit" for having a club in Palm Beach that was "open to everybody." This is a little off our topic today, but I have to once again point out that Trump's club is open to everybody with $100,000 to cover the membership fee.)

But about guns. Let's follow Trump's thought. It's easy to buy a gun in Florida and supereasy to get a permit to carry around a concealed weapon. Even the Florida Legislature, however, doesn't allow people to carry guns into bars. Trump did not specifically say that we need to uphold Americans' freedom to drink while armed. But there doesn't seem to be any other way to interpret his argument.

Also, there actually was an off-duty police officer working in the club who tried to shoot the gunman but failed. This is important, because the myth of the cool and steady shooter is one of the most cherished beliefs of the National Rifle Association and its supporters. Trump himself has bragged that if he'd been in Paris on the night of the attacks there, he would have shot the terrorists. ("I may have been killed, but I would have drawn.")

This is an excellent example of delusional gun thinking. Although Trump frequently reminds us he has a permit to carry a gun, there's no indication he's ever done so. And there's certainly no evidence whatsoever that he has any skill in hitting things.

It's very, very difficult to draw, aim and shoot accurately when you're under severe stress. It's one of the reasons that police officers so often spray fleeing suspects with bullets. They can't hit a moving target, even though they get far more weapons training than your normal armed civilian.

In Florida, people who want to carry a gun merely have to be able to demonstrate they can "safely handle and discharge the firearm." Nowhere does it say anything about accuracy.

A few weeks ago in Houston, a 25-year-old Afghan war veteran named Dionisio Garza walked up to a stranger sitting in a car at a carwash and shot him in the neck while railing about "homosexuals, Jews and Walmart," according to local reports. He fired off 212 rounds, mostly from an assault rifle, hitting a police helicopter and a nearby gas station, which burst into flames. The police said a neighbor who heard the shooting came running with a gun, but was shot himself.

People who hear this story may draw different morals. The way we've been going, it'll be a miracle if some member of the Texas Legislature doesn't submit a bill requiring employees of carwashes to be armed at all times. However, others might note that the weapon in this case was an AR-15, the same type of military-style rifle that was used in the Orlando shooting, the Newtown school shooting and the terrorist attack in San Bernardino. It would seem as if the best way to cut down on mass shootings would be by eliminating weapons that allow crazy people to rapidly fire off endless rounds of bullets.

The possibility of banning assault weapons like the AR-15 is most definitely not on the table in Congress, although Hillary Clinton supports it, and has brought it up a lot since Orlando. No, the current debate in Washington is over whether people on the government's terror watch list should be kept from purchasing arms.

The fact that even people who aren't allowed to get on a plane can buy a gun in this country is obviously insane. Yet most of the Republicans in the House and the Senate regard changing the status quo as an enormous lift. "I think you're going too far here," Senator Lindsey Graham of South Carolina told the backers during one of the bill's pathetic trips to nowhere.

Since the Orlando shooter had actually spent some time on the terror watch list, the pressure seems to be growing. Trump says he'll meet with the N.R.A. to talk over the matter. Perhaps, after all this time, we'll get some pathetically minor action. Then only apolitical maniacs would have the opportunity to buy guns that can take out a roomful of people in no time flat.

GAIL COLLINS joined The New York Times in 1995 as a member of the editorial board and later as an Op-Ed columnist. In 2001 she was appointed editorial page editor — the first woman to hold that post at The Times.

A Militia Gets Battle Ready for a 'Gun-Grabbing' Clinton Presidency

BY DAVID ZUCCHINO | NOV. 4, 2016

At a militia training camp in Georgia, it was clear that no issue motivates members more than guns — and the enduring belief that Hillary Clinton is plotting to take them away.

JACKSON, GA. — "Put the guns down!"

The order crackled over a loudspeaker from two sheriff's deputies crouched behind the doors of police cruisers, semiautomatic rifles at their sides.

Several middle-aged militiamen were toting loaded AR-15 rifles and 9-millimeter pistols at a makeshift checkpoint — two lawn chairs and a narrow board — on a dirt driveway in central Georgia. The men, members of the Georgia Security Force III% militia, grumbled but laid their weapons down on the red clay earth.

The brief standoff ended with an amicable chat, and the men retrieved their weapons the moment the lawmen drove away. But the episode further stoked the militiamen's abiding fears that their cherished Second Amendment rights were under assault.

The Georgia Security Force is one of scores of extremist militias nationwide that have rallied around the presidential campaign of Donald J. Trump, heartened by his harsh attacks on immigrants, Muslims and Syrian refugees. But no single issue motivates militiamen more than guns — and the enduring belief that Hillary Clinton, despite her insistence that she is not anti-gun, is plotting to take them away.

The Georgia militiamen mobilized in the woods here last weekend to fire weapons and train for the day when, they believe, they will be forced to defend what they call "our way of life." Two dozen armed men and women conducted live-fire search-and-destroy drills, pumping out enough rounds to saw through and topple a loblolly pine.

KEVIN D. LILES FOR THE NEW YORK TIMES

The group's members are so-called 3 percenters, who believe that just 3 percent of colonists fought in the Revolutionary War.

"We thought it was bad under eight years of Obama, but the gun-grabbing is going to get a whole lot worse if Hillary gets elected," said Chris Hill, 42, a blond-bearded paralegal who goes by the code name Blood Agent and commands the militia. He wore combat fatigues and packed a .40-caliber Smith & Wesson pistol on his hip.

When Mr. Trump says he wants to make America great again, a message that has appealed to a broad segment of the electorate, Mr. Hill and his roughly 50 local militiamen are particularly enthralled. They long for an America they believe has been stolen from them by liberals, immigrants and "the P.C. crowd." Their America is one where Christianity is taught in schools, abortion is illegal and immigrants hail from Europe, not faraway Muslim lands.

These weekend warriors form the obdurate bedrock of Trump Nation: white, rural and working class. They vote, and they are

KEVIN D. LILES FOR THE NEW YORK TIMES

Practice rounds at the militia's camp in Jackson.

heavily armed, right down to the .22-caliber derringer fired by Nadine Wheeler, 63, a retiree who calls her tiny gun "the best in feminine protection."

During two days of conversations, grievances poured forth from the group as effortlessly as bullets from a gun barrel. On armed excursions through sun-dappled forests, they spoke of a vague but looming tyranny — an amalgam of sinister forces to be held at bay only with a firearm and the willingness to use it.

They are machinists and retirees, roofers and factory line workers, all steeped in the culture of the rural South. They say Mr. Trump, a Manhattan billionaire and real estate tycoon, speaks for them.

"Within the extreme right, many of Trump's most passionate backers come from the militia movement," said Mark Pitcavage, a senior research fellow at the Center on Extremism at the Anti-Defamation League. "The militia movement is overwhelmingly behind Trump's candidacy."

KEVIN D. LILES FOR THE NEW YORK TIMES

A Trump campaign banner, a Confederate battle flag and flags bearing the words "Don't Tread on Me," in a tent at the militia's camp. There were an estimated 276 active militias in 2015.

For militias, Mr. Trump's anti-establishment views "play right into their paranoid style of politics," said Ryan Lenz, editor of the Hatewatch blog at the Southern Poverty Law Center.

The Georgia Security Force is noteworthy among militias for its acute Islamophobia, Mr. Pitcavage said. Its members are so-called 3 percenters, who believe that only 3 percent of colonists fought in the Revolutionary War. That is "a historical myth," said Mr. Pitcavage, a historian, but useful for those who believe a few people with guns can defeat tyranny.

At least 330 such 3 percenter groups have formed, in all 50 states, by Mr. Pitcavage's count. There were 276 active militias in 2015, Mr. Lenz said. The number includes some 3 percenter groups.

Mr. Trump has retweeted posts from white nationalists and Nazi sympathizers, but Mr. Hill and his followers insist they are not racists, only staunch citizens and patriots with an admittedly apocalyptic outlook. They consider Mr. Trump a bulwark against the candidate they call "Shillary" Clinton.

Teresa Bueter, 41, worked for 26 years behind a grill at a Waffle House while raising three children. Now she is an active member of the Georgia Security Force, decked out in military fatigues. She owns a .32-caliber pistol and a German-made sniper rifle.

Mrs. Bueter said Syrian refugees entering the country "scare the crap out of me." With her guns and the militia's weekend paramilitary drills, she said, she is prepared to fight for the values she has instilled in her children and three grandchildren.

"Donald Trump would fit right in with our little group," she said. "He wants America the way we want it, back like it used to be."

Firearms are central to their identities. In September, some Georgia Security Force members paraded with guns while protesting plans for a local mosque; one wore a T-shirt that read, "Islam Is of the Devil." Last year, armed Security Force militiamen rallied in support of the Confederate battle flag. At their campground, militia members squeezed off several dozen rounds before breakfast. Then they sat down to scrambled eggs and sausage amid the lingering scent of cordite. Mr. Hill asked who was voting for Mr. Trump. Everyone shouted a unanimous "Oorah!"

The militia members seem comfortable inside the same sort of echo chamber of self-confirming arguments they ascribe to the liberal elites they say denigrate and demean them. They repeat tropes gleaned from militia websites and social media. They seem convinced that either the Islamic State, or agents sent by Mrs. Clinton, or both, may soon descend on the woods of central Georgia.

In separate interviews, various militiamen shared the same conspiracy theories, almost word for word: Muslim refugees have established terrorist training camps on American soil. The liberal billionaire George Soros has rigged voting machines for Democrats.

"We're like a small military of like-minded people," said Donald Ensey, 44, a father of four and grandfather of two, who wore fatigue

KEVIN D. LILES FOR THE NEW YORK TIMES

Donald Ensey, center, said training with the militia was essential to securing everything he had worked for in his lifetime.

pants and a black T-shirt bearing a profane depiction of an Islamic State fighter and a goat.

Mr. Ensey, who has a 3 percenter logo tattooed on the back of his hand, said training with the militia was essential to securing everything he had worked for in his lifetime. Even if Mrs. Clinton is not elected, he said, surely someone else will come for his guns.

Mr. Hill, a Marine veteran, holds FTX sessions, or field training exercises, roughly once a month. Otherwise the members communicate via regular posts on Facebook. Prospective members are approved by a "review board" of current members who vet them on their compatibility with the militia's beliefs. This session was held on 14 acres owned by Devin Bowen, a machinist who was having a miserable day even before the deputies forced him to drop his pistol.

The door of his trailer — the one with a sign that reads, "If You Don't Live Here, Don't Come Here" — was smashed in that day. Three rifles,

KEVIN D. LILES FOR THE NEW YORK TIMES

When Mr. Hill asked who was voting for Donald J. Trump, everyone at the camp shouted, "Oorah!"

a crossbow, 13,000 rounds of ammunition and an 800-pound gun safe were taken — not by federal agents, but by local thieves. Worse, Mr. Bowen was coughing up blood from an unknown malady. He soothed his throat by chugging cold Coca-Colas.

Mr. Bowen's comrades urged him to see a doctor, prompting a sour discussion about yet another conspiracy they see: the Affordable Care Act. Mr. Bowen waved them off. He was more concerned about Muslim immigrants' imposing Shariah law. "You cannot come to my country and shove your religion down my throat," he said, coughing.

Phillip King, 25, who builds ductwork for a living, was outfitted in camouflage fatigues and a tactical vest holding ammunition clips. Mr. King, code name Cowboy, is the only African-American member of the Georgia Security Force.

He said he was not offended by the militiamen's affection for the Confederate battle flag. He shares their love of guns, their conservative

KEVIN D. LILES FOR THE NEW YORK TIMES

Phillip King, left, with his fiancée, Katie Hardegree, at the militia camp in Jackson last week.

values and their view of Mr. Trump as someone who will insulate them from the tyranny of the political left. "This is my family — a brotherhood," he said.

For Daniels Potts, 21, owning a gun and learning to use it as part of a well-trained militia are essential to halting what he calls "the spread of radical Islam." He appreciates Mr. Trump's fierce opposition to Muslim refugees. "Not every Muslim is ISIS, but a lot of them are," Mr. Potts said.

He proudly calls himself an infidel and a deplorable. His arms bear tattoos of the 3 percenter logo and of the Kuntry Krackerz, a group affiliated with the Georgia Security Force.

Mr. Potts earns $16 to $18 an hour as a commercial roofer. He considers himself the type of law-abiding, hard-working American he said is belittled and marginalized by coastal elites. "We've been forgotten," he said.

Mr. Hill, the militia commander, led Mr. Potts and two dozen other members through a boot camp-style obstacle course carved out of the woods. They clambered over a wall of logs and fired at imaginary enemies as they "cleared" rooms made of plywood and sheets of black plastic.

One militiaman wore a shirt with a message that read, "When Tyranny Becomes Law, Resistance Becomes Duty."

It was all part of the militia's efforts to be armed, ready and united for looming threats, especially if Mrs. Clinton is elected, Mr. Hill said. He mentioned his two children. "The security and safety of my kids motivates what I do," he said.

Mr. Hill, who calls his group a "defensive militia," predicted unrest and violence from extremists on both sides no matter who wins the presidential election. If Mrs. Clinton wins, he said, millions of gun owners will march on Washington at the first attempt to restrict gun ownership.

"If the people decide they can no longer suffer the inequities," he said, "I'd be with the people and I'd take my guns up to Washington, D.C."

Repeal the Second Amendment

OPINION | BY BRET STEPHENS | OCT. 5, 2017

I HAVE NEVER understood the conservative fetish for the Second Amendment.

From a law-and-order standpoint, more guns means more murder. "States with higher rates of gun ownership had disproportionately large numbers of deaths from firearm-related homicides," noted one exhaustive 2013 study in the American Journal of Public Health.

From a personal-safety standpoint, more guns means less safety. The F.B.I. counted a total of 268 "justifiable homicides" by private citizens involving firearms in 2015; that is, felons killed in the course of committing a felony. Yet that same year, there were 489 "unintentional firearms deaths" in the United States, according to the Centers for Disease Control. Between 77 and 141 of those killed were children.

From a national-security standpoint, the Amendment's suggestion that a "well-regulated militia" is "necessary to the security of a free State," is quaint. The Minutemen that will deter Vladimir Putin and Kim Jong-un are based in missile silos in Minot, N.D., not farmhouses in Lexington, Mass.

From a personal liberty standpoint, the idea that an armed citizenry is the ultimate check on the ambitions and encroachments of government power is curious. The Whiskey Rebellion of the 1790s, the New York draft riots of 1863, the coal miners' rebellion of 1921, the Brink's robbery of 1981 — does any serious conservative think of these as great moments in Second Amendment activism?

And now we have the relatively new and now ubiquitous "active shooter" phenomenon, something that remains extremely rare in the rest of the world. Conservatives often say that the right response to these horrors is to do more on the mental-health front. Yet by all accounts Stephen Paddock would not have raised an eyebrow with a mental-health professional before he murdered 58 people in Las Vegas last week.

What might have raised a red flag? I'm not the first pundit to point out that if a "Mohammad Paddock" had purchased dozens of firearms and thousands of rounds of ammunition and then checked himself into a suite at the Mandalay Bay with direct views to a nearby music festival, somebody at the local F.B.I. field office would have noticed.

Given all of this, why do liberals keep losing the gun control debate?

Maybe it's because they argue their case badly and — let's face it — in bad faith. Democratic politicians routinely profess their fidelity to the Second Amendment — or rather, "a nuanced reading" of it — with all the conviction of Barack Obama's support for traditional marriage, circa 2008. People recognize lip service for what it is.

Then there are the endless liberal errors of fact. There is no "gun-show loophole" per se; it's a private-sale loophole, in other words the right to sell your own stuff. The civilian AR-15 is not a true "assault rifle," and banning such rifles would have little effect on the overall murder rate, since most homicides are committed with handguns. It's not true that 40 percent of gun owners buy without a background check; the real number is closer to one-fifth.

The National Rifle Association does not have Republican "balls in a money clip," as Jimmy Kimmel put it the other night. The N.R.A. has donated a paltry $3,533,294 to all current members of Congress since 1998, according to The Washington Post, equivalent to about three months of Kimmel's salary. The N.R.A. doesn't need to buy influence: It's powerful because it's popular.

Nor will it do to follow the "Australian model" of a gun buyback program, which has shown poor results in the United States and makes little sense in a country awash with hundreds of millions of weapons. Keeping guns out of the hands of mentally ill people is a sensible goal, but due process is still owed to the potentially insane. Background checks for private gun sales are another fine idea, though its effects on homicides will be negligible: guns recovered by police are rarely in the hands of their legal owners, a 2016 study found.

In fact, the more closely one looks at what passes for "common sense" gun laws, the more feckless they appear. Americans who claim to be outraged by gun crimes should want to do something more than tinker at the margins of a legal regime that most of the developed world rightly considers nuts. They should want to change it fundamentally and permanently.

There is only one way to do this: Repeal the Second Amendment.

Repealing the Amendment may seem like political Mission Impossible today, but in the era of same-sex marriage it's worth recalling that most great causes begin as improbable ones. Gun ownership should never be outlawed, just as it isn't outlawed in Britain or Australia. But it doesn't need a blanket Constitutional protection, either. The 46,445 murder victims killed by gunfire in the United States between 2012 and 2016 didn't need to perish so that gun enthusiasts can go on fantasizing that "Red Dawn" is the fate that soon awaits us.

Donald Trump will likely get one more Supreme Court nomination, or two or three, before he leaves office, guaranteeing a pro-gun court for another generation. Expansive interpretations of the right to bear arms will be the law of the land — until the "right" itself ceases to be.

Some conservatives will insist that the Second Amendment is fundamental to the structure of American liberty. They will cite James Madison, who noted in the Federalist Papers that in Europe "the governments are afraid to trust the people with arms." America was supposed to be different, and better.

I wonder what Madison would have to say about that today, when more than twice as many Americans perished last year at the hands of their fellows as died in battle during the entire Revolutionary War. My guess: Take the guns — or at least the presumptive right to them — away. The true foundation of American exceptionalism should be our capacity for moral and constitutional renewal, not our instinct for self-destruction.

BRET STEPHENS is an Op-Ed columnist for The New York Times.

John Paul Stevens: Repeal the Second Amendment

OPINION | BY JOHN PAUL STEVENS | MARCH 27, 2018

RARELY IN MY LIFETIME have I seen the type of civic engagement schoolchildren and their supporters demonstrated in Washington and other major cities throughout the country this past Saturday. These demonstrations demand our respect. They reveal the broad public support for legislation to minimize the risk of mass killings of schoolchildren and others in our society.

That support is a clear sign to lawmakers to enact legislation prohibiting civilian ownership of semiautomatic weapons, increasing the minimum age to buy a gun from 18 to 21 years old, and establishing more comprehensive background checks on all purchasers of firearms. But the demonstrators should seek more effective and more lasting reform. They should demand a repeal of the Second Amendment.

Concern that a national standing army might pose a threat to the security of the separate states led to the adoption of that amendment, which provides that "a well regulated militia, being necessary to the security of a free state, the right of the people to keep and bear arms, shall not be infringed." Today that concern is a relic of the 18th century.

For over 200 years after the adoption of the Second Amendment, it was uniformly understood as not placing any limit on either federal or state authority to enact gun control legislation. In 1939 the Supreme Court unanimously held that Congress could prohibit the possession of a sawed-off shotgun because that weapon had no reasonable relation to the preservation or efficiency of a "well regulated militia."

During the years when Warren Burger was our chief justice, from 1969 to 1986, no judge, federal or state, as far as I am aware, expressed any doubt as to the limited coverage of that amendment. When organizations like the National Rifle Association disagreed with that position and began their campaign claiming that federal regulation of firearms curtailed Second Amendment rights, Chief Justice Burger publicly characterized the N.R.A. as perpetrating "one of the greatest pieces of fraud, I repeat the word fraud, on the American public by special interest groups that I have ever seen in my lifetime."

In 2008, the Supreme Court overturned Chief Justice Burger's and others' long-settled understanding of the Second Amendment's limited reach by ruling, in District of Columbia v. Heller, that there was an individual right to bear arms. I was among the four dissenters.

That decision — which I remain convinced was wrong and certainly was debatable — has provided the N.R.A. with a propaganda weapon of immense power. Overturning that decision via a constitutional amendment to get rid of the Second Amendment would be simple and would do more to weaken the N.R.A.'s ability to stymie legislative debate and block constructive gun control legislation than any other available option.

That simple but dramatic action would move Saturday's marchers closer to their objective than any other possible reform. It would eliminate the only legal rule that protects sellers of firearms in the United States — unlike every other market in the world. It would make our schoolchildren safer than they have been since 2008 and honor the memories of the many, indeed far too many, victims of recent gun violence.

JOHN PAUL STEVENS is a retired associate justice of the United States Supreme Court.

Ex-Justice Stevens's Call to Repeal the Second Amendment

LETTER | THE NEW YORK TIMES | MARCH 27, 2018

TO THE EDITOR:

RE "REPEAL the Second Amendment" (Op-Ed, March 27):

The retired justice John Paul Stevens is right to highlight the Second Amendment's role in the gun debate, including the fact that it is sometimes deployed as a "propaganda weapon" against gun regulation. It is also important to recognize that, as a matter of law, the Second Amendment is perfectly consistent with gun regulation.

Justice Antonin Scalia's majority opinion in District of Columbia v. Heller (from which Justice Stevens dissented) emphasized that "the Second Amendment right is not unlimited." He enumerated a wide range of "presumptively lawful" gun regulations, including bans on possession by felons and the mentally ill, dangerous and unusual weapons, and the carrying of weapons in sensitive places.

In more than 1,000 Second Amendment cases in the decade since Heller, courts have fleshed out those categories. They have struck down stringent (and extremely rare) laws like bans on public carry. And they have upheld the vast majority of reasonable gun laws.

People sometimes say they oppose gun regulation because they support the Second Amendment, or vice versa. The gun debate is difficult enough without that false dichotomy.

JOSEPH BLOCHER, DURHAM, N.C.
The writer is a professor at Duke University School of Law.

TO THE EDITOR:

This Op-Ed article is precisely why more people don't support gun control. Articles like this imply that anyone who wants sensible restrictions to prevent mentally ill teenagers from shooting up schools also wants to repeal the Second Amendment.

John Paul Stevens does not speak for me or scores of other people who support both gun rights and responsible gun sales. He is holding the gun control movement back, not pushing it forward.

SARYTA RODRIGUEZ
New York

TO THE EDITOR:

Rather than subject the country to a prolonged, deeply divisive and likely unsuccessful campaign to repeal the Second Amendment, would it not be preferable to revise its language so as to reflect contemporary social concerns (such as gun violence) while preserving the time-honored right to bear arms for legitimate purposes?

This would require us to agree on three main points: 1) gun ownership is a central part of American life; 2) all but a tiny minority of gun owners use them safely and responsibly; and 3) any restrictions on access to, as well as ownership or use of, firearms should apply only to those who might harm others (and themselves) with these weapons.

A revised Second Amendment could read as follows: "The right to bear arms for hunting, sport and recreation being a cherished and time-honored tradition, the exercise of this right by responsible persons for these purposes shall not be infringed."

JOHN V.H. DIPPEL
Salisbury, CT.

TO THE EDITOR:

John Paul Stevens has finally declared out loud what gun advocates have desperately tried to avoid: that the Second Amendment is obsolete. The National Rifle Association shouts that our freedoms are at risk, while Rick Santorum, a former senator, recommended that student protesters stop exercising their First Amendment rights and instead learn CPR.

While many of us waste time feeling outraged over the controversial statements, we lose sight of the real goal — eliminating an amendment written by founding fathers whom history has judged to be wrong about several important issues.

Recent protests provide hope that the younger generation will prioritize strict gun regulations as they mature into positions of greater influence. Meanwhile, I fear for the generation of children who have to go to school while the adults of today bask in inaction.

MARCO STARGER
Bridgewater, N.J.

TO THE EDITOR:

Three cheers for John Paul Stevens! The Second Amendment was intended to equip a militia, but we haven't had one in centuries. It is as quaint as the Third Amendment, about quartering of soldiers. How many Americans are concerned about discovering an uninvited soldier in their living room?

ARMAND W. LORANGER
Bedford, N.Y.

‘Only the Extremists Want to Ban All Guns’

OPINION | THE NEW YORK TIMES | MARCH 28, 2018

In an Op-Ed essay on Tuesday, the former Supreme Court justice John Paul Stevens called for the repeal of the Second Amendment. Readers debated it on social media and in the comments section of the piece. Below is a sample of some representative viewpoints, edited lightly for clarity.

RETIRED JUSTICE STEVENS confirms the need for conservative voices on the Supreme Court. He would change the second most important amendment based solely on his emotional lack of logic, not on history. The Second Amendment was created to guarantee the eternal freedom of the citizenry from an overreaching federal government. The same argument applies today, as history proves that one of the first steps for authoritarian governments is to remove firearms from their future serfs. Then comes free speech and religion. The founding fathers were much more wise than Stevens. — JON GALT, TEX.

Frankly, in the wake of District of Columbia v. Heller, I don’t see how any meaningful gun control could be enacted without a repeal of the Second Amendment. Heller elevated the right to own a gun to such a high level, it is right up there with freedom of speech and the right to due process. Even the most mild, seemingly sensible gun control measures can now be challenged on constitutional grounds, with a high probability of success. Heller created such an impregnable shield around the Second Amendment that tearing it out root and branch seems like the only way. — DENNIS FRITZ

Right-wing talking points aside, the Second Amendment was never written to guarantee the eternal freedom of the citizenry from an over-reaching federal government. It was written — long before we had a standing army — to guarantee a well-regulated militia to defend the country from being attacked. It is a relic we tolerate to maintain consensus and something resembling unity in this country. — **ERIC BEYER, NEW YORK**

Up to now I have been a Second Amendment supporter, but I have never been against controls on large-capacity magazines, Teflon-coated bullets, background checks, etc. I could accept repeal of the amendment, but I would need to know precisely what was replacing it. All gun owners would need to know that. — **WILLIAMIGRIFFITH, SOUTH CAROLINA**

Everyone is concerned about rights, but few chime in about responsibility. The wording of the Second Amendment is about being ready to fight for your country, with no standing army extant. You have an army now. "Militia" readiness is redundant. On another point, please remember this was an amendment. It can be modified or even repealed entirely. The issue of personal safety is a red herring. Japan has a much lower rate of gun violence. Canada, Britain, Australia and other countries are doing just fine without all the guns and some of the nuts who advocate for them. What makes America so "exceptional" that the rules of law and human nature do not apply to them? — **MDROY100, ONTARIO**

There's no need to repeal the Second Amendment, and pushing for it seems unnecessarily divisive. Courts have consistently ruled that regulating firearms does not violate it, and we've had common-sense gun regulation in the past. The last assault-weapons ban survived constitutional challenges, and there's no reason a new one wouldn't. Combine such a ban with strict background checks, training and licensing, and you can mitigate the number of mass shootings. Only the extremists want to ban all guns; clearly, there are ways to regulate weapons without taking away people's rights. Further, the process to repeal a constitutional amendment takes many years, which makes this argument even weaker. — **MARC MCCLENAHAN, ARIZONA**

I have no problem repealing the Second Amendment and believe it is a great position from which to begin. Often liberal politics start negotiations from a position of compromise, forcing us to move right when the other side screams "compromise!" If we start from a position that moves us to a fair compromise, I say go for it: Repeal the Second!

— **SARA MCELROY, NEW YORK**

It's Time to Talk About the N.R.A.

OPINION | BY NICHOLAS KRISTOF | OCT. 29, 2018

THE MASSACRE OF 11 people at a Pittsburgh synagogue a week ago was terrifyingly predictable — with an equally predictable response. President Trump and members of Congress denounced the violence but show no signs of actually doing anything.

Why is it that polls show that voters want more gun safety laws yet Congress can't pass any? One reason is the National Rifle Association, a heavyweight player in this election and every election. On Tuesday, the N.R.A. once again will help deflect what surveys suggest is the people's will to stop it.

I write this as a former N.R.A. member who grew up on a farm — my 12th birthday present was my own .22 rifle — and I acknowledge that it once was a great organization for shooting enthusiasts.

But it has been hijacked by extremist leaders committed not to their members' (much more reasonable) views, but to hard-line resistance of safety regulations. All countries have violent, hateful people, but only in America do we give them ready access to assault weapons and large-capacity magazines, and that's in part because of the N.R.A. and its political influence.

The National Rifle Association was founded in 1871 because of concern that Civil War troops had been terrible marksmen.

The Second Amendment? Few talked about it. Almost everyone, in and out of the N.R.A., accepted that there should be restrictions on firearms.

"Gun control laws were ubiquitous" in the 19th century, Michael Waldman notes in his book "The Second Amendment."

Visitors to Wichita, Kan., had to check their revolvers at police headquarters. And as for Dodge City, a symbol of the Wild West, a photo shows a sign on main street in 1879 warning: "The Carrying of Fire Arms Strictly Prohibited."

TY WRIGHT FOR THE NEW YORK TIMES

Donald Trump speaks to a crowd during the 145th National Rifle Association Convention in 2016.

In the 1920s and 1930s, the N.R.A. favored tighter gun laws, and its president, Karl Frederick, said that the carrying of weapons "should be sharply restricted and only under license." In 1934, the United States helped pioneer modern gun laws with the National Firearms Act, with the blessings of the N.R.A., and came close to banning handguns. As recently as the 1960s, the N.R.A. supported — more grudgingly — some limits on guns.

But in 1977 there was a coup within the N.R.A. that put hard-liners in charge. The group began calling for repeal of the 1968 Gun Control Act and doubled down on a full-time lobbying arm to oppose firearm restrictions. In effect, the group took an extremist turn that continues to shape American life today.

America's gun culture and Canada's had been similar in the 1950s and 60s, focused on rifles used for hunting. In 1959, a survey found that 60 percent of Americans favored a ban on handguns. Then in the post-World War II period, other countries steadily tightened gun laws, while in the United States the N.R.A. moved to emphasize handguns and personal security, building on public anxiety about crime, so the United States resisted that global trend and instead passed a series of concealed carry laws.

Leaders of the N.R.A. fervently backed a new movement to reinterpret the Second Amendment, which had been regarded as a relic having to do with state militias, as protecting individual gun rights. In 1991, former Supreme Court Chief Justice Warren Burger, a conservative, dismissed calls to reinterpret the Second Amendment as "one of the greatest pieces of fraud, I repeat the word 'fraud,' on the American public by special interest groups that I have ever seen in my lifetime."

Now that "fraud" is the law of the land.

The reinterpretation of the Second Amendment is a tribute to the undeniable effectiveness of the N.R.A. Relentless campaigning by the N.R.A. and changing American mores have resulted in a Constitutional right to bear arms, in a blizzard of concealed carry permits, and in tough stand-your-ground laws. In contrast to Canada, the United States now has a gun culture focused on handguns, assault weapons and paranoia, and that's in large part because of the N.R.A.

In fairness, let's also note that progressives have periodically driven moderate gun-owners into the arms of the N.R.A. with muddled commentary indicating that they didn't know anything about the guns they wanted to regulate. In 2013, for example, New York State banned loading magazines with more than seven rounds, with many lawmakers apparently not realizing that for many guns there are no magazines holding seven or fewer rounds.

Even now, the N.R.A.'s strategy is largely to pounce on liberal comments about "gun control" — one reason I prefer the less threatening term "gun safety" — and leverage them to frighten gun owners to become more engaged. On one of the N.R.A.'s websites the other day was a headline, "D.C. Area Witches Unite for Gun Control, Hurl Curses at the N.R.A." and "New Jersey to Gun-Owners: Hand Over Those Magazines or We Could Throw You in Jail."

Gun carrying has also become an important part of identity and self-esteem for millions of Americans, in ways that liberal city-dwellers don't always appreciate. The last few decades have in many ways demoted working class white men — their jobs have become insecure, they may no longer be the family's chief breadwinner, women and people of color have gained ground — but firing an AR-15 or packing a concealed weapon offers beleaguered men a chance to reassert their masculinity; to such men, guns provide a sense of purpose, fulfilling a traditional manly role of protecting their families and their communities. Bushmaster, the gun company, has marketed one assault rifle with a photo of it and a headline: "CONSIDER YOUR MAN CARD REISSUED."

The N.R.A. has also expanded the gun-buying constituency by reframing the purpose of firearms from hunting to personal security and by promoting the idea of empowered women — even feminists — packing handguns in their purses. Among N.R.A. programs reaching out to women are "Refuse To Be a Victim" and "love at first shot," plus a women's leadership forum.

N.R.A. spokeswoman Dana Loesch has even said that efforts to ban assault weapons constitute a "war on women." (In fact, researchers have found that having a gun in the home is associated with a huge increase in the risk of dying from murder, suicide or a gun accident; when a gun is around, husbands and boyfriends become much more dangerous in domestic violence situations.)

Fear-mongering served the N.R.A.'s interests, galvanizing donations and voting, but it also served the interests of gun manufacturers by hugely boosting sales.

Remember when President Obama tried to change the Second Amendment and ban handguns? No, neither do I. But Wayne LaPierre of the N.R.A. repeatedly warned that Obama favored "a total ban on the manufacture, sale and possession of all handguns." The propaganda worked: In one poll in 2009, 55 percent of gun-owners said that they expected Obama to try to ban the sale of guns.

The alarmism was effective. By one count, the number of Americans licensed to carry concealed weapons soared from 4.6 million in 2007 to 17.3 million today.

That raises a larger question: Has the gun industry hijacked a hunters' organization and turned it into one that drums up demand for firearms and accessories, to serve the industry's bottom line?

DOES THE N.R.A. REPRESENT THE GUN LOBBY, OR MEMBERS?

"The NRA appears to have evolved into the lobby for gun and ammunition manufacturers rather than gun owners," Adolphus Busch IV, of the Anheuser Busch beer fortune, wrote in a 2013 letter resigning his life membership in the N.R.A. "Your current strategic focus places a priority on the needs of gun and ammunition manufacturers while disregarding the opinions of your 4 million individual members. One only has to look at the makeup of the 75-member board of directors, dominated by manufacturing interests, to confirm my point."

The backdrop is several challenges faced by the gun industry. It is a mature business whose products last generations, and whose traditional constituency — hunters — is aging and shrinking, and it is also facing the kind of liability risks that struck the tobacco industry. Yet in fact, the gun industry has prospered in recent decades — in large part because it has been rescued by N.R.A. fear-mongering that drives gun owners to buy more weapons and accessories before they're banned. This is brilliant marketing.

Consider another of the N.R.A.'s current campaigns, to allow silencers. Silencers have been largely banned since the 1930s, but the N.R.A. and enthusiasts like Donald Trump Jr. argue that they should be allowed as a matter of liberty and for health reasons — to reduce hearing loss associated with gunfire.

No one takes this public health argument seriously, but allowing silencers would be a huge boon for the gun industry. If five million Americans each bought a silencer for two firearms, it could amount to $1 billion in sales.

Moreover, most firearms today don't have the threaded barrels needed to accommodate a silencer. So a gun owner who wanted both a rifle and a handgun with silencers would also buy two more firearms — a further benefit to the industry.

"The N.R.A. has policy positions and rhetorical positions that are aligned with where the gun industry makes its money," notes J. Adam Skaggs of the Giffords Law Center to Prevent Gun Violence.

Still, this doesn't necessarily mean that the gun industry has hijacked the N.R.A. Mike Weisser, a gun store owner and frequent writer about gun policy, argues persuasively that it goes too far to say that the N.R.A. is controlled by gun manufacturers; he says that the gun industry and the N.R.A. work together not out of a nefarious conspiracy but because together they can maximize both N.R.A. influence and industry revenue.

N.R.A. finances are fuzzy, and contributions to its lobbying arm are not disclosed. But a basic membership has been raised to $45 a year — higher levels are available — and those dues are a measure of loyalty, contrasting with anti-gun groups that don't even charge dues. All told, membership dues raise more than $125 million a year for the N.R.A. Major corporate donations and advertising seem to provide much smaller sums, according to the N.R.A.'s 990 non-profit filings.

Companies show gratitude in other ways. A laser sight maker called Crimson Trace donates 10 percent of certain sales to the organization, and other companies have similar initiatives.

IS THE N.R.A.'S POWER WANING?

The N.R.A. has been admired and feared for decades for its political influence. When Al Gore lost the presidency in 2000, it was widely said that the N.R.A. made the difference.

Larry Sabato of the University of Virginia says that the N.R.A.'s power is often attributed to its financial support for candidates, but that its endorsements are far more important. The key, he says, is that many gun rights supporters are single-issue voters, while historically those against the N.R.A. have also cared about the economy, civil rights, foreign policy and so on.

Charles McBurney, a Florida legislator, lamented that although he had a consistent A or A+ rating from the N.R.A., he was attacked by it because of a disagreement about one bill. In an op-ed on Jacksonville.com, he said the real message from the N.R.A. was: "You can be with me on virtually everything, but if you cross me once, even if the issue doesn't involve the Second Amendment, I will take you out."

Yet there are signs that this is changing, and that N.R.A. influence may have peaked.

The N.R.A. has raised membership dues twice since 2016, most recently a few months ago, in what could be a sign of financial challenges. Revenue from dues fell to $128 million last year, down from $163 million the previous year.

The group claims six million members, although many analysts believe that number is inflated. But even if membership is four million, that is still a huge number, and its print magazines appear to be gaining circulation. Perhaps more important, there is nothing comparable on the other side; that's why the N.R.A. wins.

Polling on the N.R.A. varies widely, and Gallup shows public opinion still net approving of the N.R.A., although trending downward in recent years. But two polls this year found that more Americans view the N.R.A. unfavorably than favorably.

A Marist poll found that 51 percent of Americans would definitely or probably vote against a candidate who received money from the N.R.A.

"Even voters in these largely Republican districts see [the N.R.A.] as another special interest against which candidates should take a stand," the Global Strategy Group concluded after polling in largely Republican-held battleground congressional districts. Some polls find a gulf between gun owners and the N.R.A., with 74 percent of ordinary N.R.A. members willing to support universal background checks that the N.R.A. ferociously opposes.

One sign of change is that members of Congress now regularly boast about how badly they are rated by the N.R.A. "I am proud of my F rating from the NRA," Representative Carolyn Maloney of New York told me. "I mention it in my gun safety town halls, releases on gun safety and campaign mailings."

A NATION WITH MORE GUNS THAN PEOPLE

Adam Winkler, a professor of law at U.C.L.A. and author of the book "Gunfight," believes the N.R.A. faces serious challenges, including demographic ones: Its core constituency of white men is shrinking. Yet Winkler is wary of concluding that the N.R.A. has peaked. He notes that after the shooting in Parkland, Fla., there was enormous pressure for federal gun measures. "The reason nothing has happened since is, I think, largely due to the N.R.A.," Winkler said.

After a shooter in Las Vegas used a bump stock to simulate automatic fire and kill 59 people in 2017, there was a widespread call to ban bump stocks. But today they remain legal around the country, and the public has moved on. This underscores the N.R.A.'s success at blocking national regulations, but also the degree to which it is vulnerable for being out of step with public opinion.

Even critics of the N.R.A. acknowledge that it also performs a significant public service that liberals rarely acknowledge: It runs gun safety classes around the country.

Every year, the N.R.A. trains some 750,000 Americans in gun safety. Sometimes these classes have an ideological tinge, and they often encourage joining the N.R.A. and fighting for Second Amendment rights, but they also train new gun buyers to use a gun reasonably safely.

It would be good to see progressive organizations teaching gun safety as well, rather than simply ceding the turf to the N.R.A.

My first encounter with the N.R.A. was in a hunter safety class in my hometown of Yamhill, Ore., when I was in seventh grade. At the end of the class, we all received a one-year N.R.A. membership.

At the time it was simply a grass-roots organization of hunters and well-meaning sportsmen. But along the way, it morphed into an extremist organization that fights any restrictions on firearms.

N.R.A. advocacy is one reason the United States diverged from the path of other advanced nations — and one reason there are now more guns in America (about 393 million) than people (326 million). A more grim indication of American exceptionalism: Americans in their late teens are 82 times more likely to be murdered with guns than their peers in other advanced nations.

There are no magic solutions to gun violence in America, but neither is reducing the toll an impossible challenge. We can do better, and one step would be to avoid demonizing gun owners, while relentlessly challenging the political influence of the N.R.A.

It has overreached and is vulnerable. If we want to tackle gun violence in America, we can start by discrediting it as an extremist organization that has been a boon to the firearms industry and a catastrophe for the American public.

NICHOLAS KRISTOF is a Pulitzer Prize-winning New York Times columnist.

Rise of the Armed Left

OPINION | BY MICHELLE GOLDBERG | NOV. 2, 2018

Threats from the right inspire a new left-wing gun culture.

ATLANTA — When I met Oso, a trash collector from rural Georgia in his late 30s, he was wearing dark shades and a black T-shirt with a silhouette of an assault rifle and the words "Piece Now." A tall and burly white man, he had a sleeve of tattoos on one arm, stubble on his shaved head, and a bushy gray beard. He looked, at first glance, like the sort of intimidating figure who'd fit in at a far-right rally.

In fact, you might see him at such a rally — among the counterprotesters. "There shouldn't be any question in anybody's mind in this country that fascism is here," he said. "It's alive and well and marching us all towards somewhere that we don't want to be." That's part of the reason, he said, that he's into guns: "I wear a pistol every day because I'm a Jewish person in the South."

It was the Sunday after the terror-filled week that culminated in the massacre at the Tree of Life synagogue. Oso was sitting with a handful of other members of the North Georgia branch of the Socialist Rifle Association, a new, swiftly growing left-wing gun group, in the backyard of an Italian restaurant in a gentrifying Atlanta neighborhood. (None of them wanted their last names used; Oso, Spanish for "bear," is a nickname.)

The mission of the S.R.A. is "to arm and train the working class for self-defense."

It launched in its current form this spring — before that there was a Facebook group of the same name — and now has several hundred dues-paying members and over 30 chapters. This Monday, 28 new people joined, the group said.

Brad, a 36-year-old math professor, is a founder of the S.R.A.'s North Georgia chapter and a member of the S.R.A.'s central committee. "Some people are scared with what's going on in the country right now," he told me. He only recently started carrying a gun, after getting death threats for the socialist organizing he was doing in his small town. "People want to be able to protect themselves," he said.

In the late 1960s and early 1970s, parts of the radical left fetishized firearms. Back then, some conservatives supported gun control as a way to disarm African-American militants; Ronald Reagan signed a bill banning open carry of loaded weapons when he was governor of California. "The Black Panthers and other extremists of the 1960s inspired some of the strictest gun control laws in American history," the U.C.L.A. law professor Adam Winkler wrote in his book, "Gunfight: The Battle Over the Right to Bear Arms in America."

Since then, however, gun culture has become virtually synonymous with American conservatism. The National Rifle Association is now perhaps the most powerful Republican lobby in the country, and its rhetoric increasingly echoes that of the apocalyptic far right. Over the last 20 or 30 years, Winkler told me, "not only has the N.R.A. become more and more associated with the right, but there's an increasingly militaristic, rebellious tone to the N.R.A. and the gun rights movement." It's become, he said, "all about arming up to fight the tyranny that's coming."

Meanwhile, most of the left has embraced gun control, something that's unlikely to change anytime soon. But it was probably inevitable that, as our politics have become more polarized and violent, a nascent left-wing gun culture would emerge.

"These are some trying times, so I do believe more black men and women are arming up," Maitreya Ahsekh, chairman of the Houston chapter of the Huey P. Newton Gun Club, told me. His group, named after the co-founder of the Black Panther Party, started in 2014. In 2016, members faced off against armed anti-Muslim demonstrators outside a Nation of Islam mosque in South Dallas. (One of the group's founders was later arrested in an F.B.I. campaign against "black identity extremists." He was imprisoned for five months before the charges against him were dismissed.)

In addition to Ahsekh's group and the Socialist Rifle Association, there are the gun-toting anti-fascists of Redneck Revolt, an organization founded in Kansas in 2009 that now has chapters all over the country, and the queer and trans gun group Trigger Warning, started last year. Left-wing gun culture has already grown enough to produce defectors; in March The New Republic published an essay titled, "Confessions of a Former Left-Wing Gun Nut."

"Everybody's afraid. Everybody's scared. They don't know what to do," said Daryle Lamont Jenkins, founder of the One People's Project, an antifa organization. "They're looking at this crowd that brags about how they have all the guns and they're going to start a second civil war and all this nonsense." Jenkins carried a gun when he went to face off against white-nationalist protesters in Charlottesville, Va., last year. He understands why most on the left still support gun restrictions, but said, "The bigger concern for me is not being protected when a threat comes your way."

As a squishy liberal, I generally find the idea of adding more guns to our febrile politics frightening and dangerous. But sometimes a small desperate part of me thinks that if our country is going to be awash in firearms, maybe it behooves the left to learn how to use them. If nothing else, an armed left might once again create a bipartisan impetus for gun control.

The members of the S.R.A. I met were more sober and responsible than I might have inferred from the group's bullet-strewn Twitter feed. Far from being cosplay revolutionaries, they've adopted bylaws banning members from advocating violence, and they have strict rules about carrying weapons at protests. As their bylaws say, they don't want to be seen as a "militia or anti-fascist action group."

Brad said they try to screen the people who are invited to their monthly range days, weeding out those who seem like "adventurers." "We don't want the John Wayne of the left showing up to our range," he said. Indeed, the S.R.A. comes off more like a wholesome civic organization than a revolutionary underground. It recently became a 501(c)

(4) nonprofit, and its members spend a lot of time on mutual aid projects like collecting funds and supplies for hurricane relief.

Part of the group's mission is to simply provide a home for people who want to shoot, or to learn about shooting, but who recoil at the right-wing trappings of mainstream gun culture. "This seems to be the antithesis of what happens at most Georgia gun ranges," said Steve, a 66-year-old paramedic and certified marksmanship instructor who recently joined the S.R.A. "Mine had a Brian Kemp day last Saturday," he added, referring to Georgia's right-wing gubernatorial candidate. "I go in there, shoot, and leave."

But even if the S.R.A. is surprisingly nonthreatening up close, much of its growth is still a response to a widespread sense of terror and vulnerability. This week, the group released a video interspersing clips of Donald Trump denouncing "globalists" with images of Nazism, anti-Semitic propaganda and anti-Semitic tweets. It ends with pictures of people firing guns, and the words, "We Keep Us Safe." In this combustible moment, some have come to feel that no one else will.

MICHELLE GOLDBERG has been an Opinion columnist since 2017. She is the author of several books about politics, religion and women's rights, and was part of a team that won a Pulitzer Prize for public service in 2018 for reporting on workplace sexual harassment issues.

CHAPTER 4

White Nationalists

White nationalists made headlines in the summer of 2017 during a "Unite the Right" rally in Charlottesville, Va., that left one counterprotester dead. While many were surprised to learn that these far-right groups had grown so prominent, those who had been paying attention had observed increased activity by white nationalists and far-right extremists surrounding the election of Donald Trump. The articles in this section describe the beliefs, actions and growth of white nationalist groups.

Law Center Finds Surge in Extremist Groups in U.S. Last Year

BY MIKE MCPHATE | FEB. 17, 2016

EXTREMIST GROUPS THRIVED in the United States last year as the divisive rhetoric of national political leaders fueled America's anxieties over the country's shifting demographics, according to a report by the Southern Poverty Law Center.

The center found that the number of hate groups organized against racial, religious, sexual or other characteristics rose to 892 in 2015, up from 784 a year earlier.

The 14 percent increase came after three years of declines in extremist groups. Mark Potok, the author of the report, portrayed the shift as a product of white Americans' heightened fears over their shrinking majority during a presidential election.

"I have been writing these year-in-hate and extremism essays for

20 years now and only very rarely, if at all, have we seen a year like last year," Mr. Potok said.

Two diametrically opposed categories accounted for the largest share of last year's surge: the Ku Klux Klan and black separatists. According to the report, the hatreds of those two groups fed in part off the same social discord — battles over the Confederate flag, highly publicized police killings and the attendant rise of the Black Lives Matter movement.

Klan groups saw a comeback in 2015, more than doubling to 190 from 72 a year earlier, the center said. The growth was linked mainly to the dissipation of two larger Klan organizations, but the center said adherents were also galvanized by efforts to lower Confederate flags in Southern states after the mass shooting at a black church in Charleston, S.C., last June.

The number of black separatist groups rose to 180, up from 113 in 2014, the center said. The organizations were driven by anger over police brutality in the same way as the Black Lives Matter movement, but they went beyond demanding reforms to demonize whites, gays and especially Jews.

The center identified 34 anti-Muslim groups, whose anger ratcheted up late in 2015 after the terrorist attacks in Paris and San Bernardino, Calif. In a year in which the battle over same-sex marriage culminated in a landmark Supreme Court ruling guaranteeing the right nationwide, the center counted 48 anti-L.G.B.T. groups that responded by redoubling their efforts toward codifying discrimination.

"Last year was an incredibly dramatic year," Mr. Potok said, "marked by very high levels of political violence, an enormous rage in the electorate, the growth of hate groups and also hate speech in mainstream politics to an extent that we have not seen in decades."

The center, a legal advocacy group in Montgomery, Ala., records only groups that are active, meaning they are more than just a website, and have turned out for protests, recruited members or showed other signs of life.

The report was published as part of the center's quarterly journal, "Intelligence Report," whose cover was illustrated with an image of Donald J. Trump holding forth in front of a microphone alongside the heading "The Year in Hate and Extremism."

The center cited the sometimes caustic rhetoric of the Republican presidential candidates as a reason for some of the blossoming hatreds. While it faulted several Republican candidates, the report singled out Mr. Trump for his remarks on Muslims and immigration across the southern border as the chief catalyst for creeping intolerance.

"White supremacist forums are awash with electoral joy, having dubbed Trump their 'Glorious Leader,' " Mr. Potok wrote in the journal. "And Trump has repaid the compliments, retweeting hate posts and spreading their false statistics on black-on-white crime."

The Trump campaign did not return a message seeking comment.

Among the states with the most hate groups were California, Florida, Georgia, New York, Ohio, Pennsylvania, Tennessee and Texas.

Hate crimes have been declining in the United States over the last decade, according to F.B.I. data. The most recent numbers showed 5,462 reported incidents in 2014, down from 7,642 a decade earlier.

Heidi Beirich of the Southern Poverty Law Center cautioned that the F.B.I. data, which relies on reporting by local law enforcement agencies, undercounted the actual number of cases. A 2013 Justice Department study estimated that cases of hate-inspired victimization occur on the order of more than 250,000 times a year.

In a separate survey released on Wednesday, the center also found an increase in so-called patriot groups, inspired in part by land use conflicts in Oregon and Nevada, where the cattle rancher Cliven Bundy led a dramatic standoff with federal authorities in 2014. The center tracked 998 such groups last year, up from 874 in 2014.

Donald Trump's Extremist Supporters Feel Like Winners Either Way

BY JONATHAN MAHLER AND JULIE TURKEWITZ | NOV. 6, 2016

TEN YEARS AGO, Jim Gilchrist was waging a lonely battle.

His organization, the Minuteman Project, which sent volunteers, often armed, to patrol America's southern border, was widely considered a fringe vigilante group with alarmist views about the dangers posed by Mexican immigrants.

Today, Mr. Gilchrist feels vindicated.

"I never thought I'd see the day where illegal immigration was included in a presidential candidate's top three issues," Mr. Gilchrist, a supporter of Donald J. Trump, said. "For me personally, my mission has been accomplished."

While Mr. Trump seems likely to lose the election, many of his most extreme supporters say they believe that they have already won. Whether the subject is immigration, military intervention, the news media or federal government corruption — and even the entire democratic process — their views, long thought to be well outside the political mainstream, have been given a voice inside it. And that voice belongs to the presidential nominee of a major political party.

Of course, Mr. Trump's populist candidacy has energized ordinary Americans across the country who previously felt alienated from the political system, but it has also emboldened extremist groups that say he has validated their agendas.

It is unclear how much legitimacy these organizations can realistically expect to gain, given the extreme nature of their views to most Americans. But if they are able to maintain even a measure of influence on the right after the election, this could be Mr. Trump's most enduring legacy.

"Trump has shown that our message is healthy, normal and organic — and millions of Americans agree with us," said Matthew

STEPHEN CROWLEY/THE NEW YORK TIMES

Donald J. Trump, campaigning in Las Vegas on Oct. 30, "has shown that our message is healthy, normal and organic," said Matthew M. Heimbach, a founder of a white nationalist group.

M. Heimbach, a co-founder of the Traditionalist Youth Network, a white nationalist group that claims to support the interests of working-class whites. It also advocates the separation of the races.

Whatever happens on Nov. 8, Mr. Trump's candidacy has brought groups like Mr. Heimbach's out of the shadows, and they say they have no intention of returning.

"For racists in this country, this campaign has been a complete affirmation of their fears, worries, dreams and hopes," said Ryan Lenz, the editor of the Hatewatch blog at the Southern Poverty Law Center, which tracks such groups from its headquarters in Montgomery, Ala. "Most things they believe have been legitimized, or have been given the stamp of approval, by mainstream American politics to the point now where it's no longer shameful to be a racist."

The biggest beneficiary may well be the so-called alt-right, the once obscure and now ascendant white nationalist movement with close ties to Breitbart News, the website operated by Mr. Trump's campaign manager, Stephen K. Bannon.

"If Trump loses, I am going to be a little bit sad, but I'm certainly not going to feel like all is lost, because he sling-shotted us a long way," said Richard Spencer, who is credited with coining the term alt-right in 2008. "We can just look at 2015 and 2016 as the beginning of a new stage."

Some on the far right say they believe the election of Hillary Clinton could prove to be its own sort of boon, further embittering and maybe even radicalizing some disappointed Trump supporters.

"There will be people who will say, 'There's nothing we can do to change this system from within,' and they are going to look to perhaps alternative options," said Nathan Damigo, the founder of Identity Europa, a California group dedicated to fighting what it calls the "dispossession" of white Americans.

TIM GOESSMAN FOR THE NEW YORK TIMES

Richard Spencer, who is credited with coining the term alt-right, in Whitefish, Mont. "If Trump loses, I am going to be a little bit sad," Mr. Spencer said, "but I'm certainly not going to feel like all is lost, because he sling-shotted us a long way."

Mr. Damigo envisions building a protest movement along the lines of Black Lives Matter — only to promote the interests of whites. Others on the far right talk about working from inside the political system, lobbying Congress or getting behind Republican candidates who espouse similar views. Some even draw parallels to the post-2008 period, when roiling anger at Barack Obama's election gave birth to the Tea Party, which ended the political careers of Republican moderates from Washington to state capitals.

In short, they say they believe that Mr. Trump's campaign has turned them into a force that the Republican establishment cannot ignore.

"What you can't say is that we're just a bunch of marginal loons," Mr. Spencer said. "The truth is that we have a deeper connection with the Trumpian forces and Trumpian populism than the mainstream conservatives do. They're going to have to deal with us."

Mr. Spencer predicted that the conservative movement's broader embrace of the far right could start with news media outlets adding what he described as "alt-lite" hosts. These would be people who did not consider themselves members of the movement, but shared the conviction that policies on immigration were threatening the country's identity and well-being.

To members of the alt-right, Mr. Trump is a transformative figure. It has been a long time since a mainstream politician, let alone a presidential nominee, talked about the mass deportation of undocumented immigrants and warned about "international banks" plotting "the destruction of U.S. sovereignty." Mr. Trump has given them the legitimacy they long craved.

"Trump reaffirms what we say," Mr. Heimbach said. "He has brought to the forefront the policies of nationalism and secure borders."

While he made headlines in the spring for shoving a young black woman at a Trump rally in Louisville, Ky., Mr. Heimbach said he had not formally endorsed Mr. Trump because "he is not a white nationalist." But Mr. Heimbach added that he and other white nationalists were grateful to Mr. Trump for championing ideas they support.

For his part, Mr. Trump has not expressed support for the white nationalist groups that have rallied to his candidacy. But neither has he distanced himself from them, with the exception of David Duke, the former Klansman who is running for Senate and whom Mr. Trump disavowed after some initial wavering last winter.

They are now beginning to grapple with how to best harness the energy that his campaign has stirred up. Mr. Spencer's group, the National Policy Institute, which says it is "dedicated to the heritage, identity and future of people of European descent in the United States, and around the world," is organizing a valedictory conference in the Ronald Reagan Building in Washington shortly after the election.

The aim is to take stock of the presidential campaign — "when our ideas began invading the mainstream" — and figure out what's next. In addition to Mr. Spencer, the speakers will include Peter Brimelow, the founder of Vdare.com, an anti-immigration website named for Virginia Dare, the first white baby born in the English colonies.

Many of these groups say they have seen a significant surge in interest in the last year. Jared Taylor, a prominent white nationalist, said traffic to his website, American Renaissance, was up 30 percent since the beginning of the Trump campaign.

Mark Pitcavage, a senior researcher at the Anti-Defamation League, suggested that these extremist groups might be trying to rationalize the growing certainty of a Trump loss for their supporters.

"They need an optimistic message for their followers, lest there be demoralization and dropouts," he said. "They are less likely to be willing to talk about how a Trump defeat might hurt their cause."

It is possible that without the organizing force and urgency of his candidacy, these groups will lose much of the momentum that they have gathered over the last 18 months. Other politicians may try to replicate his success, but Mr. Trump is in many ways a unique figure, between his name recognition and his embrace of provocative and even offensive language and ideas as a campaign strategy.

JUSTIN T. GELLERSON FOR THE NEW YORK TIMES

Jared Taylor, a prominent white nationalist, in Oakton, Va. Mr. Taylor said traffic to his website, American Renaissance, was up 30 percent since the beginning of the Trump campaign.

Whether they are able to build on the success of the Trump campaign will depend in part on what Mr. Trump decides to do after the election. It is unclear whether his America First platform was largely a product of political opportunism, or if he is truly committed to the nativist cause. It is equally unclear whether he will try to remain an active political force, most likely through his own media organization, after the election.

In the meantime, Mr. Trump's candidacy has served as a call to arms for extremist leaders who usually have little use for electoral politics.

Mr. Taylor, who has not supported a presidential candidate since Pat Buchanan sought the Republican nomination in 2000, recorded robocalls for Mr. Trump during the Republican primary. And Andrew Anglin, the founder of the neo-Nazi website The Daily Stormer, endorsed Mr. Trump days after he issued his first promise to build a wall to keep out Mexican criminals and "rapists" in June 2015.

"I basically agree with everything Donald Trump advocates," Mr. Anglin wrote in an email. He went on to say Mr. Trump has made it "socially acceptable" to talk about things that were once off limits, such as "the globalist Jewish agenda."

Even in the age of Trump, not everything is socially acceptable. The Daily Stormer recently featured a post urging its readers to make one final push for Mr. Trump via their social media feeds.

"ONLY NORMIE FRIENDLY STUFF," it specified. "NO Nazi stuff, just intense anti-Hillary stuff."

TRIP GABRIEL and **DAVID ZUCCHINO** contributed reporting.

‘White Nationalism,’ Explained

COLUMN | BY AMANDA TAUB | NOV. 21, 2016

A QUESTION HAS BEEN posed in a puzzled whisper in many of the nation’s living rooms and newsrooms ever since Donald J. Trump’s triumph in this month’s presidential election: What, exactly, is white nationalism?

Self-proclaimed white nationalists have happily embraced Mr. Trump’s victory and, particularly, his choice of Stephen K. Bannon as chief strategist, as a win for their agenda. A barrage of groups that fight discrimination and hate speech have, in turn, criticized Mr. Bannon’s appointment, warning that his embrace of the “alt-right” movement was little more than an attempt to rebrand racism and white nationalism into something palatable enough for mass consumption.

And much of the rest of the country has been left to wonder what this unfamiliar term actually means.

While white nationalism certainly overlaps with white supremacy and racism, many political scientists say it is a distinct phenomenon — one that was a powerful but often-unseen force during the presidential election and will most likely remain a potent factor in American and European politics in coming years.

Eric Kaufmann, a professor of politics at Birkbeck University in London, has spent years studying the ways that ethnicity intersects with politics. While most researchers in that field focus on ethnic minorities, Professor Kaufmann does the opposite: He studies the behavior of ethnic majorities, particularly whites in the United States and Britain.

White nationalism, he said, is the belief that national identity should be built around white ethnicity, and that white people should therefore maintain both a demographic majority and dominance of the nation’s culture and public life.

So, like white supremacy, white nationalism places the interests of white people over those of other racial groups. White supremacists and white nationalists both believe that racial discrimination should be incorporated into law and policy.

Some will see the distinction between white nationalism and white supremacy as a semantic sleight of hand. But although many white supremacists are also white nationalists, and vice versa, Professor Kaufmann says the terms are not synonyms: White supremacy is based on a racist belief that white people are innately superior to people of other races; white nationalism is about maintaining political and economic dominance, not just a numerical majority or cultural hegemony.

For a long time, he said, white nationalism was less an ideology than the default presumption of American life. Until quite recently, white Americans could easily see the nation as essentially an extension of their own ethnic group.

But the country's changing demographics, the civil rights movement and a push for multiculturalism in many quarters mean that white Americans are now confronting the prospect of a nation that is no longer built solely around their own identity.

For many white people, of course, the growing diversity is something to celebrate. But for others it is a source of stress. The white nationalist movement has drawn support from that latter group. Its supporters argue that the United States should protect its white majority by sharply limiting immigration, and perhaps even by compelling nonwhite citizens to leave.

Mr. Trump's appointment of Mr. Bannon as his senior counselor and chief West Wing strategist has, more than anything, brought white nationalism to the forefront of conversation. He is the former editor of Breitbart News, a site he described in August to Mother Jones as "the platform of the alt-right." Although the alt-right is ideologically broader than white nationalism — it also includes neoreactionaries, monarchists, and meme-loving internet trolls — white nationalism makes up a significant part of its appeal.

For instance, Richard B. Spencer, who runs the website AlternativeRight.com, is also the director of the National Policy

Institute, an organization that says it is devoted to protecting the "heritage, identity, and future of people of European descent in the United States, and around the world."

Mr. Spencer argues that immigration and multiculturalism are threats to America's white population, and has said his ideal is a white "ethno-state." He has avoided discussing the details of how this might be achieved, saying it is still just a "dream," but has called for "peaceful ethnic cleansing" to remove nonwhite people from American soil.

Mr. Bannon, the Trump adviser, told The New York Times upon his appointment that he does not share those ethno-nationalist views. But under his leadership, Breitbart News has gone to considerable lengths to cater to an audience that does. And in a 2015 radio interview that was resurfaced this week by The Washington Post, Mr. Bannon opposed even highly skilled immigration, implying he believed it was a threat to American culture.

STEPHEN CROWLEY/THE NEW YORK TIMES

Stephen K. Bannon in August. President-elect Donald J. Trump's appointment of Mr. Bannon as his senior counselor and chief West Wing strategist has, more than anything, brought white nationalism to the forefront of conversation.

"When two-thirds or three-quarters of the C.E.O.s in Silicon Valley are from South Asia or from Asia, I think ...," he said, trailing off mid-sentence before continuing a moment later, "a country is more than an economy. We're a civic society."

White nationalists, including Mr. Spencer, have rejoiced at Mr. Bannon's appointment to such a senior position in the Trump White House. But focusing on high-profile figures like Mr. Bannon may obscure the more significant way that white nationalist ideas are affecting politics — and fueling the rise of politicians like Mr. Trump in the United States as well as anti-immigrant populist movements in Britain and continental Europe.

Several studies of other countries have found that a desire to protect traditional values and culture is the strongest predictor of support for the sort of populism that propelled Mr. Trump to power in the United States.

Many of those voters would not think of themselves as white nationalists, and the cultural values and traditions they seek to protect are not necessarily explicitly racial. However, those traditions formed when national identity and culture were essentially synonymous with whiteness. So the impulse to protect them from social and demographic change is essentially an attempt to turn back the clock to a less-diverse time.

A recent working paper by Pippa Norris, a political scientist at Harvard's Kennedy School of Government, and Ronald Inglehart, a political scientist at the University of Michigan, concluded, based on an analysis of wide-ranging survey data, that populists have succeeded by appealing to the cultural anxiety of groups like older white men, who once formed the cultural majority in Western societies "but have recently seen their predominance and privilege eroded."

Elisabeth Ivarsflaten, a professor of politics at the University of Bergen in Norway, came to a similar conclusion after studying anti-immigrant policies in Europe. Their supporters, she found, were motivated by a desire to protect their national culture — suggesting they believed that immigrants posed a threat to it.

Mr. Trump's criticism of immigrants and promise to "make America great again" may have tapped into those same cultural anxieties, fueling his success with older and less-educated white voters. (Over all, he won white voters by 21 percentage points.)

Professor Kaufmann argues that anxiety over white identity and anti-immigrant populist politicians can have a symbiotic relationship, each strengthening the other. When populist politicians gain mainstream success, that can make white nationalist ideas more socially acceptable.

"It's not just a question of ethnic change and people being alarmed over it," he said. "It's also a question of what people see as the boundaries of acceptable opposition. It's about what counts as racism, and whether it's racist to vote for a far-right party."

"This is all about the anti-racist norm," Professor Kaufmann continued. "If it's weakening or eroding because people think the boundaries have shifted."

The Interpreter is a column and newsletter by **MAX FISHER** and **AMANDA TAUB** exploring the ideas and context behind major world events.

On Gab, an Extremist-Friendly Site, Pittsburgh Shooting Suspect Aired His Hatred in Full

BY KEVIN ROOSE | OCT. 28, 2018

EARLY SATURDAY, moments before the police say he barged into a Pittsburgh synagogue and opened fire, Robert Bowers's anti-Semitic rage finally boiled over as he posted one last message online.

But he did not turn to Facebook or Twitter. Instead, the man accused of killing 11 people went to Gab, a two-year-old social network that bills itself as a "free speech" alternative to those platforms, and that has become a haven for white nationalists, neo-Nazis and other extremists. There, he posted a signoff to his followers:

HIAS likes to bring invaders in that kill our people.
I can't sit by and watch my people get slaughtered.
Screw your optics, I'm going in.

— Robert Bowers (@onedingo)

The shooting in Pittsburgh came on the heels of another violent episode involving social media extremism. Cesar Sayoc Jr., the suspect in the pipe bomb mailing campaign, had a history of posting hateful and violent messages on Facebook and Twitter that were laced with misinformation and conspiracy theories.

There have long been hateful enclaves online, and chat rooms and message boards where white nationalists, neo-Nazis and other extremists have congregated. But the popularity of mainstream mega-platforms like Twitter, Facebook and YouTube has created environments in which misinformation and hate can multiply, and where extremists can attempt to convert — or "red pill," in the parlance of right-wing internet activists — a new generation to their cause.

JARED WICKERHAM/THE NEW YORK TIMES

An interfaith vigil was held on Saturday after the shooting at the Tree of Life synagogue in the Squirrel Hill neighborhood of Pittsburgh left 11 dead.

Social media platforms like Facebook and Twitter, once guided by the principle of free speech, have come to realize that an anything-goes approach is ripe for exploitation, and ultimately bad for business.

"The challenge faced by any platform that allows everything permitted under U.S. law is that if left unabated, the most objectionable content will inevitably take over," said Micah Schaffer, a former policy leader at YouTube and Snap who is now a technology policy consultant. "If an online community is dominated by porn, beheadings or white supremacists, most people aren't going to think it's a good place for their baby photos."

Facebook and Twitter's attempts to crack down on hateful and violent speech have been inconsistent, and many objectionable posts still slip through the cracks. (Mr. Sayoc, for instance, was reported to Twitter for making a violent threat against a Democratic television commentator this month, but the company declined to take action against him, a decision it has since said was in error.)

But the companies have made earnest efforts to clean up their platforms — and in the process, they have pushed some extremists to alternative venues like Gab.

Mr. Bowers's affiliation with Gab has already cost the company dearly. On Saturday, the company's web hosting provider, Joyent, said it would stop hosting the site, according to an email posted by Gab on Twitter. Gab's website went offline Sunday night and was replaced with a statement saying that its service would be temporarily inaccessible while it switched to a new hosting provider.

"We have been systematically no-platformed by App Stores, multiple hosting providers and several payment processors," the statement read.

In addition, GoDaddy, the domain name provider, told Gab it had 24 hours to move its domain name to another service, after finding content on the site that promoted violence.

The payment processing platform Stripe, which Gab has used to receive fees for its paid Gab Pro membership level, and which froze Gab's account this month for violating its terms of service, said it was suspending transfers to the company's bank account pending an investigation, according to another email posted to Twitter by Gab. PayPal, another payment processor, canceled Gab's account, saying it had been closely monitoring the site even before Saturday's massacre.

"When a site is allowing the perpetuation of hate, violence or discriminatory intolerance, we take immediate and decisive action," a PayPal spokesman said. Joyent did not respond to a request for comment. A Stripe spokesman said the company could not comment on individual users for privacy reasons.

Gab, which was started in 2016 by a conservative programmer, Andrew Torba, who was fed up with what he saw as Silicon Valley's left-wing censorship, was a controversial project from the start. The announcement of its introduction doubled as a broadside against political correctness, which the company said had "become a cancer on discourse and culture." Gab, its creator said, would be a social network where all speech would be welcome, no matter how noxious or offensive.

In an email interview on Saturday, Mr. Torba, Gab's chief executive, said that he had not reviewed all of Mr. Bowers's posts, but that the company had turned over information about his account to law enforcement agencies and was cooperating with the investigation.

"Because he was on Gab, law enforcement now have definitive evidence for a motive," Mr. Torba wrote. "They would not have had this evidence without Gab. We are proud to work with and support law enforcement in order to bring justice to this alleged terrorist."

Technically, there was nothing special about Gab at the start — its interface was buggy and unattractive, and it lacked the features of more established social networks. But the platform's intentionally slim rule book attracted a crowd of extremists, including white nationalists and neo-Nazis, who had been banned from other social platforms. Milo Yiannopoulos, the former Breitbart writer whose harassment campaigns got him kicked off Twitter, signed up for an account. So did Andrew Anglin, the founder of the neo-Nazi publication Daily Stormer, and Richard Spencer, the well-known white nationalist.

Within months, Gab had become a last refuge for internet scoundrels — a place where those with views considered too toxic for the mainstream could congregate and converse freely. The site's guidelines prohibit threats of violence, but not hateful speech.

Gab's reputation for accommodating extremism may have been what drew Mr. Bowers to the site. In January, he signed up for an account, and began sharing anti-Jewish images, conspiracy theories about Jews controlling the world, and criticism of President Trump — whom, he implied, was too accommodating of Jewish influence. He appeared to have other social media accounts, but Gab was where he aired his hatred in full. His bio on the site read, "Jews are the children of Satan," and a photo on his profile included the number 1488, a reference to Nazism that is popular among white supremacists.

After Mr. Bowers was named as a suspect in the mass shooting, Gab released a statement saying it "unequivocally disavows and condemns all acts of terrorism and violence." The company spent much of Saturday replying to its critics on Twitter, and deflecting blame by pointing out that Mr. Bowers also had accounts on other social networks. The company boasted that its website was getting a million views per hour in the aftermath of the Pittsburgh shooting.

This is not Gab's first run-in with controversy. Last year, Google banned the company's app for failing to moderate hateful content. (The app was rejected by Apple.) In August, Microsoft threatened to cut off Gab's access to its Azure cloud service after posts surfaced on the site advocating genocidal violence against Jews. The posts were ultimately taken down.

Mr. Torba insisted in his email that the shooting had not changed his mind about Gab's core mission of promoting free speech.

"Twitter and other platforms police 'hate speech' as long as it isn't against President Trump, white people, Christians, or minorities who have walked away from the Democratic Party," he wrote. "This double standard does not exist on Gab."

What did exist on Gab was a flurry of posts made by people who appeared to share Mr. Bowers's hatred for Jews.

The site, which functions like a combination of Twitter and Reddit and claims to have more than 700,000 members, is not exclusively for bigots. It has areas for various interest groups, including cryptocurrency traders, doomsday preppers and fans of Japanese-style animated pornography. But Gab's most popular posts espouse far-right ideology.

"Gab became their safe haven because it was actively recruiting the worst of the worst," said Joan Donovan, a media manipulation researcher with the nonprofit organization Data and Society. "Gab's users have complained of a global Jewish conspiracy to control the internet, where Gab is the only place online where they can network with one another."

In the past several years, as Twitter and Facebook have stepped up their enforcement of policies to prevent hate speech and abuse, some white nationalists and neo-Nazis have been forced to find other ways to communicate.

Discord, a chat app built for video gamers, became a haven of white nationalists last year, who used the service to plan and execute the "Unite the Right" rally in Charlottesville, Va. The company subsequently shut down several large far-right groups, but many have since reappeared.

On Saturday, a Discord channel populated by neo-Nazis filled with chatter and gossip about Mr. Bowers's possible involvement in a mass shooting of Jews. Several members praised Mr. Bowers, while others criticized him for jeopardizing the neo-Nazi movement's long-term prospects by resorting to violence.

"This guy just blew out the kneecaps of the movement in order to kill some no name Jews," one member wrote.

A Discord spokeswoman said the company had investigated and found some accounts that violated its terms of service, which it deleted, although she said the accounts were not directly linked to the shooting.

On Gab, however, the talk was less about Mr. Bowers and the anti-Jewish movement, and more about what was happening to the platform itself. On Saturday, as Gab's service providers began to cut ties, one of the most popular posts on the site speculated that the company was being unfairly targeted because "Gab is the free speech platform Jews want to destroy."

Asked if Gab would be changing any of its policies in response to the mass shooting, Mr. Torba gave an unequivocal answer.

"Absolutely not."

U.S. Law Enforcement Failed to See the Threat of White Nationalism. Now They Don't Know How to Stop It.

BY JANET REITMAN | NOV. 3, 2018

For two decades, domestic counterterrorism strategy has ignored the rising danger of far-right extremism. In the atmosphere of willful indifference, a virulent movement has grown and metastasized.

THE FIRST INDICATION to Lt. Dan Stout that law enforcement's handling of white supremacy was broken came in September 2017, as he was sitting in an emergency-operations center in Gainesville, Fla., preparing for the onslaught of Hurricane Irma and watching what felt like his thousandth YouTube video of the recent violence in Charlottesville, Va. Jesus Christ, he thought, studying the footage in which crowds of angry men, who had gathered to attend or protest the Unite the Right rally, set upon one another with sticks and flagpole spears and flame throwers and God knows what else. A black man held an aerosol can, igniting the spray, and in retaliation, a white man picked up his gun, pointed it toward the black man and fired it at the ground. The Virginia state troopers, inexplicably, stood by and watched. Stout fixated on this image, wondering what kind of organizational failure had led to the debacle. He had one month to ensure that the same thing didn't happen in Gainesville.

Before that August, Stout, a 24-year veteran of the Gainesville police force, had never heard of Richard Spencer and knew next to nothing about his self-declared alt-right movement, or of their "anti-fascist" archnemesis known as Antifa. Then, on the Monday after deadly violence in Charlottesville, in which a protester was killed when a driver plowed his car into the crowd, Stout learned to his horror that Spencer was planning a speech at the University of Florida. He spent weeks frantically trying to get up to speed, scouring far-right and anti-fascist websites and videos, each click driving him further into despair. Aside from the few white nationalists who had been identified by the media or on Twitter, Stout had no clue who most of these people were, and neither, it seemed, did anyone else in law enforcement.

There were no current intelligence reports he could find on the alt-right, the sometimes-violent fringe movement that embraces white nationalism and a range of racist positions. The state police couldn't offer much insight. Things were equally bleak at the federal level. Whatever the F.B.I. knew (which wasn't a lot, Stout suspected), they weren't sharing. The Department of Homeland Security, which produced regular intelligence and threat assessments for local law enforcement, had only scant material on white supremacists, all of it vague and ultimately not much help. Local politicians, including the governor, were also in the dark. This is like a Bermuda Triangle of intelligence, Stout thought, incredulous. He reached out to their state partners. "So you're telling us that there's nothing? No names we can plug into the automatic license-plate readers? No players with a propensity for violence? No one you have in the system? *Nothing*?"

One of those coming to Gainesville was William Fears, a 31-year-old from Houston. Fears, who online went by variations of the handle Antagonizer, was one of the most dedicated foot soldiers of the alt-right. Countless YouTube videos had captured his progress over the past year as he made his way from protest to protest across several states, flinging Nazi salutes, setting off smoke bombs and, from time to time, attacking people. Fears was also a felon. He had spent six years in prison for aggravated kidnapping in a case involving his ex-girlfriend, and now he had an active warrant for his arrest, after his new girlfriend accused him of assault less than two weeks earlier. On Oct. 18, the night before the event, Fears and a few others from Houston's white-nationalist scene got in Fears's silver Jeep Patriot for the 14-hour drive. Fears's friend Tyler TenBrink, who pleaded guilty to assault in 2014, posted video from their trip on his Facebook page.

There were four men, two of them felons, and two nine-millimeter handguns. "Texans always carry," Fears said later.

Gainesville would be Spencer's first major public appearance since the violence of the Unite the Right rally two months before, and the city, a progressive enclave in the heart of deep-red north Florida, was on edge. Anticipating chaos, Gov. Rick Scott declared a state of emergency — prompting Spencer to tweet out an image of his head making its way across the Atlantic toward Florida: "Hurricane Spencer." A few days before the event, the Florida Department of Law Enforcement sent out a small, bound "threat book" of about 20 or so figures, most of them openly affiliated with Spencer or with anti-fascist groups, which Stout knew from his own research meant they weren't the people to worry about. Anonymous online chatter on sites like 4chan, meanwhile, described armed right-wing militants coming to Gainesville to test Florida's Stand Your Ground law. Stout envisioned 20 white supremacists with long guns. We're screwed, he thought.

By the morning of Oct. 19, a fortress of security, costing the University of Florida and police forces roughly half a million dollars, had been built around the western edge of the 2,000-acre campus and the Phillips Center for the Performing Arts, where Spencer and his entourage arrived that afternoon. More than 1,100 state troopers and local cops stood on alert, with another 500 on standby. There were officers posted on rooftops. Police helicopters buzzed the skies. The Florida National Guard had been activated off-site, and a line of armored vehicles sat in reserve. Hundreds of journalists from around the United States and abroad were in attendance, anticipating another Charlottesville.

Some 2,500 protesters had descended on the small area cordoned off for the event, where they confronted a handful of white supremacists, most of them Spencer groupies like Fears and his friends. "Basically, I'm just fed up with the fact that I'm cisgendered, I'm a white male and I lean right, toward the Republican side, and I get demonized," Colton Fears, Will's 28-year-old brother, who was wearing an SS pin, told HuffPost. TenBrink, also 28, told The Washington Post that he had come to support Spencer because after Charlottesville, where he was seen and photographed, he had been threatened by the "radical left." He seemed agitated by the thousands of protesters. "This is a mess," he told The Gainesville Sun. "It appears that the only answer left is violence, and nobody wants that."

But Will Fears told reporters he came to Gainesville to intimidate the protesters. "It's always been socially acceptable to punch a Nazi, to attack people if they have right-wing political leanings," he said. "We're starting to push back." He went on: "We want to show our teeth a little bit because, you know, we're not to be taken lightly."

The Spencer speech turned out to be a bust, thanks to an audience so determined to drown him out that at one point they erupted in a chant of "Orange! Blue! Orange! Blue!" as if at a Gators football game. Afterward, the crowd left the auditorium and flooded back onto Hull Road, the long avenue leading toward the center of campus. Thousands of protesters surrounded the small group of Spencer acolytes. TenBrink, a sinewy young man wearing a black T-shirt and jeans, was particularly overwhelmed and jumped a barricade to escape the angry crowd. The police put him in handcuffs and escorted him into a parking garage. Then, for reasons that remain unclear, they uncuffed TenBrink and walked him out of the garage and toward the parking lot, and let him go. Neither TenBrink nor his friends were in the threat book.

There are several versions of what happened after TenBrink was released. It was about 5:15 p.m. The Texans drove down Archer Avenue, the broad street bordering the south edge of campus, about a mile from the secured area. A group of protesters were sitting at a bus stop. The men in the Jeep started shouting "Heil Hitler!" according to the police report and several witness statements. "Do you know my friend Heil? Heil Hitler? Get it?" The men started throwing Nazi salutes.

One of the protesters had come to Gainesville armed with a retractable baton. When the Texans began to harass them, he grabbed his baton and struck a window of the S.U.V. "My life and the lives of those around me was at risk," he told the police. Will Fears jumped out. "I'm about to beat this dude up with his own fricking expandable baton," he later recalled.

Suddenly, witnesses said, a man later identified as TenBrink jumped from the vehicle holding a handgun. "Shoot them!" the Texans were heard yelling. TenBrink pointed the gun at the protester.

WHITE SUPREMACISTS AND other far-right extremists have killed far more people since Sept. 11, 2001, than any other category of domestic extremist. The Anti-Defamation League's Center on Extremism has reported that 71 percent of the extremist-related fatalities in the United States between 2008 and 2017 were committed by members of the far right or white-supremacist movements. Islamic extremists were responsible for just 26 percent. Data compiled by the University of Maryland's Global Terrorism Database shows that the number of terror-related incidents has more than tripled in the United States since 2013, and the number of those killed has quadrupled. In 2017, there were 65 incidents totaling 95 deaths. In a recent analysis of the data by the news site Quartz, roughly 60 percent of those incidents were driven by racist, anti-Muslim, anti-Semitic, antigovernment or other right-wing ideologies. Left-wing ideologies, like radical environmentalism, were responsible for 11 attacks. Muslim extremists committed just seven attacks.

These statistics belie the strident rhetoric around "foreign-born" terrorists that the Trump administration has used to drive its anti-immigration agenda. They also raise questions about the United States' counterterrorism strategy, which for nearly two decades has been focused almost exclusively on American and foreign-born jihadists, overshadowing right-wing extremism as a legitimate national-security threat. According to a recent report by the nonpartisan Stimson Center, between 2002 and 2017, the United States spent $2.8 trillion — 15 percent of discretionary spending — on counterterrorism. Terrorist attacks by Muslim extremists killed 100 people in the United States during that time. Between 2008 and 2017, domestic extremists killed 387 in the United States, according to the 2018 Anti-Defamation League report.

"We're actually seeing all the same phenomena of what was happening with groups like ISIS, same tactics, but no one talks about it because it's far-right extremism," says the national-security strategist P. W. Singer, a senior fellow at the New America think tank. During the first year of the Trump administration, Singer and a colleague met with a group of senior administration officials about building a counterterrorism strategy that encompassed a wider range of threats. "They only wanted to talk about Muslim extremism," he says. But even before the Trump administration, he says, "we willingly turned the other way on white supremacy because there were real political costs to talking about white supremacy."

In March 2018, a 20-year-old white evangelical Christian named Mark Anthony Conditt laid a series of homemade I.E.D.s around Austin, Tex., in largely minority communities. The bombs killed two African-Americans and injured at least four others over the course of several weeks, terrorizing the city, yet the local authorities preferred to describe Conditt, who committed suicide, as a "very challenged young man." Also last spring, another white man, 28-year-old Benjamin Morrow, blew himself up in his apartment in Beaver Dam, Wis., while apparently constructing a bomb. Federal investigators said Morrow's apartment doubled as a "homemade explosives laboratory." There was a trove of white-supremacist literature in Morrow's home, according to the F.B.I. But local cops, citing Morrow's clean-cut demeanor and standout record as a quality-control manager at a local food-processing plant, made sure to note that just because he had this material didn't mean he was a white supremacist. "He could have been an individual that was doing research," the local police chief said.

In this atmosphere of apparent indifference on the part of government officials and law enforcement, a virulent, and violent, far-right movement has grown and metastasized. To combat it, some officials have suggested prosecuting related crimes through expansion of the government's counterterrorism powers — creating a special "domestic terrorism" statute, for instance, which currently doesn't exist. But a report released on Oct. 31 by the Brennan Center for Justice at New York University Law School argues that the creation of such a statute could easily be abused to target "protesters and political dissidents instead of terrorists," and that law enforcement already has ample authority to prosecute domestic terrorism: "Congress must require that counterterrorism resource decisions be based on objective evaluations of the physical harm different groups pose to human life, rather than on political considerations that prioritize the safety of some communities over others."

The report also calls out the Justice Department for its "blind spot" when it comes to domestic terrorism and hate crimes, which Deputy Attorney General Rod Rosenstein conceded earlier in the week. During a conference on Oct. 29, Rosenstein said that according to the latest F.B.I. crime report, "88 percent of agencies that provide hate-crimes data to the F.B.I. reported zero hate crimes in 2016." The Justice Department was reviewing the accuracy of the reports, he noted. "Simply because hate crimes are not reported does not mean they are not happening."

In 2016, the latest full year of data available from the F.B.I., more than 6,100 hate-crime incidents were reported, 4,270 of them crimes against people (as opposed to, say, defacing property). And yet only 27 federal hate-crime defendants were prosecuted that year. "The F.B.I. knows how many bank robberies there were last year," says Michael German, an author of the Brennan Center report and a former F.B.I. agent, "but it doesn't know how many white supremacists attacked people, how many they injured or killed."

More concerning to German, though, is that law enforcement seems uninterested in policing the violent far right. During the first year after Donald Trump's election, protests and riots erupted across the country, often involving men with criminal histories who, by definition, were on the law-enforcement radar. During the so-called Battle of Berkeley in March 2017, for instance, a far-right agitator named Kyle Chapman became a hero to the alt-right after he reportedly pummeled an anti-fascist counterprotester with a billy club. Chapman was a 41-year-old who had two previous felony convictions. He proceeded to travel around the country, engaging in violence at other protests, now under the online moniker Based Stickman — a cheerful reference to the Berkeley attacks.

Chapman was one of a number of known white supremacists to align with the Proud Boys, a nationalist men's movement founded in 2016 by the anti-immigrant "Western chauvinist" Gavin McInnes, a founder of Vice Media. There was also the Rise Above Movement (RAM), an alt-right group composed largely of ex-cons, many with ties to Southern California's racist skinhead movement. Over the past two years, each group engaged in violent confrontations with their ideological enemies — a lengthy list including African-Americans, Jews, Muslims, nonwhite immigrants, members of the L.G.B.T. community and the progressive left — and generally escaped punishment. This changed to a degree over the past few weeks when, after a year-long campaign by journalists at ProPublica and other media outlets, federal prosecutors filed charges against eight members of RAM, including two of its leaders. Similarly, after a pressure campaign on social media, the New York Police Department arrested and charged six members of the Proud Boys in connection with an assault after a speech by McInnes at a Republican club in Manhattan on Oct. 12. On his podcast, McInnes noted that he has "a lot of support" in the N.Y.P.D. (The police commissioner denies this.)

In at least one instance, the police have in fact coordinated with far-right groups. In 2017, a law-enforcement official stationed at a rally in downtown Portland, Ore., turned to a member of a far-right militia group and asked for his assistance in cuffing a left-wing counterprotester, who had been tackled by a Proud Boy.

"This is what public demonstration looks like in an era when white nationalism isn't on the fringes, but on the inside of the political mainstream," says Brian Levin, a former New York City police officer who now leads the Center for the Study of Hate and Extremism at California State University-San Bernardino. During the run-up to some of last year's major events in places like Charlottesville or Berkeley, he notes, "there was an unending stream of violent themed chatter and an almost choreographed exchange of web threats between antagonists across wide geographic expanses" that earned barely a nod from law enforcement.

During a congressional hearing in the wake of Charlottesville, Christopher Wray, director of the F.B.I., told lawmakers last September that the bureau had "about 1,000" open domestic-terror investigations, roughly the same number of investigations the bureau had open on ISIS. The bureau has not provided information on how many of those investigations pertained to white nationalists or other far-right extremists, as opposed to left-wing or "black-identity extremist" groups, nor whether they are full-blown investigations, preliminary inquiries or "assessments." The F.B.I. has also responded to criticism that it has failed to address hateful or threatening messages on social media. The F.B.I. said in a statement: "The F.B.I. does not and cannot police ideologies under the First Amendment." But looking at prosecutions, German says, "it's clear that many of the people targeted for investigation for allegedly supporting the Islamic State were initially identified because of something they said online."

There are serious civil liberties concerns with any broad surveillance of social media, German says. What's also true, he notes, is that the volume of white-supremacist-related content is overwhelmingly high. "There are relatively few Americans voicing their support for ISIS online. But there are millions of racists, anti-Semites, Islamophobes, homophobes and xenophobes who engage in eliminationist rhetoric about the communities of people they fear and hate every day on social media and radio talk shows. Even if the F.B.I. wanted to monitor this hate speech, they wouldn't have the resources, or any way to distinguish between those who talk and those who act."

Levin believes that the Justice Department could be more flexible in pursuing these groups without violating First Amendment concerns. Just as they do with ISIS supporters, law-enforcement agencies would be within their legal rights to monitor, analyze and share any of the publicly available intelligence on white supremacists or hate groups that suggests violent confrontations. "The problem is not that we rightly scrutinize violent Salafist extremism," Levin says, "but that we do so while materially ignoring domestic white nationalists or those on their fringes who also represent a violent threat."

When we first spoke this August, Levin noted the continued ascendance of the far right, even after many of its members went underground after Charlottesville. "The rocket ship is still twirling," he said. Levin predicted that the next big wave of activity wouldn't be around mega-rallies but around what he calls "aggressive maneuvers" by loners or small cells. A series of violent outbursts in a single week in October made his prediction seem prescient.

In just seven days, a Florida man who lived out of a van plastered with stickers, including one of Hillary Clinton's face in cross hairs, is reported to have sent a series of pipe bombs to at least a dozen of Trump's critics. Two days after the first package appeared, a middle-aged white man, having tried unsuccessfully to break into a black church near Louisville, Ky., reportedly shot and killed two elderly African-Americans at a Kroger. "Whites don't kill whites," the man reportedly told an armed white man who confronted him. Then, at week's end, a man who posted on Gab, the alt-right's preferred social-media site, about a "kike infestation" interrupted services at the Tree of Life synagogue in the Squirrel Hill neighborhood of Pittsburgh, armed with an AR-15-style assault rifle and several handguns; he was charged with murdering 11 people and injuring several more, including police officers. The Anti-Defamation League believed it to be the deadliest anti-Semitic attack in American history.

Law enforcement's inability to reckon with the far right is a problem that goes back generations in this country, and the roots of this current crisis can be traced back more than a decade. With violent political messaging emanating from the White House and echoed throughout the conservative media and social-media landscapes, Levin only expects more attacks. "What we need to worry about is the guy who is riled up by this rhetoric and decides to go out and do something on his own," he told me in August. "We have people who are ticking time bombs."

IN APRIL 2009, the Department of Homeland Security's Office of Intelligence and Analysis issued a report warning of a rise in "right-wing extremism." The department is the country's largest law-enforcement body, created after Sept. 11 to prevent and respond to various threats, most specifically those connected to terrorism. While most of its counterterrorism focus has been on preventing Islamist terrorist attacks, the department is also supposed to examine domestic threats, like those coming from violent white supremacists, antigovernment militants and single-issue hate groups, like radical anti-abortion activists.

The author of the report was a senior intelligence analyst named Daryl Johnson, who ran a small Homeland Security domestic-terrorism unit. Two years earlier, in January 2007, Johnson was sitting in his bland second-floor office when he received a call from a contact at the Capitol Police. A first-term Illinois senator named Barack Obama was planning to announce that he was running for president. "Curious if you've heard any threatening chatter," the officer said.

This was the first time Johnson had heard of Obama, and he didn't know about any threats, but that didn't mean there wouldn't be any. Though white-extremist groups had been fairly quiet in the years since Sept. 11, Johnson saw this as a temporary lull. These people never truly went away, he thought; they just needed the right motivation to energize them.

"What do you think's going to happen when the Ku Klux Klan and the neo-Nazis and other white supremacists get wind of this?" the officer asked.

Johnson didn't skip a beat: "I think it's going to be the perfect recruiting and radicalization tool for white supremacy."

At 38, Johnson spoke with the earnestness of an Eagle Scout, which he was. He was also a registered Republican who grew up in a small

Mormon community in rural Virginia where millennialism, or end-times theology, was a core concept. During the 1980s, when Johnson was still in high school, far-right separatists took to the Ozarks or to strongholds in rural Idaho, where they stockpiled food and weapons and conducted paramilitary training in preparation for the biblical "last days." Some, like the Aryan Nations, whose members embraced the racist Christian Identity philosophy, spawned domestic terror cells like the Order, which waged a brutal campaign of bombings, armed robberies and murder, culminating with the June 1984 assassination of Alan Berg, the prominent Jewish radio talk-show host who frequently spoke of flushing out the latent anti-Semitism in Denver's conservative community.

Years of law-enforcement investigation and infiltration of right-wing terror groups commenced, and by the early 1990s, many of the movement's most violent members were dead or in jail. But the government standoffs at Ruby Ridge, Idaho, and Waco, Tex., energized a new generation of separatists, Patriot militias — the forerunners of today's antigovernment militia groups — as well as individuals like Timothy McVeigh, who made his way through various antigovernment and racist ideologies and organizations under the radar of law enforcement, before the 1995 Oklahoma City bombing.

The deaths of 168 people, including 19 children, at the Alfred P. Murrah Federal Building brought the threat of domestic terrorism by white Americans into stark relief. In the aftermath, the F.B.I. added many more agents to work domestic terrorism cases, and Attorney General Janet Reno created a special task force to investigate domestic terrorism. But by the end of 2001, the dominant business of the F.B.I., as well as every other federal law enforcement body, was international terrorism. Years after the Sept. 11 attacks, the supposed threat posed by Al Qaeda and other Muslim groups continued to drive policy, notably at the Department of Homeland Security, which Johnson, who started his career in Army intelligence, joined in 2005. At the time, he later recalled, he was the only analyst exclusively working on non-Islamic domestic threats. By 2007, he had put together a small team of analysts who began to scour extremist websites and message boards. What they found alarmed them.

The militant far right was enjoying a renaissance, thanks to the internet. Hundreds of militia recruitment and paramilitary training videos had sprung up on YouTube, along with promotions for weapons training and, to Johnson's horror, bomb-making manuals. Between October 2007 and March 2008, Johnson and his unit documented the formation of 45 new antigovernment militia groups, which he saw as highly significant given that before fall 2007, these sorts of groups had been on the decline. Some white-supremacist groups, seizing upon the anti-immigration rhetoric that was then fomenting, created violent video games aimed at exploiting public fear of "illegals" streaming over the border.

By the spring of 2008, Obama's candidacy, just as Johnson predicted, had become a lightning rod for white supremacists and other hate groups. As the campaign moved into its final months, law-enforcement agencies intercepted at least two assassination plots against Obama. Other threats and racist posts flooded the internet, where Johnson's team noticed a sharp increase in membership on Stormfront, the first major white-nationalist website. The site added 32,000 new users within the first three months after Obama's inauguration, nearly double the number it added in 2008.

Johnson and his team compiled their findings into a report, which they were still working on when Obama tapped Janet Napolitano, formerly the governor of Arizona, as the new secretary of Homeland Security. Napolitano "got it" when it came to white supremacy, says Juliette Kayyem, who served as the department's assistant secretary for intergovernmental affairs in 2009 and 2010. While serving as Arizona's attorney general, Napolitano coordinated the investigation of one of Timothy McVeigh's accomplices. Now, concerned that a reinvigorated white-supremacist movement could pose a threat to the country's first African-American president and to citizens, Napolitano began asking her intelligence analysts about a rise in lone-wolf "right-wing extremism," a term commonly used in the counterterrorism world to refer to the radical beliefs of fringe players on the right of the political spectrum.

In March 2009, Johnson says he and a few colleagues from the F.B.I. briefed Napolitano on their findings, theorizing that heightened stress because of the continuing financial crisis, coupled with the election of the first black president, created a "unique driver" for individual radicalization and antigovernment and white-supremacist recruitment. Military veterans, including those returning after multiple tours in Iraq and Afghanistan, might be particularly susceptible candidates, they noted, a prediction based on a 2008 F.B.I. assessment that found 203 individuals with military experience who had joined white-supremacist groups since Sept. 11, 2001. It was a tiny number given the overall United States veteran population, which at the time was close to 24 million. It was also a small percentage of the thousands of white supremacists the F.B.I. estimated were active. But the "prestige" that those with military or tactical skills held within white-supremacist groups made their influence much greater, the F.B.I. argued.

Johnson remembers Napolitano, sitting at the conference table, soberly flipping through the PowerPoint slides and thanking the analysts for the presentation. A few days later, the Department of Homeland Security released its report, "Rightwing Extremism: Current Economic and Political Climate Fueling Resurgence in Radicalization and Recruitment," which was distributed across the government and local law-enforcement agencies.

On April 11, 2009, four days after his report was released, Johnson was at home in West Virginia when a PDF of the document was posted on the website of the syndicated conservative radio host Roger Hedgecock. A link to the PDF was also posted on a blog maintained by the Oath Keepers, the antigovernment group composed of numerous law-enforcement officials. "FORWARD THIS TO EVERY AMERICAN!" read the post, which Johnson suspected had been written by a member of the law-enforcement community. "YOU are now a dangerous terrorist according to the Obama administration."

By the next day, news of a "chilling" report from the department was making its way through far-right message boards and the blogosphere, where it was picked apart by conspiracy sites like Infowars, which deemed it evidence of a deep-state plot. More mainstream right-wing pundits like Michelle Malkin considered it, in Malkin's words, an "Obama D.H.S. hit job" on conservatives. Some progressives also had concerns about the report's "dangerously vague and speculative" nature, as a Mother Jones correspondent, James Ridgeway, wrote, warning that "civil libertarians of all stripes" should be nervous and raising the specter of government surveillance.

From the perspective of many people inside the department, the report was "exactly what the department is supposed to do, which is inform and educate our stakeholders about what we see as a threat," Kayyem says. "This was not a political document."

Congressional Republicans, answering to a nascent Tea Party movement and the American Legion, soon took issue with the label "right-wing extremism," which John Boehner, then minority leader of the House, charged was being used by the Department of Homeland Security "to describe American citizens who disagree with the direction Washington Democrats are taking our nation." Boehner was particularly bothered by the report's mention of veterans. "To characterize men and women returning home after defending our country as potential terrorists is offensive and unacceptable," he said in a statement. Several G.O.P. lawmakers called for Napolitano's resignation, as well as that of Johnson, who, in their view, equated conservatives with terrorists.

Johnson was appalled. "I never anticipated such an aggressive, vile backlash," he told me recently. It was puzzling: Just a few months before his April 2009 report was published, the department released an assessment of the cyber threat posed by "left-wing extremists," like the Earth Liberation Front and the Animal Liberation Front. Legislators, the media and the public at large — including progressives — had no objection to that terminology. But the political firestorm over "right-wing extremism" had caused such an uproar that the Department of Homeland Security ultimately avoided using ideological terminology like "right-wing." A few weeks after the report was released, Napolitano formally apologized to veterans, and after intense pressure from veterans' groups, the department withdrew the report.

Afterward, the administration tried to depoliticize the issue. Obama had been elected promising to improve relations with the Muslim world, though this soon provided an opening for conspiracy-minded Republicans like Representative Louie Gohmert, the Texas congressman who once insinuated that Mohamed Elibiary, an adviser to Obama's national-security team, was a member of the Muslim Brotherhood. During the Bush administration, the word "terrorism" had become almost synonymous with Islam. Now, as one former policy adviser recalls, "the Obama people were adamant that it couldn't just be about jihadis."

They adopted a new, less ideological lexicon. Terrorism became "violent extremism," which suggested behavior. The administration also came up with a new paradigm of "ideologically motivated violence" that ostensibly could apply to any form of extremism, not just Islamic terrorism. The Justice Department, the Department of Homeland Security and the State Department would develop "countering violent extremism" programs that focused on outreach and community engagement, not warrantless surveillance, though in practice they were still an effort to identify and root out jihadist elements from American Muslim communities, just as they had been during the Bush administration.

At the same time, most of the work exclusively focused on domestic extremism stopped at the Department of Homeland Security. "I blame an entire political apparatus led by Republicans that made calling something 'right-wing extremism' a political statement," says Kayyem, who notes the paradox of G.O.P. leaders' attacking Democrats for refusing to use the phrase "radical Islamic extremism." "They'd say if you can't say it, you can't fight it," she says. "But it cuts both ways. If you're not allowed to say that white supremacy is a form of radicalization, then how are you going to stop it?"

JOHNSON'S 2009 REPORT proved prescient. In February 2011, the Southern Poverty Law Center said that in the previous year, the number of domestic hate groups in the United States had reached more than 1,000 for the first time. The antigovernment Patriot movement gained 300 new groups over the same time period, a jump of over 60 percent. Every sphere of the far right was being energized at the same time. There was also an uptick in so-called lone wolves, who held extremist views but associated with no specific organization. In May 2010, a year after Johnson's report was released, a father and son from Ohio, members of a little-known antigovernment movement called "sovereign citizens," shot and killed two police officers during a traffic stop in West Memphis, Ark. It was the 12th attack or foiled plot by white-extremist "lone wolves" since 2009, almost all of which received little publicity.

The United States attorney from Western Arkansas, Conner Eldridge, was one of a number of Justice Department prosecutors who felt the department had given short shrift to domestic terrorism. Quietly, Eldridge began to network with United States attorneys from states with a history of white-supremacist activity. They pressed the Justice Department for more resources. "Our thesis was, hey, let's focus on domestic terrorism at an equal level as we're focusing on international terrorism, because they're both terrorism," Eldridge told me recently. "But we consistently confronted, at every level, a sort of lack of attention to domestic terrorism. The day-to-day focus was on the next potential ISIS attack."

Back in Washington, weeks would go by with the daily national threat briefings rarely if ever discussing possible domestic threats from the far right. At the F.B.I., counterterrorism agents candidly admitted that domestic terrorism was seen as a backwater and that the only path to advancement was through international terrorism cases. In a recent report on law enforcement's evaluation of Muslim versus right-wing extremism, a team of researchers at the University of North Carolina, Chapel Hill, noted that in 2008 and 2009 — the only years for which figures were made public — fewer than 350 of the F.B.I.'s 2,000 counterterrorism agents were assigned to domestic terrorism.

After a series of violent attacks by white supremacists, including on a Jewish community center and a nearby retirement home in Overland Park, Kan., Attorney General Eric Holder announced in 2014 that he was reconvening the Justice Department's Domestic Terrorism Executive Committee. The group hadn't met in 13 years. "It wasn't the same as it had been before, but it was something," says Eldridge, who was tapped to head the committee, which included representatives from about 15 law-enforcement agencies and five Justice Department divisions, including the F.B.I. and the U.S. Marshals. "But we had no budget, no staff, and we had no person whose sole job was to run the committee."

The ceaseless focus on ISIS and Al Qaeda filtered down to local law enforcement. The administration's much-touted "countering violent extremism" agenda was directed at various threats. But "the language heavily focused on recruitment and radicalization by ISIS and Al Qaeda," recalls Nate Snyder, a counterterrorism adviser to the Obama administration at the Department of Homeland Security from 2009 through 2017. As early as 2010, he says, his office was receiving calls from police officers asking for help in many Southern and Midwestern states. "They'd be like, 'Thanks for that stuff on Al Qaeda, but what I really need to know is how to handle the Hammerskin population in my jurisdiction,'" he says, referring to the white-supremacist skinhead group.

In 2011, the White House described the threat of Al Qaeda and its affiliates as the "pre-eminent security threat to our country." By 2013, a new threat had emerged: so-called homegrown violent extremists, or H.V.E.s, a category of people who, though born in the United States, were inspired by a nondomestic ideology to commit violence. H.V.E.s, who tended to be Muslim, were not to be mistaken for domestic terrorists, who by definition were not only Americans but also driven by a domestic ideology like white supremacy. And yet the two were often conflated, and therefore "homegrowns" were also perceived as domestic terrorists: the Tsarnaev brothers, responsible for the Boston Marathon bombing in 2013; the perpetrators of the San Bernardino massacre or the mass shooting at the gay nightclub Pulse in Orlando. Dylann Roof, born in South Carolina, whose homegrown racism was nurtured on neo-Nazi websites like The Daily Stormer, was not, in this context, a domestic terrorist, nor were any of his beliefs seen as indicative of "violent extremism." His shooting spree in a church in Charleston, in which he killed nine African-Americans, was interpreted as something else. What drove him, authorities said, was hate. He was a murderer.

This dichotomy plagued Representative Bennie Thompson, the Mississippi Democrat who served as ranking member of the House Homeland Security Committee. For years, Thompson pressed both the administration and fellow members of Congress to be more outspoken on domestic terrorism. "The silence was almost deafening when it came to raising any of those issues in Congress," he says. "And the administration had this do-nothing approach. They kept telling us, well, we see that white supremacy is a problem, but there's no way we can get ourselves involved in this because they won't talk to us."

It was a curious response from an administration whose "C.V.E." agenda supposedly addressed all types of ideologically motivated violence. "I really suspect they did some polling and found out that there were certain things an African-American president couldn't talk about," one former adviser said. "I think they didn't want to poke the bear."

This approach was most evident with Obama's second Homeland Security chief, Jeh Johnson, who came to the department in 2013, after a three-year sojourn as general counsel to the Defense Department, where he provided legal authority for the drone-strike program. During Johnson's tenure, Nate Snyder says, his office received calls from evangelical pastors worried about far-right recruitment in their congregations. There was also concern about reports of white supremacy in the military.

Johnson, who told me that fear of another ISIS-style attack kept him up at night, held regular round tables with imams and other members of the Islamic community. He resisted the pressure from some members of his staff, and some in Congress, like Thompson, to make similar overtures to communities concerned about antigovernment or white-supremacist groups. He thought it would be absurd to hold round tables with sovereign citizens and white supremacists. "I didn't think that would have been a very effective use of my time to try," he told me.

Johnson never called Dylann Roof a domestic terrorist, a phrase commonly applied to Timothy McVeigh. "If there was ever an opportunity to define white extremists as domestic terrorists, Dylann Roof was it," Snyder says. "But people went back and forth, and it went down the same careful deliberation that happens with active shooters: Maybe it was a mental-health issue. Maybe he was 'disturbed.' Maybe he had a predisposition to violence."

When I spoke to Johnson, he felt it was not his place to call Roof a terrorist. There isn't a crime of "domestic terrorism" to charge someone with. "There is a certain type of violent extremism that is by nature more of a matter for law enforcement, and another that is about engaging communities at the local level," he said. But the country's chief law-enforcement official at the time, Attorney General Loretta Lynch, also didn't call Roof a terrorist — though she did note that his mass shooting, which she was prosecuting as a hate crime, seemed to meet the definition of terrorism. "Hate crimes are the original domestic terrorism," she said. James Comey, then director of the F.B.I., wasn't sure. Terrorism, he stated in June 2015, was "more of a political act," and he didn't see the Charleston shooting as political. Even after a racist manifesto Roof penned surfaced online stating his intent to "protect the white race" by instigating a race war, Comey still wasn't sure it met the definition. "I only operate in a legal framework," he told HuffPost.

The refusal to name the attack as "terrorism" was, in some critics' eyes, a crucial misstep that would have far broader implications. "I was very pleased when the Obama administration started and said, We're not going to use the phrase 'war on terror,'" says Erroll Southers, a former F.B.I. agent and now director of the Safe Communities Institute at the University of Southern California. "I think the Obama people decided, O.K., we're not going to call it 'terrorism,' thinking it was a good thing. The problem was they didn't realize how much it emboldened the other side and gave them political cover."

IN THE MONTHS following Donald Trump's inauguration, security analysts noted with increasing alarm what seemed to be a systematic erosion of the Department of Homeland Security's analytic and operational capabilities with regard to countering violent extremism. It began with the appointment of a new national-security team. Like their counterparts now running immigration policy, the team came from the fringe of conservative politics, some of them with connections to Islamophobic think tanks and organizations like ACT for America or the Center for Security Policy, whose founder, Frank Gaffney, was Washington's most prominent peddler of anti-Muslim conspiracy theories.

In addition to Gaffney, whose biased and statistically flawed data on the "Muslim threat" became the premise for Trump's so-called Muslim ban, there were other ideological fellow travelers like Sebastian and Katharine Gorka, the husband-and-wife national-security team. Sebastian Gorka became a senior White House adviser, and Katharine Gorka became a senior adviser to the Department of Homeland Security. During the transition, Sebastian Gorka predicted the demise of "C.V.E.," which he suggested was a fuzzy, politically correct approach to a problem — terrorism — that needed a better fix. Shortly afterward, Katharine Gorka, who once criticized the Obama administration for "allowing Islamists to dictate national-security policy," made it clear, Nate Snyder recalls, that she didn't like the phrase "countering violent extremism." From now on, the mission would be focused on "radical Islamic terrorism," the White House's go-to phrase, which, as Sebastian Gorka later explained, was intended to "jettison the political correctness of the last eight years."

A surreal scene, replicated in nearly every department and agency, soon began to play out inside the Department of Homeland Security. George Selim, a longtime national-security expert in both the Bush and Obama administrations who headed the Office of Community Partnerships, which worked with local government and civic groups on C.V.E. efforts, noted that as the months passed, "it was clear that there were fewer and fewer of the career civil servants at the table for critical policy decisions." Some political appointees seemed to have virtually no experience with the issues they had been tapped to advise on. Katharine Gorka, as her own LinkedIn biography notes, had never held a public-sector job before joining the department, nor did she seem to have any practical experience in national security, or law enforcement, or intelligence. Another new senior Homeland Security official, the retired Navy officer Frank Wuco, had made a career of lecturing to the military about the jihadi mind-set, often while role-playing as a member of the Taliban in a Pashtun hat and kaffiyeh. "That's who was trying to tell me he understands the threat," an official said dryly.

By February 2017, after the Trump administration issued its first executive order trying to ban citizens of Muslim-majority countries from entering the United States, several American Muslim groups decided to reject federal C.V.E. grant money they were awarded under the Obama administration out of concern over the new administration's framing of the issue. That March, the White House froze the $10 million the previous administration had allotted for the grants, pending review. While that review was underway, the Department of Homeland Security and the F.B.I. issued a joint intelligence bulletin, dated May 10, warning that white supremacists might pose "a threat of lethal violence" over the next year. The report, which some analysts said reflected a fraction of the actual numbers, said that white supremacists "were responsible for 49 homicides in 26 attacks from 2000 to 2016 ... more than any other domestic extremist movement."

At the end of June, the Department of Homeland Security withheld grant money from several previously approved applicants whose focus was on studying extremists' online networks and helping both white supremacists and Muslim extremists leave their movements. Though the total budget for C.V.E. was minuscule given the department's overall grant budget, rejecting those programs nonetheless produced "a real chilling effect," as one policy analyst recalls. Some researchers withdrew from plans to brief lawmakers on far-right extremism.

In July 2017, Selim tendered his resignation. Not long afterward, a senior official on the interagency task force running C.V.E. efforts withdrew. More departures followed. The Department of Homeland Security renamed the Office of Community Partnerships the Office of Terrorism Prevention Partnerships. At the department's Office of Intelligence and Analysis, analysts specifically looking at domestic terrorism and coordinating with local law enforcement were reassigned as public-affairs liaisons, Snyder says. "So no one is looking at the intelligence and connecting the dots, which is what the Department of Homeland Security was created to do."

In the lingo of the counterterrorism world, the department's responsibility is anything "left of boom," meaning all the pre-emptive steps that might prevent an attack, from securing the borders to synthesizing and sharing intelligence to working with community leaders and local law enforcement to help them better identify risks. Today, at least for the federal government, Snyder says "left of boom is dead."

WILLIAM FEARS WAS born in 1987 and spent his childhood in Jasper, Tex., a tiny and deeply segregated town about 130 miles northeast of Houston. East Texas is Klan country, and Jasper holds a notable spot in the racist history of the region as the town where, in 1998, when Fears was 10, three white men lynched a black man named James Byrd Jr., chaining him to the back of a truck and dragging him to death.

Early in his life, Fears, searching for identity, cycled through a long list of ideologies. He was 14 on Sept. 11, 2001, old enough to absorb the patriotic fervor of that moment but too young to enlist. For a year or two, he was a Michael Moore-style populist, having been "red-pilled on 'Bowling for Columbine.'" Then, having spent a great deal of his spare time stoned and watching YouTube, Fears embraced the Sept. 11 "truthers" movement. As he spent more and more time on sites like Infowars, he was exposed to notions that the government, backed by the Illumi-nati, the globalists, the Freemasons — Jews, but not "the Jews" as he would later come to see them — had blown up the towers, crashed the financial markets and plunged the country into economic crisis. This led to his next great obsession: the candidacy of the G.O.P. presidential hopeful Ron Paul, a libertarian who had amassed a large grass-roots following of what The New York Times then called "iconoclastic white men."

But Fears eventually grew bored with Paul, just as he had grown bored with Michael Moore, and it was in this state of vague political disillusionment, and heavy drug use, that Fears kidnapped a former girlfriend in 2009 and stabbed her in the face, legs and neck before she managed to escape. In 2010, he was sentenced to seven years in prison.

Fears doesn't like to talk much about his sojourn in the Texas state-prison system, though like many young men who went from the penitentiary to the far right, he was introduced to the basic tenets of white supremacy there. "White guys got to stick together," he says, referring to an admitted friendship with members of the Texas branch of the Aryan Brotherhood, one of the most notoriously brutal white-supremacist gangs in the country. But he dropped those friendships after prison, he insists. "I didn't like the whole Nazi skinhead thing with tattoos on their face and beating up minorities for no reason," he says, implying that they represented an earlier generation: "They're like 1.0s."

Six years later, Fears was paroled and emerged from prison drug-free but otherwise largely the same. He was still a conspiracy theorist, though he was less obsessed with the government, his friend John

Canales noticed when they reconnected that summer. "Now it was all about the Jews," Canales says. At home in the Houston suburb of Pasadena, Fears submerged himself in what to him was the new, hyperconnected world of the internet, where every YouTube video he watched algorithmically directed him to others with increasingly far-right political agendas. He was fascinated by men like Richard Spencer, who fashioned himself as the second coming of George Lincoln Rockwell, the founder of the American Nazi Party. He was also intrigued by Donald Trump, the troubadour of a new generation of angry white men, the alt-right movement — white supremacy 2.0 — with its in-jokes and symbols that were mostly lost on U.S. law enforcement.

Fears believed in the power of memes, though alt-right memes, while dripping in irony, were also, in essence, hate speech, part of a propaganda war arguably intended to spread terror just as much as any ISIS execution video. Fears, his friend Canales says, was one of the first people Canales knew to understand this and promote the memes as broadly as he could, standing on street corners and "*sieg heil*-ing" at passers-by or waving a swastika-laden Pepe the Frog sign reading "Free Helicopter Rides," an allusion to the murder of political enemies, notably leftists.

In December 2016, less than six months after getting out of prison, Fears went to his first Richard Spencer event, on the campus of Texas A&M. More so-called free-speech events followed, where young white men in red MAGA hats and polo shirts descended upon college campuses or progressive enclaves in otherwise blood-red states: a clean-cut Trumpian army, marching in formation or hurling insults at activists who, outraged by their very presence, would try to fight them.

Sometimes the police would intervene, or not. Fears, for one, always felt safe with the police in Texas, though he said "they work for ZOG" — the so-called Zionist Occupied Government. "They'll take their paycheck over the country."

Cops would stand watch at events, sometimes on horseback, and while they might not have been ideologically aligned with the alt-right, they still tolerated them. Fears said the cops were far less forgiving of Antifa, a catchall term that has been used to describe dedicated anti-fascists and so-called anarchist extremists, as well as animal rights activists, immigration rights activists, members of the local Socialist movement, environmental protesters like those who had recently been blasted by water cannons and rubber bullets at Standing Rock, and Black Lives Matter supporters, whose protests have been met by dozens of cops in riot gear, as well as sometimes members of a paramilitary support unit. One Houston activist, who went to high school with Fears, recalls a rally where the police posed for pictures with members of the alt-right. "Very buddy-buddy," he says.

The same essential scenario played out across the country. At a rally in Sacramento in June 2016 organized by the white-supremacist Traditionalist Worker Party, a throng of counterprotesters showed up. "The police didn't step in really at all," a police observer and representative of the National Lawyers Guild later told The Sacramento Bee. "They basically just let people do what they wanted to do," the observer said. "In this case, someone made a decision just to let them fight it out." Ten people were hospitalized, at least five for stabbing wounds and other lacerations, most of them left-wing counterprotesters, some of whom were later charged with assault. Only one white supremacist was arrested, though court records originally acquired by The Guardian mentioned at least four T.W.P.-affiliated men who came armed with knives to the rally but were not charged. "We're looking at you as a victim," an investigator with the California Highway Patrol reportedly assured a member of the T.W.P. after the rally.

One domestic-terrorism expert who conducts hate-crimes training for law enforcement was baffled by the pushback she received from police officers who didn't seem to view white-supremacist groups as a law-enforcement problem. "They'd say things like, 'Why aren't you calling Black Lives Matter or Antifa a hate group?' The answer is, because they're not hate groups! But they didn't see it that way."

It was in this atmosphere that Fears made his progress through various protests. He traveled to Charlottesville with a backpack of dystopian gear: goggles, gloves and a helmet, though he disguised himself as a Trump supporter in a suit. It was war. It was also fun. By the summer of 2017, the media had begun to cover more far-right events, leading more people to show up in protest, which furthered the right's victimization narrative, which in turn led to more events and more violence, all of which was packaged into neat selling points for a movement whose actual real-life followers may have been far fewer than they appeared.

A person's willingness to brawl was a point of pride. Some of the most ardent fighters, many of them felons, became celebrities in their own right, offered speaking slots at rallies, where their V.I.P. status earned them police protection. The Rise Above Movement, led in part by a gang member who had gone to prison for an attack, turned beat-downs into an art form, which they promoted on YouTube, drawing recruits. Nathan Damigo, a former Marine who was incarcerated for five years for armed robbery, used footage of his punching a young woman in the face during a Berkeley protest as a recruiting video for his white-nationalist organization, Identity Evropa. The Proud Boys went as far as to create an entire culture around gang-style rituals, including initiation beatings.

On Facebook, various white men were stating their intention of going to Charlottesville for what they understood would be a huge gathering of the tribes, making plans of whom to meet up with and what to bring. Fears initially advised against carrying weapons, but he suggested keeping them close by. "It all comes down to police," he said on Facebook. "If they leave us to fight for ourselves like in Berkeley, we know to get ready for bricks to start flying."

In private communications on the chat service Discord, posted online by the progressive watchdog Unicorn Riot, organizers of Unite the Right spent weeks discussing tactics. The F.B.I. itself was limited in its surveillance capacity (though many left-wing groups argued that this did not prevent the bureau from monitoring their activities), and in the absence of comprehensive federal scrutiny, right-wing activists trawled through left-wing websites, shared photos of leading anti-fascist and racial-justice activists and infiltrated real-life gatherings. In advance of the event, leaked chats documented potential attendees openly advising their comrades to take note of any threats of violence so they could share them with the police. Erroll Southers later remarked on the sophistication of advising their followers not to bring cellphones, and sharing information among small cells of affinity groups: "From an intelligence perspective, it was very impressive."

From a law-enforcement perspective, it was chaos. Rarely did a white-supremacist event draw more than 60 people before 2016; 100 was remarkable. But Charlottesville was another galaxy, both in the sheer number of marchers and their diversity. Southers notes, "You had factions of white nationalists, white supremacists, Klan members, neo-Nazis, neo-Confederates — which was like having ISIS, Al Qaeda, Al Shabab and Boko Haram at the same rally. And they were all rallying together, shoulder to shoulder, while the police watched these people go toe to toe sort of like a modern-day 'Game of Thrones' battle."

"I PUT MY BATON on the ground and hands in the air," the protester later said of the moment when Tyler TenBrink pointed his gun directly at him. The man was terrified. TenBrink took aim and fired. One of the other protesters hid in the trees. Several more crouched behind a small wall, screaming. The bullet missed. The men jumped back into Fears's Jeep and, with Colton behind the wheel, sped away toward Interstate 75 — but not before a witness wrote down the license-plate number.

Lieutenant Stout learned of the shooting later that night, and while no one was hurt, his heart sank. In all his preparations, Stout hadn't considered that violence might occur outside the secure perimeter they had so carefully set up. That night, the Florida state police caught up with the Jeep on the highway and arrested the Texans. The city officials breathed a sigh of relief and lauded the day as a success.

Will Fears spent more than 40 days in the Alachua County Jail on $1 million bail. Depending on whom he is talking with, he and his brother and TenBrink, who both remain in the Alachua County Jail, were the "celebrities" of the jail, or maybe just Fears was. He portrayed his stay as fairly cushy, and one in which he was a very big deal, which of course he wasn't to the authorities who picked him up in December, after Texas ordered him extradited back to Houston to face charges in the supposed assault of his girlfriend last October. Along the way back to Texas, Fears tried to make conversation. "I was on the news, you didn't see that?" he remarked. When Fears arrived back in Houston, he spent two nights in the Harris County Jail, then appeared before a judge, who promptly released him on $5,000 bail.

Fears returned home to Pasadena and resumed the same life he had always led. Apparently unconcerned about exposure, he had posted his cellphone number on social media. Earlier this year, I called him. We met at a Belgian cafe in a rapidly gentrifying part of Houston. When I arrived, Fears was sitting at an outside table, drinking an Arnold Palmer.

Fears told me he had spent most of the past year celebrating the alt-right's covert domination of the news cycle. He seemed thrilled that Donald Trump tweeted about a so-called migrant caravan, which, like the supposed "white genocide" in South Africa, was mostly fiction. Yet it was effectively promoted by alt-right websites like The Daily Stormer and Breitbart, and now right-wing celebrities like Ann Coulter and Tucker Carlson were talking about it. "This idea that the alt-right is falling apart and is going to go away, it's not true," he says. "The alt-right formulates all these ideas," he went on. "What Tucker Carlson talks about, we talked about a year ago."

It was a few days after the massacre of 17 people in Parkland, Fla., and Fears had been considering the spate of school shootings in America. He repeated the rumor, widespread on 4chan and Gab, that the shooter, Nikolas Cruz, was Jewish, and so were many of his victims. It's unclear if this is true. But if it were, it would make no sense to

Fears, who, if he believes in anything, believes in the essentially tribal nature of all human beings. Jews, he said, "have a biological need to look out for their own." He had spoken a bit about what he called the J.Q., or Jewish Question, as successive generations of anti-Semites have referred to the debate over how Western nations should handle the presence of Jews in their societies. "I don't hate them for it, but I realize that their interests aren't the same as mine."

Fears's views aren't unique — roughly 22 million Americans call it "acceptable" to hold neo-Nazi or white-supremacist views, according to an ABC News/Washington Post poll taken in the wake of Charlottesville in August 2017. Roughly the same number of people, about 10 percent of Americans, said they supported the "alt-right"; about half of those polled said they were against it. Driving around Fears's neighborhood one day, I saw Confederate flags, and American flags, and sometimes a Blue Lives Matter flag, and the black-and-white "Don't Tread on Me" flag waving from shiny new trucks. I also saw row after row of McMansions, many of them with swimming pools. There were new S.U.V.s parked in the driveways, and boats: signs of money made and money spent. One former high school classmate of Fears's described the culture as "wannabe redneck."

Fears says that unlike him, the bulk of the alt-right prefers to stay in the shadows. "I see a lot of people and talk to a lot of people that people would pay a lot of money to find out who they are," he says. Some of them, he suggests, take part in his weekly Thursday-morning "fight club," practicing mixed martial arts. Some have white-collar jobs or are veterans, groups that make up a large part of the movement.

Fears was wearing a baseball cap adorned with a red, white and blue patch known as the "whomster" flag. It's "kind of a racist joke," he said, albeit one that most people won't get, as they probably have no clue what "whomster" means (it's a common meme that refers to the supposed, if baseless, fact that African-Americans say "whomst" a lot). The flag featured the Texas lone star against a backdrop of 14 red and white stripes, an allusion to a signature white supremacist slogan addressing their goal of preserving the white race. The star is centered on a large blue sonnerad, or black sun, an ancient symbol favored by white supremacists, who see it as less obvious than, say, a swastika. In recent years, even longtime neo-Nazi groups like the National Socialist Movement have rebranded by dropping the swastika for less "triggering" symbols like sonnerads or runes. The meaning is the same.

Fears has said that he was upset that his little brother, who in September pleaded guilty to accessory to attempted murder, got in so much trouble. "He's not really a white nationalist that much," he said during an interview with a right-wing podcast. "He's really only involved in anything as a result of being my little brother."

It was a bit like the little brother-big brother Boston bombing duo, Dzhokhar and Tamerlan Tsarnaev, whom Fears identifies with. He agreed to meet with me, he said, because I had written about them. "I think it's easy for our generation, or the youth, the way society is now, to feel victimized. It's like with your back against the wall, you know what I mean?"

In the Tsarnaevs' case, this led to terrorism, and for Dzhokhar, the surviving brother, it led to a stretch on death row. Fears, drinking his iced tea-lemonade concoction, considered this. "Maybe he saw a lot of things in the world that bothered him and just didn't know how to deal with it," he said. "I can sort of relate to that."

Fears munched on some bread. "You're Jewish, right?" he said pleasantly.

In fact, I am. And while I happened to be sitting across the table from an admitted fascist who admires Adolf Hitler and has advocated (he says trollishly) "white Shariah," I didn't feel threatened by Will Fears. Like so many of the movement's vague anymen, he presented himself as polite, articulate and interested in cultural politics, and though his views are abhorrent, he stated them all so laconically you might forget that he actually believes in the concept of a white ethnostate. And that's the point: The genius of the new far right, if we could call it "genius," has been their steadfast determination to blend into the larger fabric of society to such an extent that perhaps the only way you might see them as a problem is if you actually want to see them at all.

THE PURPOSE OF the F.B.I.'s Joint Terrorism Task Force is to investigate terrorism and share information from those investigations so that the law-enforcement community is able to identify the most dangerous individuals. State and local law-enforcement "fusion centers" were set up with this same goal in mind. There are perhaps half a dozen information-sharing and threat-assessment networks available to law enforcement. In an alternate universe, these networks would function efficiently. In reality, German says, "far-right violence remains a blind spot. It just isn't properly tracked or understood."

On Aug. 31 this year, his 25th anniversary on the force, Dan Stout retired from the Gainesville Police Department, in part because of the stress and fatigue he endured from the Spencer incident. "The level of resources and financial impact these types of events are now costing communities to prepare for and manage, it's just unsustainable," he says. "How much of our city do we literally turn into a quasi-police state to manage this?" Stout's study of the alt-right and left-wing movements made him an "expert," at least in the eyes of federal and state law enforcement, who, he says, began to invite him to visit their jurisdictions to share what he had learned. "They were soaking it up like a sponge," he says. And yet, in reality he feels that they had collectively dodged a bullet — "no pun intended," he says. "Just another inch to the right or the left and we'd have had a very bad situation."

In May, I called up the Harris County district attorney's office to ask why someone who had been in jail in Florida on $1 million bond had, upon extradition, been released on $5,000 bond. Joshua Phanco, a prosecutor who at the time was in charge of Fears's case, was alarmed by the call. He vaguely recalled that Fears had been in prison in Florida, but he wasn't aware that Fears had been charged with attempted murder, or that he had anything to do with white supremacy. "This is the first I'm hearing this," he told me. (Fears's charge in Florida has since been dropped.)

Phanco, who has since moved on to the district attorney's major-crimes division, spoke with me for two hours. He diagramed the byzantine system that is the Harris County criminal-justice system, one of the nation's largest, and a study in dysfunction. There is no central database, no way to share information among all the tiny police departments that feed into the clerk's office, which then divvies up crimes among 22 criminal courts, now scattered across the entire county. Basically, he said, unless someone tells him about a guy he's prosecuting, he has no clue.

"I mean, how come I didn't know what happened in Florida?" he said. "Is it my fault? Is it Florida's fault? How come there wasn't an officer in Houston watching this? How come he was on nobody's radar?" Houston has an aggressive gang task force whose investigators have deep knowledge of everyone from the street-level drug dealers to the cartel bosses. "If a fairly high-up guy from MS-13 sneezes, I get a call at 10 p.m.," he said.

If Fears were on someone's radar, Phanco doubted he would ever get off it. "But who's responsible for keeping track of these alt-right guys in Houston? Nobody. For me the question is, well, how come? If you want to look at these guys as terrorists — which I think it is when they're firing guns out of cars at protesters," he noted, "then the question remains: Who or what will prevent him from committing more crimes? And, from my chair, nobody," Phanco said. "Nobody's watching it, nobody's tracking it. And that's what's got me scared."

JANET REITMAN is a contributing writer for the magazine who is working on a book about the rise of the far right in post-9/11 America. She is also a contributing editor for Rolling Stone.

CHAPTER 5

Animal Rights and Ecological Extremists

Extremism isn't just on the right. Some favored causes of the left include animal rights and environmental protection. And as with most political movements, these causes too have their extremists, some taking actions so severe that it has landed them on terrorist watch lists. The articles in this chapter detail the beliefs, motivations and actions of those who have organized to protect animal rights and the environment.

Animal Rights: A Growing Movement in U.S.

BY WILLIAM ROBBINS | JUNE 15, 1984

PHILADELPHIA, JUNE 14 — Out of the darkness, five figures moved quietly down a University of Pennsylvania walk, entered a building, descended to a subbasement and broke into a laboratory.

What the band of intruders found on Memorial Day was an audiovisual record on 32 magnetic tapes of several years of brain-damaging experiments on monkeys and baboons. The discovery has stirred protests here, embroiled university officials in long hours of explanations in defense of their research and focused attention on new currents rippling through a resurgent, centuries-old movement to defend animals against mistreatment.

Since the 18th century, organized efforts have been under way to make more people sensitive to animals' sufferings. Groups such as the Society for the Prevention of Cruelty to Animals and the National Anti-Vivisection Society have grown with differing emphases, ranging from concerns over the treatment of pets to protests over scientific experiments with any animal.

But now, rapidly growing segments within the movement have adopted a new philosophy that began to spread in the late 1970's: that animals have inherent rights to a full life in a natural society and that it is immoral to exploit them, whatever benefits might accrue to humans.

"In the last five years we have seen a real change," said Douglas Moss, publisher of Agenda, a magazine published in Westport, Conn., that describes itself as "the news magazine of the animal rights movement."

"And in the last couple of years," he continued, "more and more people have focused on that term, 'animal rights,' rather than 'animal welfare.' They've gone beyond, 'Gee, let's be nice to animals,' to address the whole relationship between people and animals."

"It's a movement that is growing rapidly," said George Trapp, the managing director of the National Anti-Vivisection Society. "The time is ripe. It's a logical outgrowth of the push for rights for all classes of the human animal."

Older groups devoted to animal welfare have tended to work for legislative goals. But as the new organizations have grown more vocal, many have grown more militant.

Such groups as the Animal Liberation Front, which carried out the Penn break-in, the Band of Mercy and the Urban Gorillas have taken the law into their own hands. Other groups, such as the rapidly growing People for Ethical Treatment of Animals, take public positions supporting the militants' goals, although they also seek legislative gains.

Professional groups supporting animals' rights have also sprung up, ranging from Attorneys for Animal Rights to Psychologists for Ethical Treatment of Animals.

BETTMANN/GETTY IMAGES

Dr. Thomas Gennarelli, associate professor of neurosurgery at the University of Pennsylvania, looks over the damage done at the University's animal research lab here.

No one has determined how large the movement is, according to Mr. Moss, and even members of the Animal Liberation Front, which operates internationally but in secrecy, generally do not know other members beyond their immediate vicinity.

"In the last five years we have seen a real change," Mr. Moss said, reflected in smaller, localized groups that, in addition to national organizations, are springing up across the country.

DEBATE OVER ETHICS

The clash of ideas was defined the other day by Barry Cooperman, Penn's vice provost for research.

"The first question," he said, "is whether it is ethical to experiment on animals for the benefit of humans. As scientists, we say that it is. Our opponents say it is not. With them, there is simply no middle ground.

"The second question is, do you take every precaution to minimize suffering, and how far do you go down that road? That is where guidelines are needed."

A scientist working on strengthening such guidelines is Dr. Charles McCarthy, director of the Office for Protection From Research Risks at the National Institutes of Health. His office has proposed revised guidelines seeking greater assurance of humane treatment of animal subjects of research supported by Federal grants, but he expressed concern the other day over the increasing incidence of extralegal actions against such projects.

"I don't know if you could call it a crime wave," he said, "but the increasing numbers do worry me. I have been in this office for six years, and reports on break-ins in the first five years were zero. In the last year there were 10."

COMPARISON TO ABOLITIONISTS

"We may seem like radicals to you," said one of the participants in the Penn break-in the other day, a woman who identified herself only as Lauren. "But we are like the Abolitionists, who were regarded as radicals, too. And we hope that 100 years from now people will look back on the way animals are treated now with the same horror as we do when we look back on the slave trade."

She pointed to disclosures on the videotapes that her band seized as justification for the break-in.

One sequence showed a monkey strapped to a table and pulling against its bonds. The animal's head was encased in a steel cylinder attached to a pneumatic machine called an accelerator. Suddenly, a piston drove the cylinder upward, thrusting the animal's head sharply through an arc of about 60 degrees.

In another sequence, as an animal lay in a coma, a researcher's recorded voice was heard saying: "You'd better have some axonal damage there, monkey," and calling him "sucker." Axons link brain cells to one another and link the cells to other parts of the nervous system.

LETTERS CRITICIZE PENN

Excerpts from one of the tapes, shown on the news program of KYW, a local television station, and other reports generated dozens of calls and letters to the station, to local newspapers and to the university, most of them critical of the experiments.

Lauren and other militants contend that the animals' movements in the first instance show a failure to use anesthetics and that the researcher's remark in the second instance indicates callousness toward animals.

They also contend that any discoveries possible from such operations can be obtained by other means, such as autopsies on accident victims. In any event, they say, experimenters have no right to sacrifice animals for the possible benefit of people.

About 80 primates have been used in head-injury experiments at the university, according to one researcher, who said computer simulations had helped to limit the numbers sacrificed for the work.

RESEARCHER DEFENDS TESTS

Dr. Thomas Langfitt, chairman of the University of Pennsylvania Hospital's department of neurosurgery and principal investigator of head injury programs, defended the research project. He said discovery of what happened to the brain at the moment of injury was a vital step toward finding better treatment for head injuries, which are a major cause of death in the United States. Primates, he said, are the only useful subjects.

As a result of the experiments, Dr. Langfitt said, he believes his researchers are on the threshold of major improvements in treatment.

Although the animals may have shown movement before the tests, he said, they had been anesthetized to a point where they could not feel pain.

The current conflict here is one of many that have marked a surge over the last few years in an animal welfare movement regarded as beginning in 1776 with a British cleric, Humphrey Primatt, who observed, "Pain is pain, whether it is inflicted on man or beast."

SHIFT BEGAN IN 1976

Experts in the field say the new growth and a change of direction began two centuries later with the publication in 1976 of the book "Animal Liberation" by Peter Singer, a professor of philosophy at Australian National University, who equated exploitation of animals with slavery.

Now "animal rights" is heard almost as often as animal welfare, and it is heard even among members of moderate old-line organizations, such as the Humane Society of the United States.

Even longtime leaders of the animal welfare cause say they have no idea how many people are involved in their movement, but Mr. Trapp of the National Anti-Vivisection Society, which has nearly 50,000 members, said, "It's got to be many millions."

Both he and Patricia Forkan, a vice president of the Humane Society, whose membership she estimated at 200,000, said their organizations had doubled in the last five years.

ILLEGAL ACTIONS DISAPPROVED

Mr. Trapp and Miss Forkan look askance at actions of groups such as the Animal Liberation Front, the Band of Mercy and the Urban Gorillas, although she said, "We can certainly understand how people can grow frustrated enough" to resort to illegal actions.

Among other actions, the Animal Liberation Front took 12 dogs last year from a medical center research project in Los Angeles, the Band of Mercy "liberated" about 40 rabbits from the University of Maryland, and the Urban Gorillas took cats from the University of California at Berkley.

Meanwhile, other groups have sabotaged seal hunts, zoos and commercial fur farms, harassed whalers and interfered with sport hunters.

Among the new groups, one of the fastest growing is People for Ethical Treatment of Animals, which began with 18 members four years ago and now has 23,000 supporters, according to its director, Ingrid Newkirk.

"Things have changed since 1976," Mrs. Newkirk said. "It's not just 'don't beat dogs' anymore. For the first time in the United States, people are realizing that animals are creatures, too, and they have rights."

Radical Animal Rights Groups Step Up Protests

BY SAM HOWE VERHOVEK | NOV. 11, 2001

PORTLAND, ORE., NOV. 8 — The incidents have not tailed off, even since Sept. 11: a firebombing at a federal corral for wild horses in northeastern California; a fire at a primate research center in New Mexico, and back-to-back break-ins in Iowa, one at a fur farm to release more than 1,000 mink, the other to free pigeons raised for research.

All the incidents occurred in the last several weeks, and loose-knit groups like the Animal Liberation Front or the Earth Liberation Front have claimed responsibility. While many mainstream protest groups have scaled back their activism since the terrorist attacks, radical animal rights groups have not.

State and federal law enforcement officials say they are frustrated and angered by the recent acts of sabotage. Some investigators said they were worried that such vandalism could escalate because the groups involved knew that agents were already overwhelmed with reports of anthrax and terrorism.

"This is a horrible time in the nation's history," said Beth Anne Steele, a spokeswoman for the Federal Bureau of Investigation in Portland, which is looking into the incidents, "and to be adding to that with your own brand of violence just goes beyond the pale. If you look at the general public, there is even less tolerance than there might have been before for terrorism of any kind."

So far, no one has been arrested for the most recent attacks. To the degree that individuals or groups have offered any defense of the actions, they say their conduct constitutes neither violence nor terrorism.

In a statement, a Canadian-based faction of the Animal Liberation Front defended the attacks in Iowa, which took place on Oct. 17 and 18, saying that those involved were "giving these animals a fighting chance for survival."

Several other Iowa farms have been subject to break-ins and the release of animals in recent years, and the group's statement said such acts would continue until the animals' "blood stops spilling."

Several birds and mink died shortly after their self-styled liberators cut holes in fences and nets, when they were hit by cars or fell to prey, the farms' owners said. But the animal liberation group said the animals' release was preferable to the "tortures, gassings and electrocutions" they faced in captivity.

Between them, the Animal Liberation Front and the Earth Liberation Front have claimed responsibility for at least six actions since Sept. 11, and for many others in recent years, including fires at a Vail, Colo., ski resort, which they said impinged on lynx habitat, and a Long Island housing-construction site.

Several months ago, someone set fires at an Oregon tree farm and a genetics research laboratory at the University of Washington in Seattle. The Earth Liberation Front claimed responsibility.

The groups have no formal structure, but espouse philosophies, most publicly on the Internet, that support sabotage in defense of animal life or the environment. There have been few arrests in the cases.

Eco-saboteurs, as they are called, are also suspected in a Sept. 8 fire at a McDonald's in Tucson, that caused extensive damage. The initials "A.L.F." and "E.L.F." were spray-painted at the scene.

In addition, the authorities are investigating an incident last Monday at Michigan Technological University in Houghton, Mich., in which two homemade bombs were discovered at two buildings where forestry research is conducted.

The F.B.I., federal firearms agents and the Michigan State Police were called in to defuse the devices. The university said it had received e-mail threats from the Earth Liberation Front earlier this year after it received a grant for research that includes genetic manipulation of trees.

No one has been injured in the incidents, although law enforcement officials say it is only a matter of time before that happens, even if it is not the intent of the perpetrators.

In late September, vandals damaged oil-exploration equipment near Moab, Utah, leaving a postcard near the site that claimed the Earth Liberation Front was involved.

Other recent incidents include a firebombing on Oct. 15 at a corral of the Federal Bureau of Land Management, near Susanville, Calif., in protest of the roundup of the horses.

The Animal Liberation Front in Canada released a communiqué saying it was from the Earth Liberation Front, which said the firebombing was in reaction to the bureau's "continued war against the earth." It added: "In the name of all that is wild we will continue to target industries and organizations that seek to profit by destroying the earth."

One firebomb started a blaze, destroying a barn and about 250 tons of hay and causing a total of about $80,000 in damage. The vandals tore down part of a fence but failed to free the roughly 160 horses at the corral. Three other firebombs, connected to an electronic timer, did not ignite, though a nearby stretch of U.S. 395 was closed for 12 hours while the devices were removed.

While those who commit sabotage have remained anonymous, some animal rights activists have staged public protests recently. In Little Rock, Ark., on Oct. 29, animal rights protesters tried to breach a barricade at the downtown offices of Stephens Inc., a company with ties to a British company, Huntingdon Life Sciences, that conducts animal research.

Several protesters chanted "stop the torture, stop the pain" and wore animal masks, gas masks or bandanas. About 20 people were arrested on charges of disorderly conduct. The organizer, a Philadelphia group called Stop Huntingdon Animal Cruelty, says the company mistreats animals. Huntingdon Life Sciences says it complies with all government regulations on animal research both here and in Britain.

F.B.I. Calls Animal Rights Activist 'Terrorist'

BY ROBERT MACKEY | APRIL 23, 2009

THIS WEEK, THE Federal Bureau of Investigation announced that it had added a 31-year-old American animal rights activist named Daniel Andreas San Diego to its list of "Most Wanted Terrorists." Describing Mr. San Diego as a "domestic terrorist," the F.B.I. warned that he "should be considered armed and dangerous." According to the bureau, Mr. San Diego is wanted for the role he may have played in the bombings of two San Francisco-area office buildings.

The F.B.I. was careful to stress that it considers Mr. San Diego, and other extreme animal rights activists, worthy of being placed on a list headed by violent extremists like the leaders of Al Qaeda, Osama bin Laden and Ayman Al Zawahiri:

> *Animal rights and environmental extremism pose a significant domestic terror threat. To date, extremists have been responsible for more than 1,800 criminal acts and more than $110 million in damages. Currently, we are investigating approximately 170 such extremist incidents across the country.*
>
> *San Diego, known to be involved with a group called SHAC — Stop Huntingdon Animal Cruelty — is wanted for his alleged involvement in bombing two biotech facilities that did business with Huntingdon Life Sciences, a company that conducts animal experimentation for the medical and pharmaceutical industries.*

Huntingdon Life Sciences is a research company based in Cambridgeshire, England. The Times of London reports that the Stop Huntingdon Animal Cruelty campaign began "in the late 1990s when an undercover video showed employees holding a beagle puppy by the scruff of the neck and repeatedly punching it in the face." According to SHAC.net, the Web site of the animal rights group, the disturbing footage of animal abuse was captured by a woman who worked undercover at the facility while making a documentary for a British television series called "Countryside Undercover."

In the latest episode of the "Wanted by the F.B.I." podcast, available on the F.B.I.'s Web site, or on iTunes, F.B.I. Special Agent Joe Schadler says that Mr. San Diego "advocated violence in connection with animal rights issues," and may have planted a nail bomb alongside another bomb at a research facility "intended to harm or kill the first responders."

On the Most Wanted poster for Mr. San Diego, the F.B.I. says that he may now be living in Costa Rica and explains what citizens wanting to claim the $250,000 reward for finding him should be on the look out for:

> *He is a vegan, and avoids consuming or wearing anything made with animal products. He also has distinctive tattoos — one on his chest is round and shows burning hills and plains with the words "It only takes a spark."*

The F.B.I.'s character sketch also notes that he "is skilled at sailing" and "has worked as a computer network specialist and with the operating system Linux."

This is not the first time animal rights activists have been called terrorists. In 1990, The Associated Press reported that Dr. Louis W. Sullivan, then the Secretary of Health and Human Services, said before a march in Washington by animal rights groups, including People for the Ethical Treatment of Animals: "I am saddened and a bit angry... that we have to put up with major disruptions to science by so-called animal activists who are, in fact, nothing more than animal rights terrorists."

In an editorial on Wednesday, headlined "In defense of people," the San Francisco Chronicle editorial board supported the F.B.I.'s pursuit of Mr. San Diego, a Marin County native, arguing that, "Activists who resort to deadly violence are terrorists, and should be treated as such."

Scorned, Animal Rights Advocates in France Intensify Guerrilla Tactics

BY ELIAN PELTIER | MAY 25, 2018

PARIS — For years, the animal rights movement, scorned by both politicians and the public in the land of foie gras, struggled to gain traction in France, Europe's biggest producer and consumer of red meat, where one billion animals are slaughtered a year.

"Animal welfare has never really been a crowd-pleasing cause among French politicians, although the public agrees that animals shouldn't be mistreated," said Sébastien Arsac, co-founder of one of the country's most vocal animal rights organizations, L214 Éthique et Animaux.

So when Mr. Arsac and the organization's other co-founder, Brigitte Gothière, heard Emmanuel Macron, now president, pledge basic safeguards for animal welfare during the 2017 election campaign, they thought they had found an ally. Mr. Macron promised to set up closed-circuit televisions in slaughterhouses and to ban the sale of eggs from caged hens by 2022, two of L214's top priorities.

But while French lawmakers are debating a law on agriculture and nutrition this week, Mr. Macron's government has watered down the former campaign promises, dashing L214's hopes that they could make inroads with the support of political leaders.

So its activists, taking a page from the playbook of similarly minded groups in other countries, including the United States, are stepping up a campaign of guerrilla tactics, hoping to shock the Parliament into amending the government's proposed law.

They recently released a series of clandestinely recorded videos that showed the lack of hygiene on huge egg farms, and the appalling conditions in which distressed hens are kept, plucking out one another's feathers and trampling on rotting corpses in their cages.

The inspiration for these videos was Henry Spira, the Belgian-American activist who began championing the cause of animal rights in the United States nearly 50 years ago.

Mr. Spira sought to talk to companies and institutions first, but if that did not work, he would resort to exposés of animal mistreatment in shocking newspaper ads and other public campaigns.

Ms. Gothière and Mr. Arsac said their organization was part of the activist's legacy (Mr. Spira died in 1998). They founded L214 in 2007, naming it after the article of the French rural code that defines animals as sentient beings and that requires their owners to treat them with respect.

With 50 employees and 2,000 volunteers throughout the country, the organization has tried a mix of working with companies or institutions, and pressuring them through bad publicity when negotiations don't work.

While broadening public awareness, Ms. Gothière and Mr. Arsac have so far had only modest concrete victories. Their group forced two of France's 263 slaughterhouses to shut down after it shared a video showing thrashing horses, cows and sheep being slaughtered while semi-conscious.

The public outcry compelled the government to investigate the country's slaughterhouses and to acknowledge problems in 30 percent of them, including unsafe workplace conditions and a failure to follow slaughtering rules.

One of the group's most recognizable campaigns targeted the premium foie gras producer Ernest-Soulard, which they accused of mistreating geese in a 2013 video that showed many of the birds looked distressed and hurt.

In the first-ever trial of a producer of foie gras accused of cruelty against animals, Ernest-Soulard was cleared of any wrongdoing. But acclaimed chefs, including Joël Robuchon of France and Gordon Ramsay of Britain still stopped buying the delicacy from the company.

"Like Spira, our goal is to make progress one step at a time, to push the peanut forward," said Ms. Gothière, citing the Ernest-Soulard trial or the ban on battery eggs as examples of breakthroughs that "don't resolve everything yet helps reduce animal suffering."

The Australian philosopher Peter Singer, who was a friend of Mr. Spira, is publishing his biography of the activist in French in May.

"For many years, France was rather backwards in terms of its thinking of animals," he said in a Skype interview. "But L214 has made a lot of progress based on the methods of Spira, who showed the animal movement that it was possible to win against big corporations and revered institutions."

Over the past two years, L214 has pushed dozens of French supermarket chains and cattering companies to commit to stop selling battery-cage eggs by 2022 or 2025. Across the world, including in the United States, large food companies have committed to transition to cage-free eggs only.

Yet L214's methods have failed to convince politicians, and their demands have angered many who see in animal products a vital component of France's culture and economy.

"The animal industry didn't wait for L214 to tackle animal welfare," said Jean-Baptiste Moreau, a lawmaker from Mr. Macron's party, La République en Marche, and the commissionner of the agriculture and nutrition bill, referring to efforts by the livestock industry to improve animal welfare.

In many ways, Mr. Macron's backtracking is hardly a surprise. French farmers are under increasing economic stress. There has been a quiet epidemic of suicides in recent years, with hundreds taking their own lives, leading the Ministry of Agriculture to make the issue a national cause.

Unlike several other European countries, such as Portugal, Spain and the Netherlands, France does not have political parties that have made animal welfare a priority.

As a sign that L214 is fighting an uphill battle against politicians, a majority of lawmakers have chosen to ignore the organization's call for CCTV in slaughterhouses to defend those who work there.

"What kind of downward spiral are we going to have if we start filming the employees?" Sandrine Le Feur, a farmer and lawmaker of Mr. Macron's party, said on the television channel LCP.

So far, Britain is the only European country with plans to make closed-circuit TVs mandatory in all slaughterhouses by 2018.

Mr. Moreau, a former slaughterhouse manager and farmer who divides his time between the Parliament in Paris and his farm in the Creuse area of central France, where he has 100 cows, said he refused to negotiate with L214, which he called an "extremist organization" that looked to harm farmers with "fascistic methods."

His criticism of L214 echoed a widespread animosity among meat professionals, who argue that the practices the organization denounced represented a tiny minority of slaughterhouses.

"L214's cause isn't animal welfare, but the abolition of animal farming," said Marc Pagès, director of Interbev, a national organization of meat and cattle professionals.

Mr. Pagès and Mr. Moreau argued that the priority was elsewhere. "The end of animal farming would result in the extinction of any life in the countryside," Mr. Moreau said.

Indeed, L214's ultimate aims would be revolutionary in a country that so cherishes its meat. Ms. Gothière said that only a vegan society would amount to success, but that small steps were progress.

"When I see how our societies are still struggling with racism or sexism, I'm not very optimistic that I will see the end of spiecism in my lifetime," she added. "But I'm not desperate either."

For ‘Eco-Terrorism’ Group, a Hidden Structure and Public Messages

BY DAN BARRY AND AL BAKER | JAN. 8, 2001

MOUNT SINAI, N.Y., JAN. 5 — The arson committed at the upscale subdivision being built on old farmland here, just off Route 25A in eastern Long Island, will never serve as a sophisticated model for the crime. The fires that torched three nearly completed houses were all ignited by birthday candles that had been attached to the handles of plastic jugs filled with gasoline.

And the messages spray-painted on another house in the subdivision that snowy, Dec. 30 morning did not seem particularly auspicious either: “ELF” “Stop Urban Sprawl.” “If You Build It We Will Burn It.” And, finally, “Burn the Rich.”

But if the ELF acronym is mostly unfamiliar on the East Coast, it has long been a reference point in the Pacific Northwest for illegal and extreme environmental activism that law enforcement officials call eco-terrorism. It stands for Earth Liberation Front, a movement structured so loosely that trying to get a handle on it is like trying to grab a fistful of water.

For several years the people who claim allegiance to the group ELF and its partner in activism, the Animal Liberation Front, have taken responsibility for an underground campaign of destruction and fire against those they see as the earth’s enemies: lumber and construction industries, mink and fox farmers, bioengineering companies and laboratories that do tests on animals. For ELF and ALF, they all represent base capitalism.

With a lanky vegan in Portland, Ore., acting as its publicist — although he says he merely shares the information forwarded to him through means he declines to reveal — the group boasts of what it considers to be nonviolent destruction, and provides a running cost estimate of the damage wrought, now at nearly $37 million. That total includes the $80,000 in damage done in Mount Sinai, and some big-ticket destruction as well, including the $12 million arson at a new ski resort in Vail, Colo., in 1998, and the $1 million arson at a lumber company's office in Monmouth, Ore., in 1999.

Although ELF has taken credit for acts of destruction elsewhere in the country, from the burning of a luxury home on the lip of a national forest in Indiana to the sabotage of a highway construction site in Louisiana, it has largely been associated with the West. But the Mount Sinai fires, along with several smaller fires last month and the uprooting of a cornfield at the Cold Spring Harbor Laboratory last summer, have brought its message and notoriety to the quickly vanishing farmlands of Long Island and to the media market of New York.

The day after the Mount Sinai fires, ELF issued a news release that included a local angle. It said the arson, for which it took full responsibility, was partly done to show support for Andrew Stepanian, an animal-rights activist from the affluent Long Island community of Lloyd Neck. Mr. Stepanian was recently convicted of throwing a brick through the display windows of a fur store in Huntington.

This morning, just before he was sentenced to 90 days in jail in Suffolk County Court in Riverhead, Mr. Stepanian and about two dozen supporters stood outside the courtroom and expressed admiration for the ideology of ELF. They repeated the group's slogans and railed against "urban sprawl," but none admitted to being an "elf," as ELF members like to refer to themselves.

"I think what they did is a wonderful thing," said Mr. Stepanian, 22. But, he added, "we have no idea who they are."

Neither, it seems, do the Federal Bureau of Investigation, the United States Forest Service or any of the other federal, state and local law enforcement agencies that have tried for several years to stop the movement and arrest the masterminds — that is, if there are masterminds.

"Absolutely, there's frustration," said Kevin Favreau, the F.B.I.'s domestic-terrorism supervisor in Portland, which comes as close as anyplace to being the base of the amorphous group. "But people always said the F.B.I. wouldn't infiltrate the Mafia, and we did. They said we wouldn't infiltrate the K.G.B., and we did. Is it harder than your average criminal group? Yes, it is. It's not a group you can put your fingers on."

Then again, he added, "Maybe law enforcement will start getting lucky."

But Craig Rosebraugh, the publicist in Portland, said he doubted that would happen. "There's no central leadership where they can go and knock off the top guy and it will be defunct," he said. "It operates on an ideology."

He described the movement as a series of cells across the country with no chain of command and no membership roll, a structure that supporters liken to that of the French Resistance and the African National Congress. There is only a shared philosophy, he said, in taking aim at "anyone who is destroying the environment for the sake of profit."

Because he is the spokesman for ELF, Mr. Rosebraugh's pale, bespectacled face is the only one attached to the movement, even though he says he is a supporter but not a member. As a result, federal officials have raided his home, seized his computer and placed him before a grand jury investigating ELF and ALF activities. Simply put, they want to know the identities of those who keep him abreast of what ELF is doing, and the means by which they do so.

Mr. Rosebraugh, 28, has refused to cooperate with the authorities, while at the same time cultivating an air of mystery about himself and the movement. When asked how he receives the information he disseminates, he said, "I never disclose the type of communication." And when asked whether a reporter could talk to active members, he said: "The people don't want to be known to the public. They want to stay free to continue doing the action."

The movement known as the Earth Liberation Front began at a gathering of members belonging to Earth First, an environmental group, in England in the early 1990's. Some people "thought that the movement didn't go far enough, that it didn't take radical or strong enough actions," said Jim Flynn, who works for the Earth First Journal. So they began ELF, which for a while did little more than encourage people to celebrate Halloween by vandalizing bulldozers and mining equipment.

By 1997, ELF had established a presence in the United States, and formed an alliance with the Animal Liberation Front. In November of that year, with Mr. Rosebraugh as its conduit, the alliance announced that it had freed 600 wild horses and burros from a corral in Burns, Ore., and then had torched an adjacent building.

But the movement's arson attack in Vail, in October 1998, earned it the full attention of the country — and of the F.B.I. A series of early-morning fires destroyed several buildings of a ski-lift operation, causing more than $12 million in damage in what remains the country's most costly act of eco-terrorism. Mr. Rosebraugh said at the time that the development was encroaching on a habitat for lynx, adding of the arson, "As long as it doesn't harm human lives, we approve."

They claimed responsibility, and law enforcement agencies generally agreed, for a series of other actions: In Hermansville, Mich., holes were cut in the fence of a mink ranch, freeing about 5,000 mink. In Monmouth, Ore., offices of the Boise Cascade Corporation lumber company were destroyed. In Lansing, Mich., the genetic engineering research offices at Michigan State University were trashed and burned. In Niwot, Colo., a fire was set to a $2.4 million home under construction.

For all the emphasis that Mr. Rosebraugh gives to the loose, cell-like structure of ELF, there is a band of investigators who suspect that the movement has a small cohesive unit.

"From the activity that we've observed here, it appears that the core group of ELF is very small," said Bill Wasley, the director of law enforcement for the United States Forest Service, which is investigating the extensive vandalism done to its biotechnology research station in Rhinelander, Wis., last year. "They will attract local folks for specific activities and then go away. But it's very difficult to identify the total identity of the group."

ASSOCIATED PRESS

Craig Rosebraugh reads a statement from fellow activist Josh Harper in front of the federal courthouse in Portland, Ore., Wednesday, May 24, 2000.

Ron Arnold, the executive vice president of the Center for the Defense of Free Enterprise, a nonprofit agency in Bellevue, Wash., said that after researching ELF, he believes it operates as a "nomadic action group." For example, he said, a car with a couple of ELF members might leave Spokane, Wash., and drive across the country, stopping to drop off and pick up sympathizers along the way.

"You'll see these little crimes, bing-bing-bing, like ripples in a pond," he said. "This is a pattern we've seen time and again."

Teresa Platt, the director of the Fur Commission USA, which represents the interests of mink and fox farmers, generally agreed. "I don't think it's a large group; I think it's very mobile," she said. "The pattern is that it will quiet down in New York, and you will forget, and you will lose your political momentum. If they kept it up, your city wouldn't stand for it. But they move on."

Mr. Favreau, of the F.B.I. office in Portland, said the government's concern went beyond the damage done to buildings; it has to do with the dynamics of extremist organizations and the types of people they may attract. For example, he said, in 1999 some animal rights extremists, though not linked to the ALF, mailed razor-rigged letters, designed to cut fingers, to fur industry officials and scientists conducting experiments with animals.

"You start out with a large group that believes the same thing, and then it gets smaller and smaller and smaller," he said. "Ultimately, the type of thing we're trying to avoid is the lone guy who takes it to the furthest extreme."

But Mr. Rosebraugh maintained that ELF remains committed to nonviolence. "In the history of ELF, both in the United States and abroad, there have been no injuries to human life," he said. "The people take precautions so that no one gets hurt and their actions speak for themselves."

In fact, in a news release that immediately followed the fires here in Mount Sinai, the arsonists said they had made sure that no one was in the houses at the time the fires were set, and had even moved a propane tank out of the way. After apologizing for disrupting the firefighters' sleep, they added, "We encourage all citizens to donate generous contributions this year to your local volunteer firefighters."

Those sentiments did little to ease the mind of an assistant fire chief. "What if a fireman fell through the floor?" he asked. "There are just a multitude of ways that someone can get hurt like this."

The firefighter insisted on anonymity out of concern for his safety, explaining, "I don't know who these people are and how radical they are."

6 Arrested Years After Ecoterrorist Acts

BY TIMOTHY EGAN | DEC. 9, 2005

SEATTLE, DEC. 8 — The attacks have been nearly forgotten. The places that were burned have been rebuilt or relocated. The cryptic communiqués taking responsibility are distant history.

But on Thursday, after years of investigation, federal officials announced one of the biggest roundups yet of people involved in a string of ecoterrorist attacks in the Pacific Northwest dating to 1998.

Six people from five states, from New York to Washington, were arrested on Wednesday, and indicted on charges related to arson attacks and sabotage in Washington and Oregon, including the millennium eve destruction of a transmission tower owned by the Bonneville Power Administration.

The arrests are intended to strike a blow against two related groups, the Earth Liberation Front and the Animal Liberation Front, which have claimed responsibility for burning and bombing research facilities, timber operations and sport-utility vehicle dealers, among other targets.

Both groups maintain Web sites where they discuss operating as independent cells and share letters from colleagues in prison.

"The Animal Liberation Front carries out direct action against animal abuse in the form of releasing animals and causing financial loss to animal exploiters, usually through the damage and destruction of property," the group says on its Web site.

Some of the targets of those attacks expressed relief on Thursday, saying the arrests helped to close out a long period of uncertainty and fear.

"I'm gratified that that the F.B.I. has been diligent in their pursuit of these people," said Steve Swanson, president of family-owned timber company, Superior Lumber, in Glendale, Ore. The veneer and plywood plant was set on fire on Jan. 2, 2001, and the blaze caused about $500,000 in damage, Mr. Swanson said. The Earth Liberation Front took responsibility for the attack.

No one was injured in any of the attacks, but they used sophisticated fire-bombing techniques, officials said. The fires happened from 1998 to 2001.

"If left unchecked these are the kind of crimes that could really hurt someone," Mr. Swanson said.

The attacks have diminished in the Pacific Northwest of late, but they continue in California and the Rockies, where groups have targeted things like ski lifts and condominiums.

"Hopefully these arrests strike a deterrent blow, making these groups realize that the F.B.I. will come after them no matter how long it takes," said Gary Perlstein, a professor of criminology at Portland State University, who tracks ecoterrorism groups.

But Professor Perlstein said the arrests, coming after years of investigation, showed how long it took to bring domestic terrorists to justice.

Federal officials offered little on the arrests or indictments, beyond identifying those who were charged, most of them in their late 20's or 30's, and saying what the crimes were. But they touted the coordinated roundup as one of the biggest in the fight against ecoterrorism.

"This is a significant step in the government's effort to solve these crimes and to get at the activities of the E.L.F. and the A.L.F.," said Emily Langlie, a spokeswoman for the United States attorney's office in Seattle.

Although ecoterrorist groups have tried to maintain independence, Ms. Langlie said the six people arrested "were all associates, and may have been involved with each other."

The arrests did not resolve one of the biggest ecocrimes in the Northwest, the 2001 fire at a University of Washington genetics research laboratory.

The fire fit the pattern of others, in which companies, universities or government agencies that carried out different types of plant or animal research were the targets.

Animal and environmental sabotage groups pose the nation's top domestic terror threat, F.B.I. officials told a Senate committee earlier this year. The federal officials said they had 150 open investigations of 1,200 crimes from 1990 to 2004 in which ecosaboteurs had taken responsibility.

The F.B.I. identified both the Animal Liberation Front and the Earth Liberation Front as two groups that were "way out front" on different crimes.

"We have seen an escalation in violent rhetoric and tactics," John Lewis, the bureau's director of counterterrorism, said in his Senate testimony. "Attacks are also growing in frequency and size."

The arrests Wednesday were made in Charlottesville, Va., where a college student, Stanislas G. Meyerhoff, 28, was picked up, and in New York, where Daniel G. McGowan, 31, was arrested. They were indicted by a grand jury in Oregon for the arson at Superior Lumber and the May 21, 2001, fire at the Jefferson Poplar Farm in Oregon.

A 1998 fire at a government animal and plant health inspection site in Olympia, Wash., was the basis of indictments against Kevin M. Tubbs, 36, who was arrested in Oregon, and William C. Rodgers, 40, who was arrested in Arizona. Both men were indicted in Seattle.

Also in Arizona, Sarah K. Harvey, 28, a student at Northern Arizona University, was arrested and charged in connection with a 1998 arson at U.S. Forest Industries in Medford, Ore.

Chelsea D. Gerlach, 28, of Portland, Ore., was charged with two counts related to a crime that got a lot of attention during heightened terrorism fears on the eve of the millennium — the December 1999 destruction of a transmission tower near Bend, Ore.

Glossary

acolyte An assistant or a follower.

alt-right An ideological group that promotes extreme conservative beliefs, particularly related to white nationalism.

Animal Liberation Front An international activist group that promotes direct action to support animal rights.

Antifa A political protest movement militantly opposed to fascism and other types of right-wing ideology.

anti-Semitism Hostility toward or prejudice against Jews.

concealed carry The practice of carrying a weapon, such as a gun, in public in a concealed manner.

domestic terrorism The act of committing terrorism to target citizens of the perpetrator's own country.

dystopian Relating to an imagined community that is frightening, marked by suffering and injustice.

ecoterrorism The use of violence in order to advance environmentalist or ecological goals and causes.

ethnostate A state or political unit whose citizenship is restricted to members of a particular racial or ethnic group.

exceptionalism The belief or perception that a movement, country, institution, species or group is exceptional.

extradition The procedure through which a state or nation turns over someone accused of a crime to another state or nation.

federalism A mode of governance that connects distinct states with an overarching central authority.

galvanize To shock or excite someone into action, as if through an electric shock.

infidel A person who does not believe in religion or who follows a religion other than their own.

Infowars A far-right conspiracy theory website run by Alex Jones known for propagating fake news and promoting alt-right extremist beliefs.

lobbyist A person who actively attempts to influence or sway public officials and legislators toward a certain policy or decision.

militia A military force raised from the civilian population on an emergency basis.

populism A political stance that appeals to ordinary people often by positioning their interests against that of the elite.

Roe v. Wade A 1973 landmark Supreme Court decision that constitutionally established a woman's legal right to access abortion.

separatist A person who supports the separation of a particular group from a larger body based on race, religion or ethnicity.

sovereign citizen A member of a political movement that opposes taxation and questions the legitimacy of the government.

whistleblower A person who informs on a person or organization involved in illicit or illegal activity.

zealot A person who is fanatical in pursuit of their religious or political beliefs; an extremist.

Media Literacy Terms

"Media literacy" refers to the ability to access, understand, critically assess and create media. The following terms are important components of media literacy, and they will help you critically engage with the articles in this title.

angle The aspect of a news story that a journalist focuses on and develops.

attribution The method by which a source is identified or by which facts and information are assigned to the person who provided them.

balance Principle of journalism that both perspectives of an argument should be presented in a fair way.

bias A disposition of prejudice in favor of a certain idea, person or perspective.

byline Name of the writer, usually placed between the headline and the story.

chronological order Method of writing a story presenting the details of the story in the order in which they occurred.

column A type of story that is a regular feature, often on a recurring topic, written by the same journalist, generally known as a columnist.

commentary A type of story that is an expression of opinion on recent events by a journalist generally known as a commentator.

credibility The quality of being trustworthy and believable, said of a journalistic source.

editorial Article of opinion or interpretation.

fake news A fictional or made-up story presented in the style of a legitimate news story, intended to deceive readers; also commonly used to criticize legitimate news that one dislikes because of its perspective or unfavorable coverage of a subject.

feature story Article designed to entertain as well as to inform.

impartiality Principle of journalism that a story should not reflect a journalist's bias and should contain balance.

intention The motive or reason behind something, such as the publication of a news story.

inverted pyramid A method of writing a story using facts in order of importance, beginning with a lead and then gradually adding paragraphs in order of relevance from most interesting to least interesting.

motive The reason behind something, such as the publication of a news story or a source's perspective on an issue.

op-ed An opinion piece that reflects a prominent individual's opinion on a topic of interest.

paraphrase The summary of an individual's words, with attribution, rather than a direct quotation of their exact words.

quotation The use of an individual's exact words indicated by the use of quotation marks and proper attribution.

reliability The quality of being dependable and accurate, said of a journalistic source.

source The origin of the information reported in journalism.

style A distinctive use of language in writing or speech; also a news or publishing organization's rules for consistent use of language with regards to spelling, punctuation, typography and capitalization, usually regimented by a house style guide.

tone A manner of expression in writing or speech.

Media Literacy Questions

1. Identify the various sources cited in the article "How Sovereign Citizens Helped Swindle $1 Billion From the Government They Disavow" (on page 38). How does Ashley Powers attribute information to each of these sources in her article? How effective are Powers's attributions in helping the reader identify her sources?

2. In "Planned Parenthood and the Tinderbox of Abortion Rhetoric" (on page 69), Emily Bazelon paraphrases information from Cecile Richards. What are the strengths of the use of a paraphrase as opposed to a direct quote? What are the weaknesses?

3. Compare the headlines of "Why Abortion Is Not Like Other Issues" (on page 66) and "The National Regulation-Resisters Association" (on page 90). Which is a more compelling headline, and why? How could the less compelling headline be changed to better draw the reader's interest?

4. What type of story is "Among the Abortion Extremists" (on page 82)? Can you identify another article in this collection that is the same type of story?

5. Does Janet Reitman demonstrate the journalistic principle of balance in her article "U.S. Law Enforcement Failed to See the Threat of White Nationalism. Now They Don't Know How to Stop It." (on page 154)? If so, how did she do so? If not, what could Reitman have included to make her article more balanced?

6. The article "Some Extremists Fire Guns and Other Extremists Promote Guns" (on page 94) is an example of an op-ed. Identify how

Nicholas Kristof's attitude and tone help convey his opinion on the topic.

7. Does "For 'Eco-Terrorism' Group, a Hidden Structure and Public Messages" (on page 203) use multiple sources? What are the strengths of using multiple sources in a journalistic piece? What are the weaknesses of relying heavily on only one or a few sources?

8. What is the intention of the article "John Paul Stevens: Repeal the Second Amendment" (on page 112)? How effectively does it achieve its intended purpose?

9. Analyze the authors' reporting in "Trump Pardons Oregon Ranchers Whose Case Inspired Wildlife Refuge Takeover" (on page 26) and "Donald Trump's Extremist Supporters Feel Like Winners Either Way" (on page 136). Do you think the reporting is more balanced in one article than in the other? If so, why do you think so?

10. Often, as a news story develops, a journalist's attitude toward the subject may change. Compare "Some Extremists Fire Guns and Other Extremists Promote Guns" (on page 94) and "It's Time To Talk About the N.R.A." (on page 120), both by Nicholas Kristof. Did new information discovered between the publication of these two articles change Kristof's perspective?

11. Identify each of the sources in "A Militia Gets Battle Ready for a 'Gun-Grabbing' Clinton Presidency" (on page 100) as a primary source or a secondary source. Evaluate the reliability and credibility of each source. How does your evaluation of each source change your perspective on this article?

Citations

All citations in this list are formatted according to the Modern Language Association's (MLA) style guide.

BOOK CITATION

THE NEW YORK TIMES EDITORIAL STAFF. *Political Extremism: How Fringe Groups Operate.* New York: New York Times Educational Publishing, 2020.

ONLINE ARTICLE CITATIONS

BARRY, DAN, AND AL BAKER. "For 'Eco-Terrorism' Group, a Hidden Structure and Public Messages." *The New York Times*, 8 Jan. 2001, https://www.nytimes.com/2001/01/08/nyregion/for-eco-terrorism-group-a-hidden-structure-and-public-messages.html.

BAZELON, EMILY. "Planned Parenthood and the Tinderbox of Abortion Rhetoric." *The New York Times*, 30 Nov. 2015, https://www.nytimes.com/2015/11/30/magazine/planned-parenthood-and-the-tinderbox-of-abortion-rhetoric.html.

BIDGOOD, JESS. "Nashville Suspect Once Called Himself a 'Sovereign Citizen,' Police Say. What Is That?" *The New York Times*, 23 Apr. 2018, https://www.nytimes.com/2018/04/23/us/sovereign-citizen.html.

BLOW, CHARLES M. "The National Regulation-Resisters Association." *The New York Times*, 30 Jan. 2013, https://www.nytimes.com/2013/01/31/opinion/blow-the-national-regulation-resisters-association.html.

COLLINS, GAIL. "A Pistol for Every Bar Stool." *The New York Times*, 16 June 2016, https://www.nytimes.com/2016/06/16/opinion/a-pistol-for-every-bar-stool.html.

DOUTHAT, ROSS. "Among the Abortion Extremists." *The New York Times*, 7 Apr., 2018, https://www.nytimes.com/2018/04/07/opinion/sunday/among-the-abortion-extremists.html.

EGAN, TIMOTHY. "6 Arrested Years After Ecoterrorist Acts." *The New York*

Times, Dec. 9, 2005, https://www.nytimes.com/2005/12/09/us/6-arrested-years-after-ecoterrorist-acts.html.

ELIGON, JOHN, AND MICHAEL SCHWIRTZ. "Senate Candidate Provokes Ire With 'Legitimate Rape' Comment." *The New York Times*, 19 Aug. 2012, https://www.nytimes.com/2012/08/20/us/politics/todd-akin-provokes-ire-with-legitimate-rape-comment.html.

FRANK, ROBERT H. "When to Violate the Top Two Commandments of Antigovernment Crusaders." *The New York Times*, 15 Mar. 2007, https://www.nytimes.com/2007/03/15/business/15scene.html.

GOLDBERG, MICHELLE. "Affirmative Action for Reactionaries." *The New York Times*, 30 Mar. 2018, https://www.nytimes.com/2018/03/30/opinion/affirmative-action-diversity.html.

GOLDBERG, MICHELLE. "Rise of the Armed Left." *The New York Times*, 2 Nov. 2018, https://www.nytimes.com/2018/11/02/opinion/socialist-left-guns-nra-trump.html.

JANOFSKY, MICHAEL. "Two States, Two Gatherings and a Lot of Antigovernment Sentiment." *The New York Times*, 15 May 1995, https://www.nytimes.com/1995/05/15/us/two-states-two-gatherings-lot-antigovernment-sentiment-new-hampshire-common.html.

KRISTOF, NICHOLAS. "It's Time To Talk About the N.R.A." *The New York Times*, 29 Oct. 2018, https://www.nytimes.com/interactive/2018/10/29/opinion/nra-mass-shootings-pittsburgh.html.

KRISTOF, NICHOLAS. "Some Extremists Fire Guns and Other Extremists Promote Guns." *The New York Times*, 16 June 2016, https://www.nytimes.com/2016/06/16/opinion/some-extremists-fire-guns-and-other-extremists-promote-guns.html.

LEONHARDT, DAVID. "Why Abortion Is Not Like Other Issues." *The New York Times*, 13 July 2013, https://www.nytimes.com/2013/07/14/sunday-review/why-abortion-is-not-like-other-issues.html.

LOVETT, IAN. "Antigovernment Obsession Preceded Las Vegas Shootings." *The New York Times*, 9 June 2014, https://www.nytimes.com/2014/06/10/us/couple-in-las-vegas-killings-embraced-antigovernment-ideology.html.

MACKEY, ROBERT. "F.B.I. Calls Animal Rights Activist 'Terrorist.' " *The New York Times*, 23 Apr. 2009, https://thelede.blogs.nytimes.com/2009/04/23/fbi-calls-animal-rights-activist-terrorist/.

MAHLER, JONATHAN, AND JULIE TURKEWITZ. "Donald Trump's Extremist Supporters Feel Like Winners Either Way." *The New York Times*, 6 Nov. 2016, https://www.nytimes.com/2016/11/07/us/politics/donald-trump-extremist-supporters.html.

MCPHATE, MIKE. "Law Center Finds Surge in Extremist Groups in U.S. Last Year." *The New York Times*, 17 Feb. 2016, https://www.nytimes.com/2016/02/18/us/law-center-finds-surge-in-extremist-groups-in-us-last-year.html.

NAGOURNEY, ADAM. "A Defiant Rancher Savors the Audience That Rallied to His Side." *The New York Times*, 23 Apr. 2014, https://www.nytimes.com/2014/04/24/us/politics/rancher-proudly-breaks-the-law-becoming-a-hero-in-the-west.html.

THE NEW YORK TIMES. "An Abortion Ban's Bogus Arguments." *The New York Times*, 14 May 2015, https://www.nytimes.com/2015/05/15/opinion/an-abortion-bans-bogus-arguments.html.

THE NEW YORK TIMES. "Ex-Justice Stevens's Call to Repeal the Second Amendment." *The New York Times*, 27 Mar. 2018, https://www.nytimes.com/2018/03/27/opinion/stevens-second-amendment-guns.html.

THE NEW YORK TIMES. "New Frontiers of Extremism." *The New York Times*, 20 Aug. 2012, https://www.nytimes.com/2012/08/21/opinion/new-frontiers-of-extremism-from-the-gop.html.

THE NEW YORK TIMES. " 'Only the Extremists Want to Ban All Guns.' " *The New York Times*, 28 Mar. 2018, https://www.nytimes.com/2018/03/28/opinion/only-the-extremists-want-to-ban-all-guns.html.

OBERMAN, MICHELLE. "What Happens When Abortion Is Banned?" *The New York Times*, 31 May 2018, https://www.nytimes.com/2018/05/31/opinion/sunday/abortion-banned-latin-america.html.

PELTIER, ELIAN. "Scorned, Animal Rights Advocates in France Intensify Guerrilla Tactics." *The New York Times*, 25 May 2018, https://www.nytimes.com/2018/05/25/world/europe/france-animal-rights-foie-gras.html.

POWERS, ASHLEY. "How Sovereign Citizens Helped Swindle $1 Billion From the Government They Disavow." *The New York Times*, 29 Mar. 2019, https://www.nytimes.com/2019/03/29/business/sovereign-citizens-financial-crime.html.

REITMAN, JANET. "U.S. Law Enforcement Failed to See the Threat of White Nationalism. Now They Don't Know How to Stop It." *The New York Times*, 3 Nov. 2018, https://www.nytimes.com/2018/11/03/magazine/FBI-charlottesville-white-nationalism-far-right.html.

RISEN, JAMES. "Tracing the Path of a Hard-Line Foe of Abortion." *The New York Times*, 6 Nov. 1998, https://www.nytimes.com/1998/11/06/nyregion/tracing-the-path-of-a-hard-line-foe-of-abortion.html.

ROBBINS, WILLIAM. "Animal Rights: A Growing Movement in U.S." *The New York Times*, 15 June 1984, https://www.nytimes.com/1984/06/15/us/animal-rights-a-growing-movement-in-us.html.

ROOSE, KEVIN. "On Gab, an Extremist-Friendly Site, Pittsburgh Shooting Suspect Aired His Hatred in Full." *The New York Times*, 28 Oct. 2018, https://www.nytimes.com/2018/10/28/us/gab-robert-bowers-pittsburgh-synagogue-shootings.html.

STACK, LIAM. "Wildlife Refuge Occupied in Protest of Oregon Ranchers' Prison Terms." *The New York Times*, 2 Jan. 2016, https://www.nytimes.com/2016/01/03/us/oregon-ranchers-will-return-to-prison-angering-far-right-activists.html.

STEPHENS, BRET. "The Outrage Over Kevin Williamson." *The New York Times*, 30 Mar. 2018, https://www.nytimes.com/2018/03/30/opinion/the-outrage-over-kevin-williamson.html.

STEPHENS, BRET. "Repeal the Second Amendment." *The New York Times*, 5 Oct. 2017, https://www.nytimes.com/2017/10/05/opinion/guns-second-amendment-nra.html.

STEVENS, JOHN PAUL. "John Paul Stevens: Repeal the Second Amendment." *The New York Times*, 27 Mar. 2018, https://www.nytimes.com/2018/03/27/opinion/john-paul-stevens-repeal-second-amendment.html.

SULLIVAN, EILEEN, AND JULIE TURKEWITZ. "Trump Pardons Oregon Ranchers Whose Case Inspired Wildlife Refuge Takeover." *The New York Times*, 10 July 2018, https://www.nytimes.com/2018/07/10/us/politics/trump-pardon-hammond-oregon.html.

TAUB, AMANDA. " 'White Nationalism,' Explained." *The New York Times*, 21 Nov. 2016, https://www.nytimes.com/2016/11/22/world/americas/white-nationalism-explained.html.

TAVERNISE, SABRINA. "Shift in Virginia on Abortion Bill." *The New York Times*, 22 Feb. 2012, https://www.nytimes.com/2012/02/23/us/governor-of-virginia-calls-for-changes-in-abortion-bill.html.

VERHOVEK, SAM HOWE. "Radical Animal Rights Groups Step Up Protests." *The New York Times*, 11 Nov. 2001, https://www.nytimes.com/2001/11/11/us/radical-animal-rights-groups-step-up-protests.html.

ZUCCHINO, DAVID. "A Militia Gets Battle Ready for a 'Gun-Grabbing' Clinton Presidency." *The New York Times*, 4 Nov. 2016, https://www.nytimes.com/2016/11/05/us/a-militia-gets-battle-ready-for-a-gun-grabbing-clinton-presidency.html.

Index

This book is current up until the time of printing. For the most up-to-date reporting, visit www.nytimes.com.